THE HOUSE THAT HELD HER

WHAT IS THE COST OF KEEPING THE DEAD QUIET?

ELLIS HART

ISBN: 979-8-9924045-2-4 (Paperback)

ISBN: 979-8-9924045-4-8 (Hardcover)

ISBN: 979-8-9924045-1-7 (eBook)

Printed in the United States of America

For permissions or inquiries, please contact: https://www.ellishartbooks.com/

First Edition, 2025

For my Family
Thank you for always supporting my creative pursuits. I promise I
will jump on the trampoline with you now.

TRIGGER WARNINGS

The House That Held Her explores dark themes and contains scenes that may be distressing to some readers. Please proceed with caution if you prefer to avoid any of the following content:

Domestic Abuse and Violence: Includes verbal, emotional, and physical abuse within family and marital relationships.

Child Abuse and Child Death: References to a child's neglect and harm, as well as the death of a child, form part of a central plot point.

Graphic Depictions of Violence and Gore: Certain passages describe violent acts, injuries, and disturbing imagery, including human remains.

Drowning and Death at Sea: Multiple characters encounter drowning or near-drowning experiences, described with vivid detail.

Mental Health Struggles: Characters grapple with guilt, depression, and potential hallucinations; includes scenes of severe emotional distress, trauma, and anxiety.

Self-Harm and Threats of Harm: Contains moments of

self-harm behaviors and threats or implications of harm to oneself or others.

Murder and Homicide: The narrative involves acts of murder, as well as references to possible serial killings and cover-ups.

Parental Loss and Grief: Includes depictions of parental abandonment or emotional unavailability, alongside adult characters coping with traumatic childhoods.

If any of these themes or scenes could be triggering, please read with caution or consider skipping sections that may cause distress.

PROLOGUE

He watched from the shadows, still and patient, blending seamlessly into the dark. He listened to the rhythm of the couple's breath, slow and steady, feeling that same pull toward them as they slept in their bed.

They didn't belong here.

The silence was almost suffocating, broken only by the woman's soft sighs as sleep took over. He waited, unmoving, until the stillness felt absolute. Then, slowly, he moved forward like a speck of dust floating through the darkness, unheard and unseen.

He knelt beside the bed, his gaze flickering between the two figures. The room was shrouded in a dim glow, moonlight spilling weakly through the curtains while a quiet, persistent whistle of wind slipped through a crack in the window. He leaned closer, his breath ghosting the woman's ear, whispering words too faint to hear, tears slipping down his face.

They were caught in a charged stillness: an unholy balance of innocence, oblivion, and malice. He pulled back, a fleeting smile curling his lips. She murmured something in her sleep—a tiny, incoherent sound—and he leaned his head in, listening.

The specter abruptly turned, staring into the darkness

behind him. His ear tilted, listening intently, and then, as quietly as he had arrived, he faded back into the shadows as if being called back home.

The room returned to its stillness—the only trace of him a lingering chill already slipping into the sleeping woman's dreams.

1

MARGOT, PRESENT DAY

I don't know much about hurricanes. Having grown up in Maryland, I'm used to the rhythm of four predictable seasons—snow-dusted winters, humid summers, and crisp transitions in between. What I'm not accustomed to is the kind of storm that could rip roofs from houses and submerge entire streets under water. Yet here I am, barely three weeks into my new life in Florida, bracing for the arrival of a Category 4 hurricane with the deceptively sweet name of Barbara.

I stand at the window, my hands resting on the frame as I stare at the heavy, oppressive sky. Storm warnings echo relentlessly—across news stations, radios, and worried texts from family back home. And while each passing hour heightens the tension of Barbara's arrival, nothing had prepared me for my husband, suitcase in hand, ready to walk out the door as the historic storm barrels toward our new home.

"I don't understand this, Nate," I say, my voice taut, struggling to mask my frustration. "Companies everywhere are working remotely. Zoom, Skype, Teams. How is none of that feasible for your company? This is a record-breaking hurricane, for God's sake."

The strain between us is tangible. I follow him through the half-renovated house, my words reverberating in the unfinished rooms. What should be our sanctuary feels more like a battlefield, with exposed drywall and a thin layer of construction dust coating the air.

Nate pauses, his back turned to me, adjusting his tie in the reflection of a smudged window. The quiet man I once admired for his restraint now seems distant—less a partner, more a stranger passing through my life. I wait for some acknowledgment, a sign that he grasps the gravity of the situation. When he finally speaks, his words feel rehearsed, as if he's played this scene out in his mind well before now.

"We've been over this already, Margot. I carry the financial burden of our entire household on my shoulders right now. Give me a goddamn break here."

I freeze between the kitchen and hallway, dissecting his words. Arguments between us weren't new, but this one carries a sharpness I haven't felt before.

The resentment has been simmering for months. But true cracks only began to show when we moved from Maryland to Florida. I believed in our mutual decisions and our shared dreams. But now, each step toward our supposed future seems to deepen Nate's bitterness towards me, towards the new life we're trying to build—a bitterness I honestly don't understand.

There had been a time when I wasn't just Nate's wife. I'd spent a decade working in child protective services, advocating for vulnerable children. It was my calling—a mission that once defined me. But the endless battles and heartache wore me down. I had confided in Nate, yearning for something different —a family, a life where I could offer the kind of love and stability my foster children never had.

Back then, it all made sense. Nate's career at CirroSystems

was flourishing; we could finally afford our dream home. I thought I could step back, focus on building a family, and return to my career someday. Everything seemed perfect– until it wasn't.

My mind drifts to Lila, my last placement before everything unraveled. Lila—seven years old, with wild curls and a smile that could melt stone. When we first met, I saw a beautiful need to be loved in her eyes. I believed I was providing that when I placed her with Robert and Dawn Thompson. Their sprawling, picturesque home had seemed ideal—warm, inviting, the perfect environment for a young girl needing support and care.

The bruises had seemed minor. I had convinced myself they were to be expected—children fall, they bruise. Lila had been quiet and withdrawn, but that wasn't unusual for foster kids. Adjusting took time. I ignored the unease gnawing at me, the fleeting moments of doubt. I had been too preoccupied with my own life to see the warning signs.

I had convinced myself Lila was safe. I needed to believe it. But standing now in my unfinished Florida home, I can admit the truth to myself - but only silently: I prioritized myself and the desire for a family of my own over my CPS responsibilities. I let Lila down; it's my fault she's dead.

"Margot, are you even listening to me?" Nate's sharp voice jolts me back to the present.

I blink, shaking off the memory, but the pain lingers. "I heard you." My voice is soft, almost hollow.

Nate grabs his suitcase, shaking his head. "Right, of course you did. They just downgraded the hurricane to a Category 3. You'll be fine. I'll be back next week."

As Nate reaches for the door, I swallow hard, my throat tightening painfully. "I love you," I mumble, the words barely audible, fractured and weak.

His hand hesitates on the doorframe. He takes a slow, deep breath, his shoulders rising and falling before he turns to look at me. "I love you too."

For a fleeting moment, I think he may say more. I silently plead for it—for him to open up, to show something, anything. A crack in the cold wall that had been building between us. But instead, he closes his mouth, swallows whatever words had almost surfaced, and steps outside into the darkness of the oncoming hurricane.

The shadows of my past have followed me from Maryland to Florida, no matter how far I've tried to run from them.

2

The deep rumble of thunder shakes me awake. I bolt upright, heart pounding, breath caught in my throat. Hawthorn Manor groans around me, the sound of an aging house exhausted by decades of battering rain and relentless sun. Something woke me, but I don't know what.

Glancing at the clock, the hurricane was predicted to have reached its peak several hours ago. Now, all I hear is a ghostly quiet, only interrupted by the faint whistling of the wind through a crack in the window sill. My breath slows as I strain to listen, and then I notice it- the faint, rhythmic splashing of water coming from downstairs.

I swing my legs over the side of the bed, my bare feet reluctant to meet the icy wooden floor. I grab my phone and turn on the flashlight app. The beam jumps with my unsteady grip as I step cautiously toward the staircase, fingers tightening around the banister. The air inside feels thick and humid, the remnants of the storm clinging to everything, making the house feel suffocating.

The splashing grows louder, more persistent. At the bottom of the stairs, my flashlight catches on the source of the noise, and my stomach clenches. Water pools across the uneven floorboards, reflecting the dim light in broken, shimmering patterns. The storm forced its way inside.

I step forward cautiously, my slippers soaking through as cold water seeps in. The faint sound of dripping draws me toward the far wall, where a steady trickle slides down the cracked plaster. The sight takes a large bite of me; leaving behind an emerging sense of despair.

This house—our supposed fresh start—feels like a cruel joke. It isn't just the storm damage or the unfinished renovations; it's the weight of everything it represents. My fractured marriage, my guilt over Lila, the dreams I abandoned. Every flaw in these walls mirrors my own cracks, and tonight, I feel every single one of them.

The floorboards creak beneath me as I move deeper into the room, my flashlight catching on the warped edges of the wood. The water pools unevenly, collecting in the room's low points. I follow the water, my frustration mounting as I realize the extent of the damage.

Dismay claws at my throat, and before I can stop myself, I let out a scream—a raw, guttural release of everything I've been holding in. The sound ricochets through the empty house, filling every neglected corner. I grab the closest object— an old lacrosse stick from Nate's college days—and swing. The plaster gives way easily, crumbling under the force. I swing again. And again. Until the stick splinters in my hands.

Panting, I collapse onto the waterlogged floor, surrounded by darkness and the wreckage of my outburst.

For a moment, I just sit there, trembling, cold water seeping through my pajamas. The house is silent except for the faint sound of water lapping at the floor. I lean back against the damp wall and close my eyes. I've been holding everything together for so long, pretending I could fix this—the house, my marriage, myself. But tonight, the storm stripped away that illusion, exposing me.

As my breathing steadies, my gaze drifts downward. Something about the floor catches my attention. A single board, slightly raised at one corner, seems out of place. I frown, leaning forward to inspect it. My fingers brush against the edge, and with a slight push, the board shifts under my touch.

Curiosity replaces my distress as I pry the board loose. Beneath it is a small, dark space filled with murky water. I reach in, my fingers brushing against something solid. I pull it out slowly, my pulse quickening as I realize what I'm holding.

A film canister.

The black plastic shell feels strange in my hand, its gray lid loose from years of neglect. I twist it off, revealing a tightly rolled piece of paper. My fingers tremble slightly as I unroll it, the delicate fibers resisting after years of being tucked away in the dark.

A map.

A crude drawing of our new town, Mount Dora. Deliberate strokes shape the streets, while a large "X" sits near the edge of what looks like a huge body of water.

My mind races. What could this lead to? Treasure? A secret buried in the house's past? The possibilities spark something inside me—something I haven't felt in a long time: purpose.

I carefully fold the map and tuck it under my arm. The house creaks around me, as if it, too, has been waiting for this discovery. Replacing the floorboard as best I can, I climb back upstairs, my thoughts buzzing. What was the significance of the map? Who hid it, and why?

Slipping out of my wet pajamas, I crawl back into bed, fingers still tracing the edges of the parchment. The storm outside can rage all it wants. I have something new to focus on, something that makes the heaviness in my chest lift—if only a little.

My eyes drift shut, exhaustion pulling me under. Just before sleep claims me, I murmur, "Goodnight, Lila."

Somewhere in the darkness, just as I fade into the grey of sleep I almost think I hear a response—

"Goodnight, Margot."

3

The morning sun struggles against the heavy clouds still clinging to the sky in the aftermath of the storm. Humid air presses down on me, thick with the scent of wet earth and sodden wood. I step onto the porch, squinting against the unexpected brightness, taking in the devastation left behind. The lawn is a battlefield of fallen branches, uprooted shrubs, and scattered debris. A small tool shed lies in pieces across the gravel driveway; it remains a casualty of the hurricane's fury.

Behind me, Hawthorn Manor looms, standing defiantly against the shifting sky. The once-imposing gothic structure bears new scars—streaks of rain-washed decay and fresh wounds where the storm has taken its toll. Ivy clings desperately to the stonework, stretching hungrily upward as if trying to reclaim the house entirely. The steeply pitched roof, framed by towering chimneys, seems to glare down at me in silent accusation. This house has survived worse. But today, it feels tired, battered, as if even it knows how close we came to ruin.

Hawthorn Manor sits atop the highest point in Mount Dora, a commanding presence at the crossroads of Sixth Avenue and Donnelly Street. From here, the entire town unfolds below—brick-lined streets winding through historic shops, cafes, and colorful buildings that have stood the test of time. The manor's vantage point offers an unobstructed view of Lake Dora, its vast, rippling waters stretching across 4,385 acres. The largest lake in the Harris Chain it dominates the landscape, hugging the town's edges like an ever-present guardian. Spanish moss drapes from the cypress trees along its banks, and in the morning, mist hovers just above the water's surface, lending the place an otherworldly calm.

From this height, I can see where the storm has left its mark—boats tossed haphazardly against the docks, debris floating along the shoreline, and the usually pristine lakefront park now littered with broken limbs and overturned benches. With its old-world charm and sleepy Southern elegance, Mount Dora wears the storm's scars like fresh bruises, but I know the town will recover. It always does.

I pull out my phone, hoping for a message from Nate. A simple text to say he made it to DC, maybe even an acknowledgment that he thought of me at all during the storm.

Nothing.

"Surprise, surprise," I mutter, turning the screen off. "Husband of the Year right here!"

With a dramatic flourish, I throw one hand in the air, the other pointing at my phone in mock celebration. I spin slowly, mimicking the cheers of an imaginary crowd, giving them the performance of a woman so very amused by her husband's disappearing act. But the moment passes, and the silence swallows me whole. The bitter humor fades, leaving behind only disappointment.

I scan the estate. Beyond the storm-torn yard, the land stretches endlessly—wild and unkempt, once a thriving citrus grove, now a tangle of weeds and forgotten trees. A crumbling fountain stands dry and useless near the drive, its basin filled with leaves instead of water. Further back, past the remnants of a greenhouse long past its prime, an old carriage house sags under its own neglect, doors barely clinging to their rusted hinges. My eyes land on a familiar figure beneath an ancient oak, methodically clearing away fallen limbs.

Walter.

He moves with the deliberate precision of a man who has done this a thousand times before, his pruning shears slicing effortlessly through tangled branches. The storm, the damage —it doesn't faze him. He's seen worse. He's always been here, like part of the foundation itself.

I watch him momentarily before making my way down the porch steps, my shoes crunching on the damp gravel. As I approach, he straightens, wiping sweat from his brow with the back of a weathered hand.

"Morning, Margot," he greets me, his voice carrying that familiar warmth. "Storm did quite a number on the old place, didn't it?"

I offer him a small, weary smile. "It really did. I don't know what we'd do without you, Walter."

He chuckles, a soft, knowing sound. "Well, I can't just let her fall apart now, can I? She's got good bones, this house. Worth every bit of care."

His words settle over me, stirring a pang of guilt for the rage I had unleashed on these very walls last night.

I glance back at the house. "You know, I've been thinking about the history of the place. I've heard stories, but... I don't really know much about the Hawthorn family. Do you?"

Walter pauses, considering my question. He pulls off his Yankees cap, running a hand through silver hair before settling it back in place. "Sure, I knew them, as did my father before me. Mr. Hawthorn was a good man, but after his wife passed... Well, he was never the same."

"How did she die?" I ask, watching as his gaze drifts toward the lake.

"Heart attack. Out on Lake Dora," he says quietly. "It was a tragedy. The whole town mourned her. After that, Mr. Hawthorn changed. He stopped attending town events, made fewer appearances, kept to himself. Folks would occasionally catch glimpses of him on his porch, staring down towards the lake, but over time, even those sightings became rare. One day, people realized they hadn't seen him at all in months. The town whispered about what might have happened—some say he left the town to escape the memories. Others think he took his own life. No one really knows."

Walter idly nudges a rock with the toe of his boot, lost in thought. "One day, I had a good, kind man that I worked for. The next, the city of Mount Dora labeled this house a historic site and started paying me to maintain it. The checks kept coming, so I kept showing up."

He exhales, shaking his head with a wry smile. "Truth is, I would've kept showing up with or without the money. I just love this old house too much to see her fall apart."

I study him; the deep lines on his forehead roll down to his thick gray beard, with unwavering dedication in his eyes. He means every word.

"It's safe to say the house and I are happy to have you here, Walter," I say, lowering my voice slightly. "And I'm also happy Nate isn't around to hear me say that, because he thinks I'm wasting my time trying to bring this place back to life."

Walter turns his gaze back to me, his expression soft but knowing. "Your husband is a practical man. But sometimes, history is what matters most. The things that connect us to a place, to each other. Don't let anyone make you feel like what you want isn't important."

Something in my chest tightens. "Thank you, Walter. That means a lot."

He nods, smiling once more. "Anytime, Margot. Old houses tend to reflect their owners. Might be a little rough around the edges now, but give it time. She'll shine again. Just you wait and see."

I turn back toward the house, Walter's words lingering in my mind. He's right. This house is more than just rotting wood and broken dreams. There's something here—something waiting to be uncovered.

A sense of determination surfaces as I step back into the house, my mind buzzing with questions. Who was Mr. Hawthorn? What had happened to him after his wife's death? And why the hell was there a treasure map hidden under my floorboards? The curiousness of it all pushed me to dig deeper.

I head straight for my laptop, typing in every variation of "Hawthorn Manor," "original owner," and "Lake Dora tragedy" I can think of, yet the search results are infuriatingly sparse. It's like the man had been erased from history—vanished into the folds of forgotten time.

"Come on," I mutter, slamming the laptop shut. Leaning back in the creaky wooden chair, I try to steady my breathing, but frustration claws at me.

I stand up, stretching until my back pops. The satisfying release does little to calm the storm in my head. With a pencil dangling between my teeth, I start to pace, but then—movement. A flicker across the sitting room. I freeze, my heart pounding.

I stare hard, waiting. Was it my imagination? Probably. But then, a shadow sweeps past the window.

My pulse jumps, my throat tightening. Logic whispers it was just Walter moving around the house, but something about it doesn't sit right.

I creep toward the window, my footsteps feeling ridiculously loud against the old boards. Pressing my hands against the glass, I cup them around my eyes, leaning in until my forehead touches the cool pane. Nothing. Just condensation diffusing the afternoon sun. I let out a breath, fogging the glass.

"You're losing it, Margot," I whisper, beginning to turn away.

That's when the face appears. Squashed against the glass, its nose flattened comically, wide eyes blinking straight at me.

I gasp, stumbling backward with a strangled yelp.

"Hello!" the woman calls out, her voice muffled but sharp enough to make me flinch. She jabs a finger toward the back door before disappearing from view.

A knock rattles the doorframe a heartbeat later.

"What the-" I breathe, my pulse still racing as I hesitate, then yank open the door.

There she stands—an explosion of bright purple and chaos. She has to be pushing seventy, her stiff bob dyed a harsh red, lips smeared in a shade of violet that bled onto her teeth. A cigarette dangles from her fingers, a thin ribbon of smoke curling up into the humid air.

"Well! Aren't you a sight?" she practically shouts before brushing past me like she owns the place. Her heels click across the old tiles.

"I—wait, who—"

"Phyllis Brendamore. You must be Margot. Heard you bought this old place." She waves her hand dismissively, her sharp eyes scanning the dusty corners of the house with something close to disgust. "Oh, it's worse than I thought."

"Nice to meet you, Phyllis," I said dryly, still reeling. "Can I help you with something?"

"Oh, I just had to see the new owner," she chirps, pausing

to finger a dusty drape. "George and Cecilia Hawthorn were practically family. I was in and out of this house constantly. Well, not literally, but close enough."

Something about her feels off—too bold, too intrusive—but there appears to be some history in her words, and I'm looking for information.

"You knew them well?"

"Oh, darling, of course. The Hawthorns practically ran Mount Dora. They were the biggest donors for the Mount Dora Winter Gala—thirty grand every year." She pauses, eyeing me with a grin that was all teeth. "And now that you're here, maybe you'd like to keep that tradition alive?"

I blink. "Thirty thousand dollars? Yeah, that's not exactly in the budget."

Her smile falters for a second before snapping back into place. "Oh, I get it, I do. Times are tough. But maybe we could host the gala here? Since Georgie left, we've had to use the community building off Baker St. Can you imagine anything more depressing? I'm sure we could spruce the ol' girl up a bit. It'd be perfect!"

Before I can respond, she's already gesturing wildly. "We'll need new drapes, of course. And the floor, what happened to the beautiful oak? Hate this new color, much too dark. And a deep clean. God, the dust in here could kill someone."

"Seriously, Phyllis, that's not—" I cut in, but her voice bulldozes over mine.

"Phyllis, please!" I snap louder this time, but it's like yelling into the wind.

Finally, my patience wholly unravels, and I step directly in front of the woman, unloading a barrel of a yell. "Phyllis!"

She freezes mid-gesture, turning back to me with wide eyes.

"I'm not hosting a gala. I'm not making a donation. And I need you to leave. Please."

The words hang in the air, heavier than I intended, but happy to have paused the rude onslaught nonethesame.

Phyllis's expression doesn't crack. Instead, she chuckles, patting my arm, and mutters, "No harm done, dear."

She makes her way toward the door, and my pulse begins to return to its normal rate. But I can't stop myself.

"Wait– since you knew the Hawthorns... would you mind sharing some insight? I'm trying to learn more about them myself. Feels a bit odd to own a house with so much history without knowing much about the people who built and lived in it."

Phyllis brightens immediately. "Oh, darling, I could tell you stories all day, but for the real dirt? Talk to Paula Hastings. She knows this place inside and out—unappointed town historian; probably has files on files."

"Paula Hastings?"

"Mount Dora Historical Museum. Can't miss her."

With a dramatic wave, she disappears through the doorway, leaving nothing but smoke and the faint scent of menthol in her wake.

I lock the door behind her while my mind races with possibilities. At least now I have a lead—Paula Hastings. Maybe she can shed some light on the mysteries surrounding this place.

4

The heavy wooden door of the Mount Dora Historical Museum creaks as I push it open, the faint scent of black tea and old wood curling into my nose. Cool air sweeps over me, a welcome relief from the sticky Florida humidity clinging to my skin like a second layer. The building, once the town jail, carries an eerie charm. Three of the original jail cells stand intact, their iron bars stretching like skeletal fingers, now housing relics of the past. The other three have been demolished to make way for storage, a restroom, and more display space.

The museum is small, almost cozy, but its walls brim with the town's layered history. To my right, a wooden bookcase holds local history books and glossy Mount Dora Historical Museum merchandise. Opposite, a glass display case showcases keychains, postcards, and more books about the town's past. I step forward, my shoes scuffing softly against the worn floorboards.

Behind a small desk, a woman shuffles through a stack of papers. She looks up as I approach—short, likely in her late sixties, with a gray bob and thick, black-rimmed glasses perched on her nose. A kind smile deepens the soft lines of her face.

"Hi there, sweetie. Welcome to the Mount Dora Historical Museum," she greets, her voice lilting with a honeyed Southern accent. "Unless you're a student, it'll be $2 today. Anything you're interested in learning about?"

I fish two crumpled bills from my pocket and place them on the counter. "Just thought I'd check out the museum and maybe learn a bit more about the town's history."

Paula's eyes light up as she slides a blue photocopied leaflet across the desk toward me. "Well, you're in for a treat. This here's our little scavenger hunt—walks you through the town's past using artifacts around the room. Although they change things on me all the time; someone donates something new, and all the numbers get screwed up. If you need help, just ask. Oh, and if you need the restroom, we finally got one put in. Big deal for us, you know?"

I chuckle, clutching the leaflet. "Good to know. Thanks."

Paula steps out from behind the counter, gesturing for me to follow. "Now, take your time, but I'll hover a bit. Can't help myself," she says with a grin.

The first artifact is a cracked headstone propped against a wall, its engraving half-erased by time. Black-and-white photos line the walls, capturing snapshots of Mount Dora's earliest days. A horse-drawn fire hose sits in one corner, its giant red wheels rusted but still intact. Nearby, an assortment of hand-powdered tools sits on display: a sausage maker, an orange cleaner—bristles stiff with age—and a juice press, all reminders of the town's agricultural roots.

I wander deeper into the space, pausing at a full display case of Mount Dora police and fire patches, their vibrant colors dimmed by the glass. Paula drifts nearby, occasionally adding a tidbit about the town's history—who donated the artifacts, which families still live in town—but it's her familiarity with the place that fills the room with life.

Following the scavenger hunt's numbers, I weave my way to the museum's back left corner. Three jail cells, bars still intact, have been repurposed into mini-exhibits, each packed with dusty boards and relics from past displays. I step inside one, feeling the heavy air of its former purpose, then move toward the back wall.

A large glass display case dominates the space and inside is a meticulously crafted model of Hawthorn Manor. Every gabled rooftop and tiny shutter is there. My chest tightens. Next to it, old polaroids show the house mid-construction—its skeletal frame rising from the dirt, scaffolding clinging to its sides. A yellowed newspaper clipping sits beneath the photos, its headline bold: "Ballooning Lumber Prices Double Cost of Hawthorn Estate."

"Biggest project Mount Dora ever saw," Paula's voice floats over my shoulder. "George Hawthorn spared no expense. They say the whole town stopped to watch it go up. Still one of the largest and most expensive projects 'round here."

I stare at the photographs. Filthy laborers stand with the house behind them, working away on a dream that Nate and I now own. It's an odd, surreal feeling that fills me with a surprising sense of pride. Our house is important, and by proxy, we could be too.

"They planned to fill it with kids, you know," Paula adds, her voice softening. "Didn't quite work out that way."

A lump forms in my throat, but I swallow it down. "Do you have anything about what happened? To them, I mean?"

She hesitates before answering. "Not much on the official record. But folks talk. You should—"

The museum door opens with a gust of warm air and a tall man steps inside. His silver hair gleams under the overhead lights, streaks of dark gray cutting through the silver. His sharp gray eyes sweep the room before settling on me.

"Well hello there!," Paula whispers before pausing, her eyes narrowing slightly as if realizing something. "You know, I didn't even get your name."

"Margot," I reply. "Margot Bennett."

The moment my name leaves my lips, something shifts. Recognition flickers across Paula's face. "Doctor, this is Margot Bennett. Margot, this is Doctor Raymond Whitfield, he owns a practice right here in town."

The man closes the distance with a kind smile on his face and an extended hand. "So, you're the new owner of the beloved Hawthorn Manor, huh? Congratulations. Beautiful home."

I shake his hand, the grip firm, almost clinical. "Thank you so much. The wild part is my husband and I actually bought Hawthorn Manor without ever stepping foot inside. We found the listing online while still in Maryland. We needed a fresh start, so we called the realtor and made an offer. Honestly, I didn't know much about the house—certainly not how beloved it seems to be here."

Paula beams. "Well, it's wonderful to have someone new in town, especially someone willing to take care of that house. The way things ended for the Hawthorns was sudden and tragic, but we're all pretty excited to see it lived in again."

Dr. Whitfield nods. "It's a part of the town's soul, in a way. Seeing it empty for so long was hard on folks."

Paula leans closer, pointing to a small window in the museum's front door. "You can even see it from here—up on that hill."

I step closer to the glass and, sure enough, through the trees and over rooftops, I spot Hawthorn Manor's steep gables rising above the town.

Turning back, I ask, "Did either of you know the Hawthorns well? Like I said, I don't know much about them or the house when we purchased it, and clearly—" I point to the display case featuring a model of my new home. "I should better understand the history we've inherited."

Paula sighs. "We both went to elementary school with George and Cecilia. We stayed friends into adulthood. After Cecilia's death, George became a recluse. No one saw him, but sometimes, late at night, you could see lights on in the house, hear tools clanging—he was always tinkering with something. He loved building things, always went big for Halloween decorations or the Fourth of July parade floats."

"But then," Dr. Whitfield adds, "the lights stopped. No sounds, nothing. The police did a wellness check but found the place empty. No note, no trace. Instead of losing one friend, we lost two."

I hesitate before asking, "What do you think happened to him?"

Paula speaks first.

"I don't think anyone knows for sure, but I like to think he simply packed up a few things and left. He may have felt that he needed a fresh start somewhere without Cecilia's death tainting everything around him" she said.

I nod in agreement before turning to Dr. Whitfield for his theory, but his gaze is drifting, clearly not present.

"Doctor?" I say gently in an effort to draw him back into the conversation. But he remains far away, somewhere else.

I feel awkward now, uncomfortable, like I've overstayed my welcome here. I pull the treasure map from my pocket, thank Paula for the experience and consider the Doctor one more time before I turn away. I'm two steps away from the door when Dr. Whitfield touches my shoulder, light but deliberate.

His sharp gray eyes flick to the map in my hand, a cold curiosity visible in them. "Where did you get that?"

His newfound intensity puts me off balance and I struggle to form the right words. "Found it in some documents at the house. It's my next mystery."

He stares between me and the map for a moment too long before Paula breaks the silence with a chuckle. "Well, if you find any treasure, be sure to cut us in!"

I laugh, pleased to be exiting the odd exchange. I thank them both again, and head out into the sun. The map feels like electricity in my hands. Wherever it's leading me to, I'm getting closer. I can feel it.

5

The Florida sun is unrelenting, its golden rays baking the streets of Mount Dora as I follow the map's directions toward the lake. The humidity clings to my skin, thick and suffocating, turning even the simplest movements into a slow, sticky effort. My grip tightens around the crinkled map, its edges soft from handling. I walk past the quirky charm of Mount Dora's streets, where pastel-colored homes and swaying palm trees stand in contrast to the mystery I'm chasing.

I enjoy my stroll through the beautiful, historic town. Charming shops like this no longer exist in big cities; it makes me happy that Amazon has yet to claim this slice of paradise from the world.

I pass by a curious little trinket shop, screaming for attention. Its large display window is crammed with a strange but cheerful collection—potted plants, baskets of fruit, gardening tools, and a spinning wire rack filled with bingo cards and dabbers. Glossy magazines featuring strong, shirtless men, shelves stacked with books, and a row of colorful watering cans catch my eye. Tucked between them are old camera antiques and framed photographs—JFK in Dallas, a serene beach at sunset, and a black-and-white photo of Mount Dora's town square.

A wooden sign swings above the entrance, painted in bright, playful letters: *Frankie's Favorites.*

I step inside, the soft chime of the door announcing my arrival. The air is thick with the scent of blooming flowers and old paper. Shelves lined with snacks, drinks, and an impressive collection of antiques stretch along the walls. Among them, I spot a sturdy metal bingo roller and a set of old metal reusable punched bingo cards. A goofy sign hangs nearby, depicting a burly cartoon bouncer with the words *"Bingo or Bounce!"* and a thumb pointed to the exit. Against the far wall stands an old Coca-Cola dispenser, its red paint faded but still gleaming under the store's warm lighting. The blend of vintage and eccentricity makes me grin.

Behind the counter stands an older woman with charming glasses, long black hair, and a bright yellow apron covered in embroidered flowers. She wipes her hands on a dish towel and eyes me with a playful sparkle.

"Hi there, I'm curious—what kind of store is this, exactly?" I ask, unable to hide my smile.

She grins, then gestures dramatically toward the sign outside. "This, sweetheart, is *Frankie's Favorites.* Everything you see here is something I love. I'm Francesca Jeann Pruitt, but everyone calls me Frankie." She winks. "I love gardening. I love reading. I love bingo. I love history. I love strong, half-nude men. Oh, and I love eating." She pats the countertop. "So, voilà, I made Frankie's Favorites."

I chuckle, wandering through the aisles. I grab a cold bottle of water from a vintage cooler and a packet of sunflower seeds —something bright and cheerful. Then, my eyes land on a sturdy garden trowel on a nearby shelf. I glance down at my own hands, and the realization hits—even if I actually find the location of the X on the map, I have nothing to dig with! Feeling sheepish but incredibly lucky, I pick up the garden trowel.

As I approach the counter, Frankie eyes my selection approvingly. "Good choices. Nothing like a little digging to uncover life's best surprises."

I laugh, handing her the cash. "I have a feeling you're right."

With my purchases in hand, I step back into the Florida sun, Frankie's quirky charm lingering with me as I continue toward the docks.

As I approach the shoreline, the wind blows my hair in every direction. A foldable sign sits halfway down the dock, its paint chipped but bold: "Rusty Anchor Boat Tours—Explore Mount Dora's Beautiful Waters!" Beneath it, the board lists various tours: *Sunset Cruise: $40, Private Lake Tour: $60, Wildlife Adventure: $50.*

A man stands on the dock, squinting out over the lake, a faded baseball cap shading his face. He appears right at home with tanned skin and broad shoulders. I clear my throat.

"Hi there! I'm looking for Donald?" I ask.

He turns, his face crinkling into a smile before spitting into a stale-looking coffee cup. "That's me—your fourth-generation Native Floridian boat guide. But you can just call me Donny. You looking for a ride?"

I pull the map from my pocket and unfold it, smoothing it out in front of him. "I'm hoping you can take me here," pointing to the X.

Donny leans over the map, his brow furrowing. "Interesting. This doesn't look like any of my usual tour spots. What's out there?"

I hesitate. "Just... following a scavenger hunt."

He chuckles, but his eyes stay sharp. "Huh. Well, alright. Normally, a short trip like that's forty bucks, but with this wind picking up, gotta charge you an extra ten."

I wince at the markup but nod before handing over two twenties and a ten. "Done."

We set off in a sturdy pontoon boat, the engine sputtering to life as it pulls away from the dock. The lake stretches wide, glittering under the afternoon sun, its surface rippling in the breeze. As we cruise forward, I glance to my right. Hawthorn Manor looms above the treetops, its towering gables clearly visible—even from here—sitting at about four o'clock from our direction.

The shoreline passes by, and I notice massive concrete tunnels fixed into the retaining walls along the water's edge. They yawn open like hollow mouths.

"Storm run-offs," Donny says, catching my stare. "Keeps the town from flooding during hurricane season."

I nod, but my focus drifts when I spot something near the water's edge—a broken, overturned rowboat wedged among the tall sawgrass. My chest tightens.

"That's the old Hawthorn rowboat," Donny notes. "The wife drowned out there some years ago. Folks say the hubby might've gone out in that same boat and never came back. If you ask me, gator got him."

I force a polite smile, more out of courtesy than amusement, and push away the unsettling thought.

Moments before we dock, Hawthorn Manor vanishes behind the dense forest, the steep hill between it and us resembling more of a cliff than a hill.

"Twenty more, and I'll wait for you," Donny offers.

I shake my head. "I'll take the long way back."

He raises an eyebrow and shrugs. "Suit yourself."

As the boat putters away, I turn toward the dense foliage. The hike will be long, but I have the energy to burn.

I trek through the woods, tracing the map with careful precision. Sunlight filters through the trees, dappling the undergrowth. After what feels like hours, I spot the landmark I'm looking for—a peculiar-looking tree with red, peeling bark and naked limbs.

"This is it," I whisper.

My heart hammers in my chest as I glance around, making sure no one's watching before I step into the secluded patch next to the iconic tree. It's quiet here—eerily so—tucked away from the buzz of tourists and the hum of town life. The air smells damp and earthy, heavy with the storm's aftermath. I pull the small garden trowel from Frankie's Favorites out of my bag and kneel, brushing aside a layer of slick, fallen leaves.

The soil is soft, the storm's gift, and I work quickly, my fingers moving with a sharp, eager rhythm. Each scrape of the trowel cuts deeper, the earth peeling back like layers of some long-forgotten story. I dig with purpose.

Chunk.

My mind starts to drift. The steady rhythm of metal-biting soil drags me backward.

Smack.

Lila's terrified eyes flash in my mind, wide and pleading. Her tiny body flinching as the blow lands.

Chunk.

I freeze, the past bleeding into the present. The dirt in front of me isn't dirt anymore—it's the stage of every failure I've tried to bury. My breath stutters, shallow and quick. I dig harder.

Smack.

The sounds tangle together. My trowel scrapes deeper,

faster. I tell myself it's the thrill—the hunt—but the lie is thin, breaking beneath the pressure of my pulse.

Chunk.

Lila's cries echo in my head, raw and sharp. My hands tremble as I dig, the soil giving way in jagged chunks, the rhythm turning frantic.

Then—

Rustling.

I freeze. The trowel is still gripped tight in my hand, its warm handle grounding me. My ears strain, the world narrowing into that single sound. It comes again—closer.

And then the hiss.

I whip my head towards the water. A massive alligator slides forward, its scaled back barely cresting the surface.

Its glassy eyes fixed on me.

Panic slams into me. I scramble to my feet, mud sucking at my shoes. The alligator surges closer, its powerful tail cutting through the water like a blade. I stumble, my foot snagging on a root, and hit the ground hard. The trowel flies from my grip.

The hiss deepens. The gator's wide jaws gape, and it lunges.

Adrenaline rockets through me. I push up, legs scrambling for purchase and bolt. My feet slip on wet leaves as I tear through the trees. Branches claw at my arms and face, but I don't stop. I can hear it—crashing through the underbrush behind me.

The trees are thin. I break into a clearing, legs burning, heart thundering in my ears. The alligator halts at the tree line, its cold eyes locked on me.

I collapse into the grass, my body trembling, my chest heaving. My vision blurs, nausea curling low in my gut. I sit there, breathing hard, until my hands stop shaking. Slowly, I rise, my limbs heavy with exhaustion, embarrassment radiating from my face. Each step towards home feels like an epic failure, a childish treasure hunt that almost killed me.

I make my way through historic Mount Dora, the embarrassment continuing as I pass others on the street, certainly staring at the muddy mess I am. By the time Hawthorn Manor comes into view, my legs ache, and my breath comes in shallow gasps. The house looms, cold and still. I walk the last stretch, the gravel crunching underfoot.

Walter is in the driveway, tinkering with something, but his head snaps up when he sees me. Concern darkens his features as he hurries over.

"Margot, what on earth happened to you?"

"I... I was down by the lake," I manage, my throat raw. "An alligator came after me."

His face pales. "Margot! That's no place to be this time of year. The females nest along the shore—get too close, and they'll kill to protect their eggs."

"I didn't know." My voice is small, the weight of my stupidity sinking in.

"You're lucky to be standing here, goodness gracious," he says, his voice softer now. Promise me you'll stay away from that lake."

"I promise."

His features relax a fraction. "Good. You look like hell. Go clean up."

A weak laugh slips out. "Thanks, Walter."

Inside, the cool air hits me like a wave. I sink onto the couch, my body aching. I grab my phone, my thumb hovering over Nate's contact before I press call.

It rings. Once. Twice. Voicemail.

I hang up, the hollowness settling deep. I could've died today, and he didn't even pick up.

My hands shake as I unfold the map from my pocket. The

thrill that once tugged me into this game is gone, stripped away by the raw edge of reality. I fold it back up, stand, and return it back to its hidden resting place beneath the floorboard.

The hunt can wait.

For now, survival is enough.

6

I sit on the edge of my bed, my heart heavy, my phone cold and useless in my hand. I reach Nate's voicemail again—just as I expected. The silence in our master bedroom is suffocating, pressing against my chest like the heavy air before a storm. I'd been hoping, foolishly, for something more than his curt text: *"Stuck in a meeting. Will call later."* No warmth, no concern, just empty words on a screen.

I set the phone down, the screen fading to black as if it had even given up. Outside, I hear the rhythmic thudding of Walter working on the roof, each hammer strike like a heartbeat in this hollow house. The storm had ripped through the place, leaving the roof battered and the rooms damp with the smell of wet wood. Walter had done what he could, patching things here and there, but the house was like me—barely holding together.

The damp scent drifts upstairs, mingling with the faint buzz of oscillating fans Walter must have set up. I try to focus on the sound, but my mind races. I need to do something, anything, to break through the oncoming cloud of depression I can feel seeping into my chest.

"Come on, Margot. No one likes a pity party," I mutter, forcing myself to my feet.

I head downstairs. The kitchen tempts me with the half-eaten pint of Ben & Jerry's Gimme S'more, whispering promises of sweet, mindless comfort. But the living room—soggy boxes, overturned tables, chaos—demands my attention. I eye the ice cream longingly, but the living room wins.

"Not fair, Ben and Jerry," I smirk. "We'll hang out later—you, me, and our friends from 90 Day Fiancé."

I tackle the mess, setting the side tables upright and drying off my lamps. The boxes, though—so many damn boxes—are a different beast. They shouldn't even be here. Thanks to the movers' mix-up, my office boxes ended up here instead of in the study. I heave one onto the table, the cardboard soggy and heavy, dust and water stains streaking its surface.

The tape gives way under the box cutter, the flaps springing open to reveal my past—case notes, memos, CPS paperwork—my old life—the one I left behind. Or maybe the one that left me.

I shouldn't do this. I shouldn't dig through this stuff. But I can't help it. I rifle through until a name jumps out—*Lila Griffith.*

I freeze. Her case file sits right there, ink smudged from water damage, but the words are still legible. I trace my finger over the notes I wrote—hopeful, stupid notes. *"Warm, stable foster home. History of long-term placements. Ideal environment for adjustment."*

I swallow hard. I remember how confident I was in placing Lila with the Thompsons. I'd been so sure they were perfect. But the bedwetting, the avoidance, the broken eye contact—it had all been there. I'd seen the signs and convinced myself they were just part of the adjustment period. I wanted it to be fine. I *needed* it to be fine.

But it wasn't.

The reality of it crashes over me again. Lila was hurting. And I failed her.

I shove the papers back into the box, my throat tightening, fighting back unshed tears. It's too much. I can't—

But then, that feeling—that prickling, spine-tingling sensation like something is watching me. My breath catches. I turn, my eyes scanning the dim room.

Nothing.

Still, the feeling lingers, heavy and cold.

"Jesus, Margot. Pull it together," I whisper.

But I can't shake it. It's that childhood fear, waking up at night, certain there's something at the foot of your bed. Your eyes haven't adjusted yet, but you *know* something's there.

I force a shaky laugh. "You're fine. You're fine."

I turn to leave, to leave this room and its ghosts, but my foot lands on a familiar warped floorboard. It groans under my weight, and I slowly stare down at the unspoken dare - *try again, Margot*. Slowly, I kneel and pry it up. My fingers brush against the brittle paper once again as if it always knew I'd come back.

I stare at it for a long time, my eyes tracing the lines I walked, the bold red "X" and the naked Indian tree. Then the alligator with its yellow eyes, hovering above the water, its snapping jaws, and the mud sucking at my legs—it all floods back, my pulse quickening. I fold the map halfway shut, my hands shaking. I should put it back, forget I ever found it, bury it again for the next owner to find.

But I don't.

Instead, I sit there on the cold, warped floor, the map open in my lap, my mind unraveling. Nate isn't here. He hasn't been here, not really, for a long time. Every ignored call and hollow text is a reminder that I'm alone in this house. And worse, I feel untethered, floating without purpose. My career is gone. My pride is gone. And whatever version of me that existed before, the one with purpose and drive, the one with reasons to really live—she's gone, too.

The emptiness is terrifying. It's always been here, floating just outside my peripheral vision. I've fallen victim to it at various times throughout my life, though I've always had something to anchor me, to keep me going. But now, sitting alone in a giant house that still feels strange and foreign... it feels like the kind of darkness that could swallow a person whole for good.

"What am I even doing here?" I whisper to no one.

I trace the X on the map with my fingertip, circling it repeatedly.

The thought claws at me, sharp and unrelenting.

If people exist without purpose, they stop existing altogether.

The words sit heavy in my chest. And for a split second, I wonder if that's already happened to me.

But then the house groans around me, the wind rattling the windows, and something shifts. Not outside, but inside me. A flicker—weak but present.

I look at the map again. Maybe it's stupid. Maybe it's dangerous. Hell, I almost died last time. But at least that day, I *felt* something. Adrenaline. Terror. Purpose.

I refold the map, slipping it into my pocket.

The house creaks again, almost like it's cheering my recommitment like it needs its secrets revealed.

"I'm still here," I whisper. "And as long as I'm still here, I'm going to keep searching—for answers, for purpose, for whatever parts are left of me."

7

I stare at the map, its worn edges curled from the sticky Florida humidity, the red "X" almost taunting me—daring me to try again. Walter's warning rings in my ears, his low voice reminding me of the gators, the danger. He made me promise not to go back to the lake. But here I am, already plotting my way there. I don't even know why I care if he finds out. But I do. There's something about him—the way he genuinely seems to care—that makes me want to keep that promise. But I can't, not today.

I peer out the kitchen window. Walter's out front, orchestrating the arrival of the contractors, his hands gesturing as he talks to them about the new hardwood install. Perfect. I slip out the back door, staying low, my heart hammering with a childlike mix of fear and excitement. The house looms behind me, its dark windows hollow and knowing, like it's watching.

I dart to the remains of the old shed, where tools are scattered around like forgotten relics. My fingers close around a shovel handle, cold and rough against my palm. I glance back—Walter's still out front, distracted. Good. I wrench the shovel free and take off across the yard to my car, my breath coming in heavy waves.

I pull out the keys to my old, yellow VW Beetle, the shovel hidden beneath a tattered blanket in the backseat. The engine sputters to life with a familiar, comforting rattle. Rolling down the window, I spot Walter out front, still deep in conversation with the contractors. I lean out and shout, "Running into town for some groceries!"

Walter barely looks up but gives me a thumbs-up before turning back to his clipboard, scribbling signatures onto work orders. Perfect.

I pull out of the gravel driveway, my heart racing. The tires crunch over the drive as I steer toward the narrow road leading back to town, back to good 'ol Donny at the Rusty Anchor. The Florida sun cuts through the trees in sharp beams, dappling the windshield as I descend the winding road.

I park the Beetle behind a thick cluster of trees by the shoreline, tucked far enough to hide it from casual view. Even though I'm an adult, fully capable of handling what I'm about to do, the thought of Walter finding out sends a ripple of anxiety through me. I can't face his disappointment. So, I leave the car there, hidden, just in case.

I step out, pulling the shovel from beneath the tattered blanket in the backseat. I head back toward the dock, where I hope I'll find Donny. The scene is exactly as it was yesterday—same creaking boards, the same faint smell of gasoline and lake water—but today, the air is different. The wind's died down, the sky a flawless stretch of blue.

Donny spots me before I even call out. "Back again, huh?"

I give him a half-smile. "Can you take me to the same spot as yesterday?"

He squints at me, running a hand down his weathered face. "Forty bucks this time."

I hand him sixty.

He frowns, holding the bills up like he's checking for counterfeits. "I said forty."

"The extra twenty's for you to stay this time."

His eyes flick to mine, gauging whether I'm serious, and then he shrugs. "You got it."

I climb into the boat, the lake's stillness stretching out before me, beautiful and unnerving all at once. I don't say anything else as Donny cranks the engine, steering us toward the far shore. I grip the shovel's handle tighter, bracing myself for what's next.

The shoreline finally comes into view, with the Hawthorn's overturned boat to my right, with Hawthorn Manor still jutting out above the trees for another few moments before disappearing. Donny slows the boat, cutting the engine with a low grumble.

"Hang tight, Donny," I say, gripping the handle of the shovel tighter. "Hopefully, I'll be back in just a few minutes."

He tips his cap back, squinting at me. "You got it. But don't take too long—on a nice day like this, someone else is bound to want a tour."

I offer a small grin before hopping out. My boots sink slightly into the damp shoreline as I make my way inland. I am grateful for the larger shovel in my hand this time, as opposed to the tiny trowel I left behind yesterday.

I follow the same path I took before, weaving through the tall grass and low-hanging branches, each step stirring the familiar scent of wet earth and moss. The sun filters through the canopy above, casting fragmented shadows on the ground, and the stillness of the day feels both peaceful and unnerving.

Before long, I find it—the gumbo limbo tree, its red, peeling bark unmistakable against the green. And there, right beside it, is my freshly dug hole from yesterday, the dirt still loose and dark around its edges.

This time, I don't jump right in. I crouch low, my body tense as I scan the area. My ears strain for any sign of movement, any low hiss that might betray a gator lurking nearby. Minutes stretch thin as I wait, the air soft with the faint rustle of leaves.

Nothing.

Releasing a slow breath, I rise and plant the shovel into the dirt. The blade sinks deep, and I begin to dig, muscles straining as the ground gives way under the steady rhythm of my efforts. The sun climbs higher, its heat heavy on my back, but I keep going—this time without hesitation.

My hands blister, dirt wedges under my fingernails, but I keep going, the same relentless rhythm as before. And then—

Thud.

Metal hits wood. My pulse skyrockets. I drop to my knees, clawing at the dirt until the edges of a chest emerge. It's real. My hands tremble as I clear more soil, revealing the ornate metal fittings. Worn but elegant—like something out of another century.

But it's locked. Of course, it is.

I grab a stone and slam it against the old, thick padlock. The clang echoes across the clearing way too loudly. I freeze, listening. Nothing but the quiet lapping of water. Good. Another hit and the lock holds firm.

I yank the chest onto firmer ground, my muscles screaming. It's heavier than I thought, awkward and unbalanced. But I can't leave it here—not where anyone could stumble across it. With sheer will, I drag it back toward the shoreline, the chest scraping over roots and rocks, leaving a rough trail behind me.

When I finally reach the dock, Donny's still there, leaning against the side of the boat, chewing on a toothpick. His eyes widen as he catches sight of me, dragging the chest.

"What in the world is that?" he barks, straightening. "What are you doin' out here, lady?!"

I don't answer. Instead, I dig into my pocket and pull out another twenty, waving it in the air. "Help me get it into the boat."

Donny blinks but snatches the bill. "You're trouble, you know that?" Still, he jumps down, grabbing one side of the chest as I grip the other.

Together, we heave it into the boat with a heavy thud. The wood creaks under its weight, but it holds. We sit in silence as Donny starts the motor and steers us back across the water, the stillness only broken by the soft churn of the engine. I can feel Donny's eyes flicking between me and the chest, the questions hanging thick in the air—but he keeps his mouth shut. A lovely trait I won't soon forget about him.

When we dock, I hop out before he can say anything, hurrying up the dock toward the road. My VW Beetle is still hidden between the trees, its bright yellow paint nearly glowing against the green. I get in, throw it into reverse, and let it roll backward down the steep hill, arriving gently at the dock's edge.

I pop the hatch and jog back down. Donny's already got the chest halfway out of the boat, grumbling under his breath. We each take a side, heaving it toward the Beetle. As we lift it into the hatch, the car sinks a few inches under the weight, the suspension groaning in protest.

"If there's gold in there, you owe me a few nuggets," Donny mutters, wiping sweat from his brow.

"Thanks, Donny," I say, slamming the hatch closed. I hand him another twenty before sliding into the driver's seat.

I give him a quick wink. "You didn't see me today."

He tips his cap and returns the wink. "Wouldn't dream of it."

With that, I peel away, the weight of the chest pressing heavy in the back, but somehow, even heavier is the storm of questions now swirling in my head.

When the spires of Hawthorn Manor peek through the trees, I could cry with relief. Almost there. I drive my old yellow VW Beetle along the winding road, pulling alongside the incoming truck before swinging around and backing behind the manor.

I back the Beetle up to the door, the tires crunching over gravel as I ease it into place. The chest in the back shifts slightly with the car's movement, its weight pressing heavy against the hatch.

Glancing toward the front of the house, I see Walter still engrossed in directing the truck, his clipboard waving in the air. Good. I throw the car into park, jump out, and pop the hatch. With a grunt, I drag the chest out, its metal fittings scraping against the car's interior.

I haul it through the mudroom, every thud of wood against tile echoing like a siren in my ears. My heart races as I shut the back door behind me, the chest now safely inside, hidden from any wandering eyes.

The climb upstairs is brutal. The chest is incredibly awkward to carry myself, its rectangle shape awkward and punishing, the metal edges digging into my palms as I drag it step by agonizing step. I time each pull with the loud clatter and banging from the contractors below, using the cover of dropped tools and shouted instructions to muffle the scraping sounds echoing through the manor.

Sweat pours down my back, my breath coming in ragged gasps as I brace my foot against each step, yanking the chest upward. It slams into the risers with dull thuds, the old wood creaking beneath the weight. My arms burn, my hands slick with sweat, but I can't stop—not here, not where anyone could stumble across me.

The contractors shout something to Walter outside, and I seize the moment, heaving the chest up the last few steps just as a hammer strikes metal, masking the final crash. I barely make it to the landing before my legs give out, and I collapse beside it, my breath wild and uneven.

I hook my fingers under the rough metal fittings and drag it inch by inch down the hallway, each tug sending a dull thud through the old floorboards. With one final grunt, I reach my bedroom door and haul the chest inside. It scrapes loudly against the hardwood as I drag it into the center of the room. I kick the door shut behind me, the soft click of the latch sounding impossibly loud in the sudden stillness.

The chest sits there, muddy and ancient, like it belongs here. Like it's been waiting.

But I need the key. I found the chest through clues hidden in this house, so logically, the key is likely to be here, too. George Hawthorn wouldn't have buried it somewhere random. It would be concealed, just like the map.

I scan the room, my mind racing. My thoughts snap back to the map hidden under the living room floorboards. Could the key have been there, too? My stomach sinks. The contractors. The torn-up floor.

I bolt downstairs, every step a hollow thud echoing in my ears. The living room is stripped bare, the subfloor exposed, and the wooden boards are gone, hauled off as construction debris. My heart pounds as I dart to the nearest contractor, my voice rough and desperate.

"Where's the trash from the demolition?"

He barely glances up from his clipboard, jerking a thumb toward the driveway. "Dumpster out front."

I don't hesitate.

The metal dumpster towers like a rusted beast, filled with splintered wood and rusted nails. I scramble up the side, hauling myself in, my hands clawing through the debris, breath tight in my chest. The sharp stink of old wood and metal fills my lungs, but I keep digging.

Minutes stretch, my pulse pounding in my ears, until—

A glint.

I dive for it, but my foot slips. Pain explodes as a nail pierces my sneaker, driving deep into my foot. I cry out, tears springing hot and fast, but I yank my foot free, blood slick against the torn fabric. I don't stop. I can't. My fingers close around cold, heavy metal.

The key. Except, it isn't a key at all; it's a nail plate—rusted and jagged. My heart sinks.

For a moment, I just stand there, my breath shallow, blood still seeping from the hole in my sneaker.

The ache in my foot sharpens, reality crashing back in. I look around the dumpster—splintered boards, shards of wet wood, the head from a broken hammer—but nothing else gleams beneath the debris. Nothing that could be the key.

Defeat coils tight in my chest. I'm bleeding, tired, and the damn chest is still locked. Crawling to the edge, I haul myself out of the dumpster, boots scraping against rusted metal, every movement sending sharp jolts of pain through my foot.

I land heavily on the pavement, staggering before limping toward the house, utterly embarrassed. The cool air inside barely registers as I drag myself through the foyer, the weight of failure pressing in heavy. I rest a hand against the wall for balance, feeling the warm trickle of blood through my sock.

No key. No answers. Just me—lost, bleeding, and more confused than ever.

I'm half-hunched over the sink when Walter appears, his face a perfect blend of concern and disapproval.

"Oh no, what happened this time?"

I hesitate, the sting in my foot sharp and unforgiving, but I muster a smile. "Lost something in the dumpster," I lie, my voice light despite the throbbing pain shooting through my ankle. I wince as I shift my weight, the pain betraying me.

Walter's brow furrows, and before I can wave him off, he steps in closer. "Sit down," he instructs, his tone soft but unarguable.

I don't fight it. I sink into a dusty chair as he crouches in front of me. His hands, rough from years of manual work, surprise me with their gentleness as he inspects my foot. Every dab of the cloth, every careful swipe cleaning the wound, makes my throat tighten. This was the kind of care Nate should be giving me—the kind of presence I miss. But here I was, with Walter, the landscaper, the stranger, showing me more kindness than my own husband had in months. My chest aches, and I blink hard, refusing to let the tears win.

Looking for something, anything to distract me, my eyes fall on Walter's baseball cap. It dawns on me that I've never seen him without it. "Walter, without sounding rude, can I ask about your hat? It's the Yankees, but I always assumed you grew up here in Florida."

A small smirk crosses his lips. "Born and raised here, yes ma'am. But my dad was a huge baseball fan, adored Babe Ruth. 'Love a team for its players, not its location, son' is what he'd always tell me."

He pulls the hat from his head and flips it upside down for me to see. "He even met Babe once, had him sign this very hat right here." He points to a faded marking that says "Bambino."

I don't care about baseball at all, but seeing Walter cherish something of his father's adds another layer of depth and kindness to the man in front of me.

"But enough about me. *You*, Mrs. Margot, shouldn't be

digging through dumpsters," Walter teases, a smile tugging at the corner of his mouth.

I let out a soft laugh, the tension easing for a beat. "Yeah, clearly not my brightest moment."

He wraps the bandage neatly, his hands still steady and sure, before rising to his feet and dusting off his khakis. A wave of gratitude washes over me, but it comes laced with sadness —how starved I'd been for even this simple, human connection.

I bite my lip, debating whether to speak up as Walter starts gathering his things. But curiosity claws at me, the thrill of the hunt outweighing caution. "Walter?"

He pauses, glancing down at me. "Yes, ma'am?"

I swallow. "What was George Hawthorn like?"

Walter's expression shifts, softening into something nostalgic. "George? He was a good man. Real generous. Kind. But there was always this... weight on him. Had a rough childhood, lost a lot early on. I think that's why he loved games and puzzles so much—like he was trying to reclaim something he'd been robbed of."

My heart beats faster. "What do you mean by games? Like children's games?"

Walter chuckles under his breath. "No, no. He'd turn everything into a mystery. Loved hiding things, leaving riddles. It was his way of making life more interesting. Like, one time, there was this roadside library in town—you know, those little book boxes? —and one morning, all the books inside were gone. Instead, there was a single note left behind, and before noon, half the town's kids were running around, solving riddles, trying to find the missing books. Took them hours, but they finally found them stashed in a P.O. box at the post office. And get this—every single book had a dollar bill tucked inside as a reward."

Walter's stories paint such a vivid picture that I couldn't help but laugh, the sound escaping me before I could stop it. "George sounds like a great person," I say, the warmth of admiration threading through my voice. "Creative, generous... a mind that loved giving as much as it loved the mystery."

"Absolutely," Walter confirms with a nod. "It was like a constant treasure hunt around here."

I force a grateful smile. "Thanks, Walter. That really helps me understand the legacy Nate and I have inherited here."

He studies me for a moment, a flicker of pride warming his features. He doesn't say it outright, but it's there— the small, almost imperceptible smile in the way his eyes soften. He was proud to have known the Hawthorns. Then he pats my shoulder gently. "Just... be careful, alright? And stay outta dumpsters."

I laugh more genuinely this time. "I'll try. Thanks for everything, Walter."

As he leaves, my mind is already racing. George Hawthorn loved puzzles. If he'd hidden the map beneath the floorboards, perhaps the key was never under the floor to begin with. Maybe it was hidden somewhere equally clever. Somewhere, he'd want someone worthy to find.

I push myself up, limping toward the stairs, each step a dull throb in my foot. I scan the living room—the aged bookshelf in the corner, the ornate wooden fireplace, the old grandfather clock near the window. So many possibilities.

George wouldn't make it obvious. He'd want it to be a challenge. My gaze drifts over the intricate carvings on the front entrance's doorway—maybe one of the flourishes twists or slides open to reveal a hidden compartment. The heavy curtains hang awkwardly near a vent—could something be tucked behind them? I scan the chandelier overhead, wondering if George had ever tampered with its base, hiding something in plain sight. Even the old grandfather clock seemed suspicious; perhaps its hollow base held more than gears and springs. The possibilities multiply, each one more tempting than the last.

I can feel it in my bones—there is a puzzle here waiting to be solved. And I am going to solve it.

8

With a renewed sense of determination, I dive into my search. If George Hawthorn had hidden the key, it would have been somewhere clever, somewhere that fit a man who thrived on mysteries and games —just like the map.

I start in the library. It's grand—towering bookshelves stretch to the ceiling, dark wooden panels gleaming under dust-speckled sunlight that filters through heavy curtains. The scent of old paper and varnish lingers in the air. The shelves are a blend of the Hawthorns' books, left behind when George disappeared, and the ones Nate and I brought with us. Making this library my space was the first thing I did when we moved in. I wanted somewhere that felt like mine, somewhere I could breathe. I run my fingers along the spines, a mix of dusty old volumes and my own well-loved favorites, feeling the weight of two histories colliding. I randomly pull out a few titles, hoping for that telltale click of a hidden mechanism. Nothing. I sigh, replacing the books, and step back, scanning the room.

This house is stunning. It radiates a kind of elegance from a long-gone era—intricate moldings, hand-carved details in the woodwork, stained-glass windows painting fractured rainbows on the floor. Even as I move through the halls, there's this sense that the walls remember everything. I trace the graceful curve of the banister, run my hand over the delicate carvings framing the doors, and I can't help but admire the craftsmanship. The Hawthorns loved this place. It's obvious. And somehow, that only deepens my pride in being this home's latest owner.

Next, I head to the study—smaller and cozier. A heavy oak desk dominates the room, its surface littered with papers. I push them aside, rifling through drawers, my fingers hunting for anything out of place. I yank open the central drawer, my hand brushing inside, searching for something, anything different. I freeze as my fingertips roll across a foreign shape. It's smooth and round, much like an old-fashioned doorbell, recessed in its metal housing.

Heart hammering, I press it.

A faint click echoes in the silence. The right side of the desk slowly crawls open, revealing a hollowed-out compartment. I can't help but think about how insane this actually is—a treasure hunt in my own home. I dig inside—there's a worn baseball glove, probably George's from his childhood, a photo of a little girl with "A.H. 1976" scrawled on the back, and a stack of old newspaper clippings about George's citrus grove business. It's like holding pieces of his life, fragments of someone I never met but somehow feel connected to.

But this isn't what I need.

I replace everything carefully and keep going. I'm not about to stop now—not after finding a hidden compartment tucked away in plain sight. My hunch was more than just a feeling— I'm actually onto something. If there was one secret here, how many more are waiting for me? I mentally scan the house, picturing every nook and cranny that could hold the next surprise.

I find myself in the next room, where giant windows flood the space with soft light. A built-in bench stretches the length of the far wall, with a backdrop of rich, deep red brick. I run my hands along the rough mortar binding the bricks, running my fingertips along the uneven lines, feeling for anything out of place. One brick shifts under my touch—a subtle, almost imperceptible give. My pulse spikes. I wedge my fingers in and work it loose, dust swirling in the air as it comes free. Tucked behind it, in a hollow pocket, sits a tiny, carved wooden box.

I pull it out, my heart racing, and pry it open. Inside, there are only a few tarnished coins and a delicate, dried flower pressed between brittle parchment. Not what I was hoping for, but still, it tugs at something deep inside me. Every discovery here feels like unlocking the past, peeling back layers of lives that once filled these rooms with laughter, love, and loss.

Hours slip by. I lose track of them, following hunches, studying the house like it's a living, breathing thing. I circle back to the study eventually, frustration tightening in my chest. I sit at the desk, fingers drumming out a restless rhythm. I have to be missing something. I scan the room again—my gaze lands on the bookshelf. I checked the library's many shelves, but not the two large bookcases here.

I stand, moving toward them.

A specific book catches my eye on the top shelf, almost out of reach. Its spine is marked with a golden towering tree. I reach out with the intention of pulling it down for further inspection, but the book stops before it can be pulled out entirely. Instead, the top corner pulls towards me about an inch, followed by an audible click.

Bingo.

I scan the room, searching for any change. What shifted when I pulled the book? What was different? I search high and low, but nothing stands out. Frustration creeps in. There's something I'm missing—I can feel it. I take a step back, eyes narrowing at the bookcase.

I skim through the other titles: *The Princess Bride, The Adventures of Huckleberry Finn, The Divine Comedy,* and even *The Hitchhiker's Guide to the Galaxy.* Then, tucked between two hefty encyclopedias, I spot another book like the one I pulled before. But instead of a flourishing tree on its spine, this one shows a withered, skeletal version. Of course—it's a sequence.

Adrenaline kicks in. I scramble across the two cases, scanning the shelves, until I spot a third book—this one showing a tiny sapling. Perfect. I push them all back into place, then pull them in order: sapling, full-grown tree, dead tree.

A deep click echoes through the room. A hidden gear shifts, followed by the low creak of the bookshelf as it slowly swings open, revealing a dark passageway. My throat tightens as I stare into the black void. My hand trembles slightly as I pull out my phone and flick on the flashlight, the narrow beam slicing into the shadows.

Holy shit, this is really happening.

I step through.

The passage is narrow, stale air brushing against my skin. It leads to a small room—musty, forgotten. The walls aren't plastered; instead, the laths are visible, featuring exposed wiring, cobwebs, and dust. Newspapers hang from the walls, yellowed and curling at the edges, mixed with faded photographs and handwritten notes pinned in a chaotic collage. It honestly feels a lot like the Mount Dora Historical Museum—endless layers of history hanging on the walls. But I barely give it a second thought.

Instead, my eyes are drawn straight to the center of the room. There, resting on a low pedestal is a box—almost identical to the chest I dug up earlier. There's no question—it's linked to the larger chest. My pulse races as the pieces fall into place.

I approach slowly, my heart in my throat. My fingers tremble as I lift the lid.

Inside—

Two items.

The first is a Polaroid picture featuring a young woman standing proudly in front of Hawthorn Manor. Debris from the building still litters the front yard, marking it as a moment frozen in time—probably Cecilia Hawthorn, captured before she ever took her first step inside this very house.

The second—a thick, hefty key.

I gasp, snatching it up. The cool metal presses against my palm, sending pure electricity down my spine. It has to be a match for the chest's padlock. Relief and excitement collide inside me, and my chest tightens as I realize this could be it— the end of a hunt that's dragged on for days.

I don't waste a second.

I bolt out of the room, my footsteps echoing in the dark passage. My mind races. I'm so close—so damn close. The study blurs past me as I sprint up the stairs, the house groaning and creaking beneath my hurried steps.

My bedroom door slams shut behind me.

The chest sits in the center of the room, waiting.

I drop to my knees, the key clutched tight. My breath comes fast, ragged. I hesitate—just for a heartbeat—then shove the key into the lock.

It turns with a soft click.

The lid creaks open, and–

The stench hits me first—rot, decay, something ancient and foul. It's overwhelming. My stomach lurches. I gag, my throat tightening, but I force myself to look.

I shouldn't have.

The bile rises fast—I turn away, retching violently onto the floor. My body shakes as I wipe my mouth with the back of my hand, eyes watering.

I glance back into the chest.

Horror anchors me to the spot.

Whatever I expected—it wasn't this.

9

I know the human skull is made up of twenty-two distinct bones: eight cranial and fourteen facial. If I were to count the number of bones now staring up at me from the treasure chest, it would be roughly three hundred and fifty-two in total—or rather, sixteen skulls.

For a moment, I can't breathe. The foul smell is sharp, sour, and unmistakably human. It claws its way down my throat, forcing me to gag again. I stumble backward, my hand covering my mouth, but my eyes refuse to look away. Hollow sockets gape up at me, dark and empty, like open mouths mid-scream. Some of the skulls are yellowed, brittle with age, edges crumbling like dried leaves. Others look... fresher. Thicker. The kind you'd expect to see perched on a doctor's shelf, polished and clinical—only these aren't plastic.

One skull, near the top, bears the violent signature of blunt force trauma. Cracks spider out from a quarter-sized hole near the rear left, radiating like the jagged legs of an ant trail converging on a forgotten crumb.

The stench of decay claws up from the chest, metallic and heavy. Dark, congealed blood stains the inside. My stomach twists violently. I swallow hard, tears pricking at my eyes as I force myself to turn away.

These aren't just bones. They're people. Men. Women. God —some of them are small. Kids. Even without formal training, I can see the decades etched into them. A few still hold entire rows of teeth, grinning grotesquely up at me, while others have snapped jaws, their smiles fractured and incomplete. These bones tell a story, or sixteen separate stories, that I don't think I ever want to know.

My legs give out. I slide down the wall, the world tilting violently. Moments ago, I was having the time of my life— exploring this new charming, historic town, meeting new faces, peeling back layers of this house's rich heritage. I had been proud of what I'd found. A lovely couple had built this home, lived here, thrived here. It had been their legacy.

But now? Now I'm staring at sixteen human skulls. Death —violence—right here, buried within these walls.

How could this place be connected to something so horrific? My mind fixates on the cracked skull near the top— the one with the gaping wound, the jagged spiderweb of cracks. Were all of these people... murdered?

The shift from light to dark is too fast, too jarring. I can't make sense of it. I feel the significance of it pressing down, the cruel irony that the same house I had seen as a fresh start was actually a graveyard all along. How did it go so wrong, so quickly? I press my palms into the cold floor, trying to ground myself, but the question keeps looping in my mind: Who were they? And why are they here?

The image is seared into me now. I'll never unsee it. And deep down, a chilling certainty blooms—I don't think I want to know their stories, because knowing means accepting the truth: this house isn't what I thought it was, what I needed it to be.

I need help.

Nate. He's my first thought. We've been distant lately, wires crossed more often than not, but he's still my husband. The co-owner of this house. He has to know. My hands fumble for my phone, fingers trembling, but I freeze. He's miles away. This needs immediate action. The police. I need the police.

I scramble to my feet, everything spinning as I stagger to the door, lungs clawing for air. The house feels like it's closing in—walls too tight, air too thick. I can still smell it—clinging to my skin, my clothes. The rot. The death.

I burst outside, gasping, fingers shaking as I claw for my keys. The metal slips through my grasp, clattering onto the driveway.

"No, no, no," I whisper, bending down—but someone beats me to it.

"Margot? Are you alright?"

Walter's hand closes around the keys, his face lined with worry as he hands them back.

I shake my head, the words falling apart in my mouth. "The chest... the skulls... I need the police."

His brow furrows, confusion knitting deep lines into his weathered face. "Slow down. Skulls? What're you talking about?"

"Upstairs. In the chest. Sixteen skulls. Blood." My voice cracks, the sheer horror of it tightening around my chest like a vice, making it hard to breathe.

Walter's jaw works silently for a moment. "Margot, what the heck are you saying right now?"

"Listen to my words, goddamn it!" I snap, before reeling it back. "Please, listen to me. There's a chest upstairs in my bedroom. It is full of human-skulls. I have to go. I have to get help."

Walter stumbles over what to say. His eyes flick between

me and the house, jaw tightening as he debates his next move. He takes a step toward the house, then stops, turning back to me. His mouth opens like he's about to speak, but no words come out. Instead, he lets out a sharp breath, shoulders rising and falling as if he's forcing himself into action. Finally, he digs into his pocket, pulls out his own keys, and meets my eyes.

"Okay. But let me drive. No way in hell you should be behind the wheel right now."

The ride to the Mount Dora police station is a blur—Walter glancing at me every few seconds, me staring out the window, hands clenched so tightly my nails dig half-moons into my palms.

The station sits tucked behind a forgettable, white-paneled building. Its plainness almost making it invisible from the main street. Ambulances and police cruisers intermingle in the lot, their flashing lights occasionally cutting through the stillness, though right now they sit asleep.

I step out of the truck slowly, my legs stiff and my heart heavy. My eyes feel vacant and unfocused as I struggle to imagine explaining what I've uncovered. I drift toward the entrance, Walter trailing behind, his boots scuffing against the pavement.

The bell above the door jingles softly as I step inside—a sound that feels far too cheerful. I approach the front desk; my hands limp at my sides. My voice comes out low, flat, almost a whisper.

"I... I need help."

An officer looks up from the paperwork scattered across the desk. His eyes widen instantly as he scans my face. Alarm flickers across his features as he begins to reach for the phone.

"Ma'am, are you alright?

I open my mouth to explain, but no words come out. My throat feels tight, dry. I manage only, "It's... bad. My house."

Before the receptionist can respond, Walter steps forward, his voice steady but urgent. "We need to see Chief Miller. Something's been found at Hawthorn Manor."

The officer straightens instantly, the easy slouch in his posture vanishing. He grabs the desk phone, his sharp eyes never leaving me as he dials.

Moments later, the back door creaks open. Chief Miller steps out, his silver hair catching in the harsh fluorescent light. His sharp eyes flick from me—pale and shaken—to Walter. Walter steps forward, extending a hand. They shake firmly, old familiarity passing between them.

"Andy," Walter says, his voice low but steady.

"Walter," Miller replies, giving him a nod before his eyes drift back to me. There's a subtle shift in him now—a tension, a nervous energy humming under his calm exterior. These kinds of things don't happen in Mount Dora, bad things, and it shows. He glances around the lobby, making sure no one else is nearby before turning his full attention to me.

"I'm Chief Miller," he says, though there's a thin edge of strain in his voice. "You'd better come back with me. We'll talk in my office—somewhere private."

Walter moves to sit, but I grab his arm. "He's coming, too."

The Chief raises an eyebrow but doesn't argue. "Fine by me."

His office is cramped—walls lined with commendations, an old map of Mount Dora hanging lopsided behind his desk. The scent of stale coffee and old paper clings to everything. I sink into the chair opposite him, Walter sitting beside me, his broad frame tense and still.

"Okay," the Chief begins, fingers steepled under his chin. "So, what's going on? You look like you've seen a ghost."

I tell him about the map, the chest, the key—every insane detail. Halfway through, I see the disbelief creep onto his face.

When I finish, he leans back, his fingers drumming nervously against the desk. "So... a hidden map. A buried chest. Sixteen human skulls." He swallows hard, glancing toward the closed door as if worried someone might overhear. "You do understand how this may sound, right? This—this kind of thing doesn't happen in Mount Dora".

I shift uncomfortably in my seat, my hands twisting in my lap. My voice is small when I speak. "I know how it sounds. It's insane. But... I'm telling you the truth." I glance down, feeling the heat of embarrassment flush through me.

Chief Miller doesn't immediately respond. Instead, he turns to Walter, his brow raised. "And you? Did you see this chest of skulls?"

Walter looks down at the floor, his boots scuffed and still. "No," he admits quietly. "I didn't. I just... she wasn't in any shape to drive herself." He jerks his thumb toward me. "I thought getting her here safe was the best move."

That's when the frustration in me boils over. "I can show you!" I blurt, my voice louder now, raw with emotion. "I'm not making this up. Just—come see it for yourself."

His skeptical smirk fades slightly. "Alright then. Let's take a look."

He glances toward the doorway just as a tall officer steps inside, his badge reading "Jenkins." Without missing a beat, Miller leans forward, mutters something low to Jenkins, who responds with a sharp nod before disappearing back down the hall.

"Jenkins is my deputy here in Mount Dora," Miller tells me, his voice sliding into something softer. "Best officer I have. He'll help us sort this out." He flips open his notebook, fresh page ready, the faint scratch of pen against paper the only sound for a beat. "Walk me through it again. Slowly this time."

I swallow hard. My throat feels raw as I force the words

out, rehashing every gruesome detail—the weight of the skulls, the hollow eye sockets, the rancid stench that still clings to my memory. My voice trembles, but I push through it.

Miller jots down notes, his face carved from stone, giving nothing away. "Alright, Mrs. Bennett. We'll take a look. Jenkins is gathering some of the guys, and we'll meet them there." He stands, as Walter's hand appears in my line of sight, steady and grounding. I let him pull me up, his grip warm and sure.

Outside, the cool air slaps me awake, cutting through the haze of panic. Mount Dora hums around us like nothing's wrong—cars pass, people talk, shop windows glow soft against the encroaching dark. Somewhere out there, life is still normal. But not here.

Walter's truck waits at the curb, its battered red frame flanked by a police cruiser. I hesitate as he opens the door for me. My mind flashes forward—to the house, the chest, the skulls. Panic surges hot in my chest, rooting me to the spot.

Run. Just leave.

The thought is wild and fast, gone almost as quickly as it came. I grit my teeth, push the fear down, and climb into the seat.

The drive blurs past. I barely register the streets as they slide by. Walter's hands are firm on the wheel, but there's tension there too—the slight whiteness of his knuckles, the set of his jaw.

"Margot," he says, his voice breaking the heavy silence. "Whatever happens when we get there... just know I've got your back."

I want to accept it. I want to lean into the promise. But for some reason, the words feel paper-thin. I stare at his profile, the hard line of his brow caught in the dashboard glow, and say nothing.

Gravel crunches beneath the tires as we pull up to

Hawthorn Manor. Its dark silhouette looms ahead, the porch light casting long, warped shadows. Behind us, Chief Miller's cruiser pulls in, headlights flashing over Jenkins leaning against his car, arms crossed.

I step out of the truck, my legs shaky beneath me. The house looks the same, but the air feels wrong—thicker, heavier.

Walter hovers close as we approach the porch. Jenkins steps forward. "Perimeter's clear, sir. No one's been in or out."

Miller gives a tight nod before turning to me. "Alright. We're following you, Mrs. Bennett."

The weight of the key in my pocket feels like lead. Every step inside is harder than the last. The house groans around us, floors creaking under boots, the smell of dust and something older, deeper, filling my nose.

When we reach my bedroom, I freeze. The door looms in front of me, the memory of what I saw behind it stark and raw. My fingers tremble as they hover over the knob.

"Margot?" Walter's voice is gentle, coaxing.

I force myself to move. The door swings open.

The chest sits exactly where I left it. The lock dangles, open. The lid gapes wide.

Empty.

I blink. Once. Twice.

No. No.

"They were here," I whisper. My voice cracks on the last word. "They were right here."

I rush forward, dropping to my knees. The inside of the chest is the same—old wood, a dark stain in the corner—but the skulls are gone.

Chief Miller crouches beside me, his pen tapping against his notepad. "Mrs. Bennett... are you sure you—"

"I'm not crazy!" I shout, heat flooding my face.

Miller's face is hard to read, somewhere between concern and skepticism. "I don't think you're crazy, ma'am. But right now... there's nothing here."

His voice trails off, heavy with implication.

Desperation claws at my chest as I turn to Walter, needing —aching—for someone to believe me. But his eyes falter, flicking away from mine, his jaw tightening with something raw and brutal. Embarrassment. Not for me—by me. The realization hits like a slap, sharp and cold.

"Walter—" I try, but my voice breaks before the rest can form. Nothing comes out. I stand there, mute, my throat locked with panic, unsure how to make them see.

I lunge toward the chest, my hands scrambling inside, pushing past splinters and dust until my fingers find it—the dark, sticky smear against the wood.

"See!" I cry, turning to face them. "There's blood! You need to test it for DNA. It'll match someone from Mount Dora—I know it!"

Chief Miller steps forward, peering into the chest. His expression is unreadable as he studies the stain. "If that is blood, it would have to match someone's DNA we already have on file—which would mean a known criminal."

The words drop heavy between us, thick with finality. My hope fractures.

I turn away, my arms wrapping around myself as Chief Miller does a final glance around the room.

His movements are slow, methodical. He checks under the bed. Peeks inside the closet. But then, just as I rub my forehead, willing away the pulsing headache forming behind my eyes, I catch it—his hand brushing over the nightstand, fingers subtly lifting the lid of the drawer. My stomach twists as I realize what he's doing.

"Are you looking for something?" My voice is sharper than I intend, the accusation laced within it unmistakable.

Chief Miller barely hesitates, but I don't miss the fleeting moment of surprise that crosses his face before he schools his features back into something neutral. He turns toward me, his lips pressing into a thin line.

"Just making sure there's nothing that could explain what you saw," he says evenly.

My skin prickles, anger clawing its way up my throat. "You mean like medication?"

The room is quiet. Too quiet. The two other officers shift awkwardly near the door, avoiding eye contact, their postures suddenly tense. Chief Miller exhales through his nose and nods.

"I have to consider every possibility, Mrs. Bennett."

I let out a sharp laugh, humorless and bitter. "So, let me get this straight. I tell you I found a chest full of skulls, and instead of considering that someone might have taken them, you think I hallucinated the entire thing?"

His silence is answer enough.

My chest tightens. This is a dead end, I realize. Even if I scream until my voice breaks, it won't matter. They don't believe me. And worse, they've already made up their minds.

Walter looks at me, something soft and sad in his eyes. "I believe you, I do" he says quietly. But we both know it's a lie.

The words cut deeper than I expect. I nod, swallowing the lump in my throat.

I want to scream. Instead, I stand, my hands curled into fists again. He turns toward the door, signaling the men to leave.

Then I'm alone.

The room feels cavernous, hollow. I stare at the empty chest. Doubt slithers in, cold and sharp.

What if I did imagine it?

My breath comes in shallow gasps as I drop to the floor, curling my arms around my knees. The key digs into my palm, the metal cold and real.

I know what I saw.

Don't I?

10

I sit on my bed, the old external hard drive clutched tightly in my hands as I plug it into my laptop. The hum of the drive spins to life, warm and familiar, grounding me in a reality that feels like it's slipping through my fingers. I need comfort—something, anything, to pull me back from the edge of whatever nightmare I'm teetering on.

The hurricane outside passed days ago, but its chaos lingers, tangled in my mind. Nothing—none of Walter's carefully chosen words or Chief Miller's flat reassurances—can untangle it. I know better. Something is wrong.

I need Nate. I need to feel him again, even if only through the thin veil of memory. The hard drive clicks and whirs, the screen filling with thumbnails—birthdays, vacations, holidays—all versions of a life that feels so far away now. My fingers hover before I click into the folder marked *Early Days*.

The first video loads—a trip to the Smoky Mountains. The camera jostles slightly in Nate's hands as he stretches his arm out, his grin wide and boyish. My heart aches watching it. Then, there I am, my younger self appearing on screen, cheeks flushed with excitement, laughter bubbling from my lips. I smile through the sting of tears, letting the moment wash over me.

For a beat, the weight on my chest lifts. I'm not trapped in this house or tangled in fear. Instead, I'm the newly minted Mrs. Bennett—happy, loved. I let the video finish before hesitating, my cursor hovering over the next file. I want to hold onto that feeling a little longer.

The next video flickers onto the screen—Nate and me dancing in the kitchen on a lazy Sunday morning, still in our pajamas, Sinatra crackling from the old thrift store vinyl. I can almost smell the coffee brewing, feel the worn kitchen tiles under my bare feet.

Then I hear it.

A soft, rhythmic thumping—barely noticeable at first. My finger hovers over the spacebar. I pause the video, but the sound doesn't stop. It continues, hollow and slow, seeping through the house.

I freeze, my heart pounding as the sound grows louder, more insistent. It reminds me of something heavy being dragged up the stairs. My mind snaps to the chest—the effort it took to haul it inside, the weight of it. But it's right here, in my room.

The laptop slides onto the bed as I stand, my bare feet hitting the cold wood floor. The thudding echoes, vibrating through the walls. I creep toward the hallway, my pulse thudding in my ears, each step tightening the knot in my chest.

The noise guides me down the flight of stairs and then to the basement door.

The handle is cold under my trembling fingers as I twist it. The door creaks open, darkness spilling out like ink. The smell hits me—earthy, metallic—stout with the unmistakable stench of decomposition.

I descend the stairs slowly, the wood groaning under my

weight. The gnawing sound grows clearer—wet, tearing, something primal. Halfway down, my foot slips into something cold and slick. I look down, the faint light from above catching a crimson smear.

Bile claws at my throat.

At the bottom of the stairs, in the center of the basement, sits an old, stained tub. A hunched figure crouches inside, shoulders jerking with grotesque movements. The gnawing grows louder, more frantic. My hand shoots to my mouth, choking back a scream.

The figure twists slightly, and I see its face—sunken eyes and blood-slicked lips stretched into a twisted snarl. The torn body it hovers over is a ruin of flesh and bone, the head barely hanging on.

I stumble backward, my foot slipping on the blood-slicked step. My body crashes into the railing, pain flaring as I scramble for balance. The gnawing stops.

A low, guttural growl fills the space.

I bolt up the stairs, the growl following me, thick and heavy in the air. I slam the door shut behind me, my breath ragged, my heart a hammering drum in my chest.

I need help. Walter. He will believe me. I scramble upstairs, grabbing my phone with clammy hands. My thumb hovers over his contact.

But then I stop.

I remember the humiliation—the empty chest, the looks from the officers, the pity in Walter's eyes. I can't do it again, not without proof.

I switch on the camera, the flashlight cutting through the dark as I make my way back to the basement. The house feels heavier now, the walls pressing in as I retrace my steps. I grip the doorknob hard, steeling myself before pushing it open.

The basement yawns open beneath me, silent. I take a

shaky step down, then another, my camera trembling in my hands. I sweep the light across the floor.

Nothing.

No tub. No blood. No figure.

The space is empty.

I sway on the stairs, my knees buckling beneath me. A broken sob claws its way out as the phone nearly slips from my fingers. I *saw* it. I *heard* it.

Hadn't I?

I collapse onto the cold cement, my back against the wall, the weight of it all crashing down. If it wasn't real, then what is happening to me?

A sharp laugh breaks from my throat, edged with panic. My hands tremble as I wipe at my face, but the tears keep falling.

I'm losing my mind.

11

The hot water scorches my skin, but I don't care. I need it—the sting, the burn—something tangible to ground me. Steam fills the room, dense and suffocating, but I let it cocoon me as I stand beneath the relentless stream, eyes closed, my hair plastered to my scalp. I haven't slept. Not a damn wink. The night terrors claw at the edges of my mind—twisted flashes of the basement, the bloated body in the tub, and that gnawing sound, still burrowing deep in my ears. I tip my face into the spray, hoping it will wash the images away. It doesn't. They cling to me, just beneath the surface, waiting.

I think of Nate. God, I need him. His voice. His arms. Some tether to reality. I remember calling him last night, my hands shaking, but the phone just rang and rang. No answer.

I'm not stupid. I know what this is. Nate is probably with someone else—has been for a while now. The distance between us hasn't just crept in; it has carved itself out, bit by bit, over time. I know that. I just don't want to admit it.

My mind drifts, thinking about the last few years. My push to start a family, Nate's big promotion at CirroSystems, Lila's death—and the brutal legal battle that follows. I'm not sure when exactly Nate stopped loving me, but I have a suspicion. It was probably right after I failed to protect Lila. I mean, what screams 'unfit mother' more than letting a child get abused for months under your watch?

Shame curls tight in my chest. I feel... unlovable. Broken in a way I can't fix. And this move—from Maryland to Florida—is our last-ditch effort to salvage something that's already rotting. Nate's idea, actually. A clean slate. A fresh start. And for a few brief weeks, it feels like he's all in.

But then the storm. His disappearance. The hollow, half-hearted efforts at communication. He's not here. Not really. And deep down, I know it. Our marriage is over. Has been for a while now. I just haven't had the guts to say it out loud.

The water cools, snapping me back. I twist the tap off and step out, the cold air prickling my wet skin as I grab a towel. The house is too quiet. Heavy with it.

I wipe the fog from the mirror, my reflection pale and hollow-eyed, before reaching for my phone. A notification blinks—voicemail from Nate. My chest tightens as I hit play.

"Good morning! I don't know about you, but I slept like a baby last night. Being with you always helps me rest easy... I love you, Margot."

Click.

I blink back tears, the lump in my throat swelling until I can't swallow. His voice is everything I need, soft and grounding in a way that twists the incoming guilt tighter in my chest. Here I am, ready to throw in the towel on our marriage, and I step out of the shower to this—his voice, his warmth, like he still cares. Maybe he does. Maybe his head is just caught in its own storm, same as mine.

I call him back. Once. Twice. No answer.

"Dammit," I mutter, slamming the phone onto the night-stand. I can't stay here—not today.

I dress fast, yank on jeans and a sweater, and grab my keys. The Hawthorns—the house—there's more to this place, layers I haven't peeled back yet. And if no one else will help me, I'll dig until I find the truth myself.

Sunlight spills across Mount Dora, illuminating the cobblestone streets and century-old lampposts with a golden glow that feels almost too pristine. The town looks like a preserved postcard from another era—brick storefronts with ivy creeping up their sides, wrought-iron benches tucked beneath towering oak trees draped in Spanish moss, and flower boxes bursting with petunias and marigolds. The gentle clink of wind chimes echoes from a nearby café patio, where early risers sip coffee beneath striped umbrellas. The air is crisp, carrying a faint hint of lake water and freshly baked pastries from the bakery down the block. It's all so charming, so picture-perfect—far too cheery for what I'm setting out to prove today.

I walk through town until the Mount Dora Library comes into view—small, brick, with a faded "OPEN/CLOSED" sign swaying in the breeze. Inside, it smells of old paper and something burnt, maybe coffee. I approach the front desk, my voice barely there.

"Hi. I'm looking for anything you might have on the roots of Mount Dora—town records, deeds, newspapers."

The librarian, an older woman with kind eyes, tilts her head, her smile soft. "Local history's in the back room, dear. Help yourself."

"Thanks," I whisper.

I make my way through the stacks, the hum of fluorescent lights overhead buzzing in my ears. My head pounds, exhaustion digging its claws deep. The skulls claw their way back into my mind—the hollow sockets, the twisted grin of desiccated flesh clinging to bone. I rub my temples, trying to force the images out. Not now. I need to focus.

The records room is small, dusty, and cluttered with binders, old ledgers, and rows of metal filing cabinets. Wooden shelves groan under the weight of town archives, thick with decades of local history. A series of tall drawers house microfilm canisters, each labeled by decade—1920s, 1930s, 1940s—some even older, their paper labels curling at the edges.

I flip through the drawers, my fingers trailing over dusty canisters labeled with events—"Founding Families," "Mount Dora Citrus Boom," "Lake Dora Regatta 1966"—but none of them seem specific enough to help. I open another drawer, this one packed with newspapers meticulously organized by month and year, their edges beginning to yellow. I start scanning, flipping through front-page stories, sifting through decades of town history—parades, festivals, scandals—each headline a breadcrumb from another life.

The hours blur as I comb through paper after paper, the soft shuffle of pages and the distant hum of the library the only sounds around me. My stomach growls a low reminder that it's probably time for a break. Moments before I give up, I stumble across an article that stops me cold: "The Tragic Death of a Town Icon."

I skim the article, my eyes racing over the grim details. Cecilia loves the lake, often taking the boat out alone to read or simply drift in the stillness. But one summer afternoon, she doesn't return. They find her hours later, slumped under the relentless sun, her skin blistered and split, her hair tangled in lake weeds. A bird has pecked out one of her eyes, leaving her face frozen in a twisted mask of agony. It's George who finds her, and from that moment on, he is never the same.

The article lacks photos of Cecilia or George—just a stark image of the Hawthorn rowboat, one I recognize all too well. In the picture, the boat sits upright, tied neatly to the pier, its hull pristine and intact. Not a scratch, not a crack. Nothing like the battered wreck I've seen lodged in the tall marsh grass on my way to and from the chest's hiding spot.

Another article catches my eye: "Respected Business Owner Missing After Wife's Death."

George vanishes days after Cecilia's death, just as Walter said. The town searches, scours the woods and the lake, but he's never found.

I sit back, the paper trembling in my hands. There's more. I can feel it—a thread tying it all together. The chest. The dreams. The goddamn house.

I leave the library, surprised to see the sun now dipping low, casting beautiful pink and red across the Florida skyline. A spark of orange flickers across the street—Dr. Whitfield, cigar in hand, the ember pulsing with each slow inhale.

He catches my eye and waves me over.

I hesitate, then cross the street.

"Evening's the best time here," he says, patting the bench beside him.

I sit, the smoke heavy and sweet, dragging up old memories of my dad smoking on summer nights.

"How's our little town treating you?"

"Strangely," I admit.

He chuckles, low and dry. "Most folks feel that way at first. But Mount Dora's got layers. You'll figure it out."

I study him. "Have you been here your whole life?"

He nods. "Most of it. Stayed for love. Stayed longer out of habit."

There's something wistful in his tone, but I don't pry. "Doctor, have you ever... noticed anything odd about this place? Or rather, about my house?" The words feel awkward coming out of my mouth. Even though Nate and I own Hawthorn Manor, it doesn't feel like ours—not with everything that's happened.

The doctor chuckles softly, a warm sound, not mocking. "There are plenty of odd things about this town, Margot, including that house on the hill. But it sounds like you're hinting at something more specific. What are you really asking me?"

A wave of familiar embarrassment settles over me, one I'm growing fairly tired of. I stare at the ground. "I... I don't really know. I've been seeing strange things at the house. Things that can't be real—things I can't logically explain."

He regards me calmly, waiting for me to go on.

"I... it..." The words tangle on my tongue. "Sometimes it feels like I'm being watched. I see and hear things that make no sense. I guess what I'm really asking is... do you believe in ghosts?"

The doctor raises an eyebrow, taking a long drag from his cigar before releasing the smoke into the growing dusk. "Sure, I believe in ghosts. I've never experienced what it sounds like you're describing, but that doesn't mean it isn't happening to you."

His honesty is grounding. "I'll be more direct—did something bad happen at Hawthorn Manor? Something that might explain what I've been experiencing?"

His expression shifts, curiosity flickering in his eyes. "A lot happened at that house, but if you're looking for tales of brutal murders or secret cults chanting in the basement, I think you'll be disappointed. It was just a house, lived in by a couple who had their fair share of misfortune and pain."

For the second time during this conversation, I feel an opening to dig deeper—and this time, I take it.

"Doctor Whitfield, how well did you know George and Cecilia Hawthorn?"

He stares into the distance, the glowing embers of his cigar illuminating his face in the Floridian dusk. "I knew Cecilia better than I knew George. She and I came up in school together. I was also their primary care physician. In fact, I was the primary for most of the historic district before I began to scale back my practice."

I nod, reading between the lines of his responses so far. "And how was your... personal relationship with them both? Would you say you were friends?"

A small, sad smile slowly appears on his face. "Truth be told, Cece was my best friend growing up. Although, I'm afraid she likely wouldn't say the same about me."

He pauses, something resting just on the tip of his tongue. I wait, choosing my words carefully. I need more—whether or not Whitfield's story will give me what I'm looking for, I don't know, but I have to try.

"Did the two of you have a falling out or something?" I ask gently.

It's hard to tell in the fading light, but I think his eyes are misting over.

"Or something—yes," he finally says. "I suppose it doesn't matter much now, with both of them gone, but it still feels wrong to speak ill of the dead." He takes a deep breath, trying to steady himself. "I'll preface this by saying I know my opinions are clouded by how I felt about Cecilia. Still, facts are facts."

I wait, pulse quickening, while he sits in silence—cracking his knuckles, shifting on the bench, dragging slowly from the cigar. Just as I begin to wonder if he's changed his mind, he speaks again.

"I was in love with Cecilia Doyle from the moment I met her as a boy. She was kind and gentle, patient and smart. She never said a bad word about anyone. She saw the good in everything and everyone. Unfortunately for me, that included George Hawthorn."

He glances at me, then continues.

"George had a darker side. I knew it even then. He was older, loud, rich—always the center of attention. But Cece liked him. I believe it's because she saw that darkness and thought she could fix it. She fell in with the 'cool kids'—those Bugs—and our friendship slowly faded. It never ended outright, just faded. Which, in my opinion, hurt more than any big blow-up ever could."

Tears slip down his face now, catching the last light of the sun like falling orbs of sorrow. He doesn't wipe them away. He just lets them fall.

"Losing a friend hurts. Being replaced hurts. But losing the person you love—to someone cruel and secretive—breaks you."

My heart aches for him. But the moment he mentions secrets, sympathy turns to curiosity. I draw a breath, ready to push for more, but he speaks again unprompted.

"Again, I won't speak ill of the dead. But truth persists, even after death—Cecilia always wanted children, but they struggled. My assumption, as George's doctor, was that he was infertile. We never tested it, but it was my prevailing theory. Until..."

He trails off, shaking his head in disbelief.

"Until what, Doctor?" I prompt.

He straightens and stands, brushing ash from his lap. "I can confirm to you that George fathered a child outside his marriage. But it feels wrong to say more."

I rise, instinctively ready to protest, but he lifts a hand gently—wordlessly asking me to let it go.

"Regarding your question about the oddities in your home... you should have it checked. Mold, asbestos, radon. Sometimes things in the air make people sick. Headaches, dizziness, hallucinations—even paranoia. Have you experienced any of that since arriving?"

I swallow hard. Every single symptom he listed... I've been dealing with all of them. The realization hits like a stone: a mix of relief and embarrassment.

"Honestly, yes. All of it." Nate said the house had been inspected before we moved in, but I don't actually know what that covered. "Yeah, I'm feeling pretty sheepish for not thinking of that explanation myself, Doctor."

He nods firmly. "No need to feel that way at all. I'm a doctor. It's how I'm trained to think." He pats my shoulder kindly and turns to walk away—but then stops, draws a breath, and turns back.

"About what I said earlier, Margot—the mother and child are unimportant. What matters is that you understand George Hawthorn was not the golden boy most of this town makes him out to be. It doesn't change anything now, not after all this time, but it's important to me that *someone* knows the truth. George had a cold, selfish side that few ever saw. Now go home and get some rest."

He smiles—a faint, gentle expression—but I don't catch it. My eyes snag on something else, something across the street, barely visible in the fading light. A figure moves with purpose, his head turned away, but I know that silhouette. That messy, pushed-back hair—the way he walks, I'd know it anywhere.

"Nate?" The name slips out, barely a whisper, my heart suddenly thrumming against my ribs. I shoot to my feet. "Nate!" I call, louder this time, my voice cracking in the cold air.

But he's gone. Just like that—around the corner, swallowed by shadows before I can even think to run.

"Margot?" Dr. Whitfield's voice snaps me back. I flinch,

realizing he stands just a few steps away, his brow creased in concern. "Are you alright?"

I force a smile, brittle and hollow. "I'm fine. Just... tired."

His eyes linger on me, skeptical. "If you're sure. And please remember what I said, get the house tested." There's a softness in his tone, almost fatherly, but it slides right off me. I'm too restless, too rattled.

"Tested, yeah," I mutter, already watching him walk away.

Then I bolt.

I cross the street fast, my boots slapping against the pavement, heading straight for the corner where I saw him vanish. My pulse roars in my ears.

I round the corner, chest tight with hope—and then it caves in.

Nothing. The street stretches out, empty and quiet. A streetlamp buzzes overhead, its pale light casting long, lonely shadows. No sign of him. No hurried footsteps. No fading silhouette.

"Nate?" My voice cracks this time, softer, desperate.

Silence answers.

I push forward, scanning the alleys, the doorways, every darkened corner. But there's nothing. No one.

By the time I hit the end of the block, the truth is obvious. It wasn't him. Or worse—maybe there was never a man there at all.

Frustration claws at me. I drag my fingers through my hair, tugging hard, trying to snap myself back to reality. But what is reality anymore? Since Hawthorn Manor, nothing feels solid. Every answer unravels into more questions, and now—now I'm seeing ghosts in the dark, thanks to what... mold?

I turn back the way I came, my shoulders sinking. And the question claws at me again, sharper this time, impossible to ignore: *What the hell is happening to me?*

12

The humid Florida night clings to my skin, and the stars above cast long, deep shadows across my path. My foot throbs with every step—a dull, persistent ache radiating from the wound where that damn nail punctured it. It's worse than I want to admit. What was sharp, searing pain the day it happened has now sunk deeper, dragging at my energy, turning every movement into a significant effort.

My mind twists and turns, replaying the conversation I just had with Doctor Whitfield. Two things stand out, both unsettling in different ways. The first is straightforward—if George had a child with someone else, who was she, and where is she now? Could she still be in Mount Dora, or did she leave long ago?

The second detail is more troubling. Whitfield spoke with confidence—certainty, even—about George being dead. But most people in Mount Dora say George disappeared, at least entertaining the possibility he could still be alive somewhere, leaving Mount Dora and it's tragedies behind. Why is Doctor Whitfield so sure he's dead? And isn't it more than a little disturbing that the man so sure of George Hawthorn's death also happened to be in love with George's wife?

I'm no detective, but I've watched enough crime documentaries to know that when someone talks about a missing person in the past tense—and has a motive as powerful as love—there's a pretty good chance they're involved.

I think back on my two interactions with Doctor Whitfield. He was pleasant, even charming. He seems sweet and knowledgeable. But my judgment of character hasn't exactly been flawless the past few years. Which leaves me worrying– is it possible Doctor Whitfield had something to do with George's disappearance?

Before I can continue my thought process, headlights swing wildly across the yard, jolting me to a stop. A car rumbles over the gravel, moving with careless, jerky swerves that kick up clouds of dust. My pulse quickens. Whoever is driving doesn't seem to care about the narrow path—or anything in their way.

I tense, preparing to dive out of the path if I have to. But the car slows as it nears, its engine growling before settling into a purr.

A metallic purple PT Cruiser.

It coughs to a stop beside me, its headlights cutting sharp lines through the dark. The driver's window rolls down with a whine, revealing a cigarette jutting from lipsticked lips.

"Evening, darling!" Phyllis Brendamore coos, smoke curling into the night air.

She is all chaos and color—oversized round sunglasses at night, a polka-dot headscarf flapping in the breeze, and an offensive floral perfume battling the cigarette smoke. Her lipstick is a violent shade of pink, clashing spectacularly with the deep purple of her car.

"Phyllis," I say flatly, my patience already fraying.

Then I notice him. The man in the passenger seat. Late forties, maybe, with a heavy beard and olive skin. His dark shirt clings to broad shoulders, but it's his eyes that pin me—deep, intent, and unsettlingly hungry.

"Ah! Where are my manners?" Phyllis chirps, following my gaze. "This is my son, Patrick."

Patrick doesn't speak. He just watches me, head tilted slightly as if trying to read something I'm not saying. His eyes linger, too long, too deep.

I force a polite smile. "Nice to meet you."

He nods once, the barest acknowledgment.

Phyllis waves her cigarette in a wide, smoke-trailing arc. "I was just popping by, dear, thought maybe you'd changed your mind about hosting the Winter Gala at Hawthorn Manor. It'd be perfect!"

"No, Phyllis. I haven't."

"Oh, Margot, come on. You're sitting on a goldmine of local history! The town would love it."

"No, and I don't appreciate these unannounced visits," I snap before I can stop myself.

Phyllis's smile flickers, then rebounds even brighter. "Well, excuse me! Mount Dora's always been a pop-in kind of place. We're neighbors, after all."

I catch her glancing into the rearview mirror, her gaudy rings glinting as she adjusts it. She scans behind her like she expects someone—or something—to show up.

"Where exactly do you live, Phyllis?" I ask, the question sliding out before I can second-guess it.

Her jaw twitches, a tiny tell, before she answers, "Oh, just down the way."

Vague. Deliberately vague.

"Well, maybe I'll swing by sometime. You know, neighborly and all."

Her laugh is too loud, too forced. "Of course, darling. Anytime."

Patrick still hasn't spoken. His gaze hasn't shifted.

"Alright then, we really must be going," Phyllis declares, hitting the gas. "Ta-ta!"

The PT Cruiser lurches away, dust billowing in its wake. I stand there for a beat, watching the taillights flicker into the distance, my mind racing.

Shaking my head in disbelief, I start toward the house, my steps slow and uneven, the throbbing in my foot fading beneath the swirl of questions buzzing in my head. Phyllis and Patrick. What are they doing here before I arrive? They couldn't have just been sitting in the car waiting. Have they been snooping around the grounds? The thought itches at me, refusing to settle. And that look Patrick gave me—too intent, too knowing. There's something more there, something off. Phyllis seems to be circling Hawthorn Manor with a kind of desperation. Why does she keep showing up?

"Evenin', Mrs. Bennett."

I nearly jump out of my skin. Chief Miller's voice slices through my thoughts, yanking me harshly back to reality.

I haven't even seen him—but there he is, sitting against his cruiser, arms folded, watching me with a steady, patient stare. How long has he been there, waiting?

"Chief, hi," I reply, forcing calm. "What...uh, what's wrong?"

"Just checkin' in." His eyes drop to my limp. "What happened there?"

"Renovation injury," I mumble. "Stepped on a nail."

"Yikes. Hope you got a tetanus shot."

I give a weak smile.

He hesitates. "Margot... about last time I was here. The, uh, skulls."

I stiffen.

"I don't want to press," he continues, "but you know how things are around here. Folks talk. And it seems like—"

I stare at him, waiting

"Seems like you're asking a lot of questions." He kicks at the gravel with the toe of his boot. "Which in itself is fine, but I'm worried it may alarm some of the residents here."

"Alarm them how exactly?"

He runs a hand through his hair, searching for the right words. "What happened to the Hawthorns was tragic. I knew Cecilia and George well—better than most. The town still misses them dearly. And while I understand your curiosity about the history of your home, dredging up Cecilia's death and George's disappearance only drags the town back to one of its darkest times. Things are... stable now. Tourism keeps the town's income steady, and we've weathered the past few hurricanes just fine. Everything is... good. I don't want folks getting restless over old ghost stories."

"Ah, so you talked to Dr. Whitfield, I see. Well, I appreciate your concern and I'll take your request into consideration," I say coldly.

His eyes acknowledge the hint. "That's all I'm asking." He turns to return to his cruiser but pops his head over the door. "One more bit of advice, not that you want it—steer clear of Phyllis Brendamore. That family's... complicated."

"Understood."

He climbs into his cruiser, the engine sputtering as it rolls away.

The quiet that follows is more solemn somehow, my frustrations bubbling.

Inside, I lock the door, leaning against it for a beat before heading to the kitchen. Hunger nibbles at me—until I hear it.

That wet, rhythmic gnawing.

My whole body tenses. Not the basement this time.

Upstairs.

Knife in hand, I creep toward the stairs, each step of the climb shooting pain through my foot. The sound grows louder, more grotesque, vibrating through the house like a heartbeat.

My bedroom door looms ahead.

I throw it open.

Nothing.

No bathtub, no monster in the dark, no headless body.

Except...

I drop to my knees, ear to the treasure chest in the center of the room.

The sound is coming from inside.

Hands trembling, I flip it open—preparing myself for this house's latest trick on my tired mind.

Empty. Of course, it's empty.

Like the room, the chest is empty, and the maroon fabric lining the interior is untouched. I kneel there, my fingers gripping the edge of my chest, my eyes wide and unfocused. Tears blur my vision, the frustration and fear overwhelming me.

I'm losing my mind. Maybe it's the death of a child in my care or the ache of wanting and failing to have my own family, feeding into this bottomless pit of inadequacy. Perhaps it's the loss of home, back in Maryland, needing to run away to find some semblance of peace again. Or maybe it's Nate's absence, the long silences between us stretching thinner each day, leaving me to wonder if he's already gone in spirit.

A sob claws its way out, raw and ugly. I bury my head into the crook of my elbow, my right arm resting against the cold edge of the chest. The significance of everything—this house, the grief, the hollow ache of being left behind—presses in on me, suffocating.

When I finally open my eyes, something catches my attention. The corner of the maroon fabric at the base of the chest is pulling away—just slightly as if it's been disturbed. I sniffle, wiping my face with the back of my hand, and lean in closer.

There are faint but undeniable wear marks near the fabric as if fingers have clawed at it repeatedly.

I grab the knife from the floor, slipping the blade beneath the fabric, prying it loose. It peels back with a reluctant hiss, revealing words scratched deep into the wood beneath—dark, jagged letters:

The Darkness stirs, ever hungry but never satisfied.

Below it, a neat row of tally marks—sixteen, stark and accusing.

Sixteen tallies. Sixteen skulls.

I stagger back, the breath punched from my lungs, my body collapsing into a seated heap as the words burn into my mind.

The Darkness stirs, ever hungry but never satisfied.

This is it—finally, proof! I haven't imagined the skulls. Miller, Jenkins, Walter, they have seen the chest here in my room; it's real. And now these words, these tallies inside the chest, are also in my room. There's no mold making me hallucinate. I'm not fucking crazy. I found sixteen skulls buried in this town, and I'm going to find out why.

13

I try Nate's number again, the familiar ringtone echoing in my ears, each unanswered call tightening the knot in my chest. Six days. That's how long he's been gone. Though he told me it was a week-long work trip from the start, it still feels like a month—each day stretching wider with his absence. My thumb hovers over the redial button before I sigh, letting the phone fall onto the table. I need him, now more than ever, and yet he isn't reachable.

Frustration prickles at my skin as I flip open my laptop. My fingers hesitate over the keys, trembling slightly before I start typing.

Nate,

I've been calling. I don't understand why you're blowing me off like this, but I need you to reply. Things are happening here at the house that you need to know about, things I can't explain. I need your help. Please, just call me.

Love you, Margot

I hit send and stare at the glowing screen. A bitter mix of

anger and loneliness swells inside me, heavier than I can push down. I don't have time to drown in it. I have to keep moving forward—alone if I have to.

Since Lila, I've been barely holding it together. Nate has been my crutch, my anchor. Now, stripped of that, I can feel something hardening inside me. A shift. Maybe I don't need him as much as I thought. Maybe I'm capable of standing on my own. The idea is both terrifying and liberating.

The clock on the wall ticks steadily, its hands pushing me to do something. I grab my coat and sling my bag over my shoulder. The house feels heavier today, its shadows deeper, its walls pressing in. I need fresh air.

The Florida sun hits me like a soft slap, warm and grounding as I step onto the path. Mount Dora bustles in its usual small-town rhythm—shop doors creak open, the scent of fresh bread drifts from a bakery nearby, and someone laughs in the distance. Life moves on out here, even if I feel stuck inside my own storm.

Frankie's Favorites comes into view, its storefront cluttered with antique trinkets and dusty books. Frankie waves from behind the window, rearranging a row of mismatched vases. I manage a small wave back before veering toward the Mount Dora Historical Museum.

The brick building looms ahead, its facade worn but proud. Inside, the comforting scent of black tea and aged paper wraps around me. Paula glances up from her cluttered desk, her round glasses slipping down her nose. Her face lights up when she sees the bagels and chai teas in my hands.

"Well, if it isn't my favorite local historian-in-training," Paula quips, brushing aside a stack of papers. "And you brought treats! Smart girl."

I set the bag down, offering her a smile. "Figured it might earn me another hour of your expertise."

She chuckles, taking her tea. "You're lucky I'm a sucker for carbs."

Sliding into the chair across from her, I waste no time. "Paula, I need to know more about the Hawthorns. I've been digging, but I'm missing pieces. I know George built the manor and that Cecilia died on the lake, but isn't there more? Why did they have such a huge house but no children? Were there any questions around Cecilia's death, maybe something more nefarious?"

Paula's smile fades, her fingers tracing the rim of her cup. "Oh my, those are big questions for so early in the morning, sweetie!"

I smile but press on. "Please, Paula. I need to understand what I'm living in. It feels like... it feels like I'm an imposter in a place that isn't actually mine."

Paula's eyes grow softer before she leans in. "Cecilia struggled with fertility. It weighed on her—on both of them. Hawthorn Manor was supposed to be filled with children; with laughter and love. Instead, it just stood empty. For a while, I think it held promise. But near the end, I think it was only a reminder, at least to Cecilia, of what she couldn't give her husband."

Something heavy twists in my chest. "And her death?"

"Heart attack, pure and simple." Paula's voice drops. "January 2008. On the boat. Alone. How horrible to be out there unable to get back to shore. No one really knows how much she suffered, if at all. George chose to believe she was gone well before the sun and birds destroyed her body."

I hesitate, my fingers drumming on the edge of the table. Paula wipes crumbs from her napkin when I lean forward.

"Paula... have you ever experienced anything odd around here? Something you couldn't explain—spiritual, maybe? Or otherwise?"

"Spiritual? Well, I believe in our Lord and Savior Jesus Christ if that's what you're asking, Margot." She makes the sign of the cross.

I smile. "No, nothing like that—I wonder..." I try to get the words out just right. "Have you ever heard of anyone... going missing here in Mount Dora?"

She stiffens, her fingers pausing mid-wipe. The air between us crystallizes, and for a moment, I think she might ignore the question altogether. Instead, she glances at her watch, her eyes widening in exaggerated surprise.

"Oh! Would you look at that—I didn't realize the time. The museum's supposed to close soon, and I've got errands to run before I pick up my grandkids from school." Her words come fast, a nervous energy filling the space.

Before I can respond, she's already shoving the leftover bagels into the trash bin and gathering her papers in a flurry. "You should get going too. Don't want to keep you longer than I should."

"Paula—"

"Come on now, out you go," she interrupts, practically ushering me toward the door.

The museum door shuts behind me with a hollow thud, and I stand staring at it, bewildered. The glass rattles slightly from the force, the dangling sign on the door catching my eye.

9AM–4PM Monday through Saturday.

I glance at my phone.

11:13 AM.

The lie lingers in the air, leaving a sour taste in my mouth. I consider Paula's reaction—her sudden urgency, the way her eyes darted to her watch as if it held the answer she needed. It feels like fear, a raw, knee-jerk instinct to flee. But what is she afraid of?

As the museum's caretaker, Paula is bound to hear her

share of small-town gossip and half-truths dressed up as urban legends. But this isn't gossip—this is something deeper, something she doesn't want to talk about. Maybe she's heard things, truths so unsettling that even mentioning them is risky. The thought prickles unease down my spine.

The streets blur around me, my mind spiraling as I walk aimlessly back to Hawthorn. Sixteen skulls. Buried chest. Sixteen tallies. Ghosts. Paula's warning echoes, sharp and evasive. *The Darkness stirs, ever hungry but never satisfied.* Disappearances. Secrets. Phyllis. Patrick. Strange, knowing glances. Nate. The way Paula bolted like I'd uttered a forbidden word.

"Afternoon, Margot!"

I startle, spotting Walter in the garden, his hands deep in the soil. He waves me over.

"Hey, Walter," I call out, my throat dry, mind still trying to return to full attention to the here and now.

"How're you feeling today?" He wipes the back of his hand across his brow, leaving a streak of dirt. "Been sleeping any better?"

There it is—the polite concern laced with quiet disbelief. He doesn't believe me, not entirely. But I push the thought aside.

I sit down, bringing a glass of lemonade to my lips, condensation trailing down my fingers. Walter's words come back to me, and I sit up straight as the facts collide in my brain.

August 2009.

Not January. Not 2008.

If Cecilia died in August 2009, it wasn't seventeen years ago—it was sixteen.

Sixteen skulls. Sixteen tallies. Sixteen years.

It's all connected. I don't know how and I don't know why. But Cecilia Hawthorn and that chest of skulls are connected, and I'm going to find out how.

14

My half-conscious mind pulls me from sleep. I lie here, staring at the ceiling, my thoughts tangled in a haze. A familiar sense of dread weighs on my chest, pressing me deeper into the mattress.

I push myself upright, wiping the sleep from my eyes. The house sits in a heavy, empty silence. It reminds me of a museum after hours, every corner and hallway pregnant with memories that don't belong to me.

I have to admit, I never planned to call this place Hawthorn Manor. Naming a house—even a grand, sweeping one—has always felt pretentious to me. However, after closing, the agent reminded us that it was legally a historic site and that any renovations would require city approval.

"I'd recommend calling it by its legal name," the agent had said, "as all the townsfolk already do. It'd be rather time-consuming redoing all that paperwork, don't you think?"

That day feels so distant now—like a dream that slips away the moment I try to remember it.

What doesn't feel like a dream is the torment I'm experiencing in this house. It's a strange limbo: part psychotic breakdown, part full-blown poltergeist haunting. For every minute I feel sane, there are two where I'm convinced I've lost my mind and another three where I believe I'm being haunted by something—or someone. I need to break out of this cycle. I need a clear head. I need coffee.

I've never been much of a cook. Honestly, I have no idea if the stovetop in this place is gas or electric. Nate and DoorDash usually have me covered on that front. But when it comes to coffee, I know how to make a serious cup of joe.

Back in college, I paid for my entire education as a barista at the only Starbucks in town. That was when you had to shout, "calling bar!" through the chaos, The Avett Brothers blasting way too loud in the background. The barista on bar duty would shout "calling!" back, letting you announce the order for everyone to hear. It was high stress for terrible pay, but at least I honed some authentic coffee-making skills.

Now I sit at the bay window in the kitchen, cradling my mug of Death Coffee, a blend I first discovered in a tiny café years ago. The espresso crema is perfect—bittersweet and strong. The name is grimly fitting, considering the current atmosphere around me, but it works miracles on my foggy brain.

I stare out at the grounds of Hawthorn Manor. The day is light and breezy, and I can just barely return to how I felt when Nate and I first decided to buy this massive old place. Gazing across the lawn, I realize I've been a passenger in my own life for too long, letting this house and its mysteries pull me along.

I set my coffee on the windowsill and move into the living room, rummaging through cardboard boxes until I find my old CPS ID badge. The edges are frayed, and the laminate is yellowed, but my name is still right there. Simply holding it puts me in a different frame of mind.

Standing in front of the hallway mirror, I slip the badge around my neck, tighten my ponytail, and give two gentle squeezes to my biceps, toes flexing in my shoes. It's the same ritual I used to do when facing difficult cases.

Sixteen skulls. Sixteen lives. I can't keep thinking of them as just bones. These were people with stories and families. Their absence is like a weight in the air, an echo in every silent corner of this place. If the skulls are gone now and the police refuse to help, I need to track down other proof—evidence that can't disappear so easily.

I open my laptop, fingers flying as I scour missing persons reports, articles, and community forums for any lead. Hours pass as I overwork my espresso machine, my eyes growing gritty from the screen's glow. But the search yields little—mostly far-flung disappearances I can't connect.

Then, finally, something. A fifteen-year-old article about a local boy, age six, who vanished without a trace. Michael Lark. No forced entry, no leads. He lived not far from here, just outside Mount Dora. Excitement and dread tighten my chest. It's not conclusive, but it's a start.

I lean back, running my fingertip over the boy's photo on my laptop screen. Michael Lark. The name feels like a puzzle piece. I snap the laptop shut, the quiet hum of the house amplifying the sudden rush of my thoughts.

I grab my keys and slip on my shoes. If Michael's disappearance is linked to the sixteen skulls, I won't solve this stuck behind a screen. I need to see where he lived, breathe the air of that place, and try to feel what happened.

The Lark residence is easy enough to find. Its paint is chipping, and the grass is left to grow wild like no one's cared for the property in years. My heart thrums as I knock. I can't predict what I'll find or what I'm supposed to say.

For a long moment, silence. Then the door creaks open, and a middle-aged woman peers out. Exhaustion etches her face, her eyes sunken in with dark shadows beneath them. She looks at me like she's trying to guess if she's seen me before.

I manage a polite smile. "Hi, my name's Margot, and I'm looking for Ms. Penny Lark. Have I got the right address?"

She hesitates, then nods. "Yes." Her voice is guarded. "What do you want?"

I keep my tone gentle, producing my old CPS badge just enough for her to notice. It's unethical—maybe outright illegal —but I need her to talk about Michael. "I'm investigating a missing persons case, and I think it might be tied to your son's disappearance. I was hoping you could tell me about the day Michael vanished."

Her eyes widen, and I see pure fear behind them. She shakes her head, voice trembling. "I don't know what you're talking about. I don't have any children."

That hits me like a punch. I blink, fumbling my words. "I'm sorry, but you are Penny Lark, right? Isn't Michael your son? He disappeared from here fifteen years ago. Please, I only want to help. I know what it's like to lose someone."

Penny's expression hardens. "You need to leave. Now." She tries to shut the door, but I press my hand against it, desperation in my voice.

"Please, Ms. Lark. He was your son. Something is happening in this town."

"No!" she snaps, her voice breaking. "You don't know anything. I never had a son, and I don't know who Michael is."

She forces my hand away, slamming the door. I hear the bolt and chain lock behind it.

I stand there, stunned, staring at the notes in my hand and the printed article. The address clearly matches. Penny Lark must be so overcome by PTSD that she's erased the memory of her own child's existence. I've seen survivors do strange things, but never to this extent.

I walk back toward my car in a haze, my mind replaying the look on Penny's face when she denied ever having a son. That look wasn't defiance—it was terror.

Through my dusty windshield, I watch the battered house. It looks like a sad house full of sad secrets, hiding an even sadder woman.

I hover a moment, my hand on the key, but I can't turn the ignition. I feel that same surge of focus I had at home when I put on my CPS badge. The last time I ignored a gut feeling like this, a child paid the price. I can't do that again.

Quietly, I slip out of the car and circle around to the left side of the house.

At the first window, I can just barely see into what must be a dim kitchen. I hear Penny moving somewhere inside, her footsteps echoing in the hush. I follow the sound until I find a second window, this one taller than the last.

A small paper sailboat is taped to the bottom of the sill as if riding the window frame. My heart beats faster. Cautiously, I peer inside.

It's a little boy's room. There's a bed with a blanket covered in bright cartoon rockets. Toys spill across the floor. On a small desk, crayon drawings are strewn about in disarray. The walls are decorated with pictures of a bright-smiling blond kid, his name—Michael—drawn in cheery letters above the bed.

It's like a time capsule, frozen in place from the exact day he vanished. My pulse thuds in my ears. I'm staring at a life left in limbo, and for the first time, I feel the cold chill of realization that I may be on the brink of something bigger than I've ever imagined.

15

I run my fingertip along the painted seam of the window, testing for any give. It's sealed tight. I slip my car key out of my pocket and carefully wedge its edge between the window frame and the casing, digging into the layers of latex paint. The paint clings stubbornly, and sweat breaks across my forehead as I work it loose.

I know I'm exposed like this, perched on the side of Penny Lark's house with nothing but a half-baked lead. If anyone drives by, they'll see me immediately. And given my previous run-ins with the local police chief, I doubt he'd believe anything I have to say. I push harder, prying at the frame, feeling the paint finally crack. The window groans in protest as I ease it open, an ugly shriek of old wood and Florida humidity. But it budges enough for me to squeeze inside.

I pause, listening. My heart hammers, but I force myself to be patient, to make sure Penny isn't about to come rushing in. After a few seconds of silence, I pull myself up and through.

Squatting low, I take in my surroundings. I wait, body tense, but no footsteps approach. Slowly, I straighten and move deeper into the room. A child's bedroom. The sight of it tightens my throat. My fingertips brush over the crayon drawings scattered on a small desk. One of them shows a little boy playing with a sailboat—Michael; I recognize him from the news article. He was real, and he lived right here. But why would his own mother pretend he never existed?

My unspoken question is answered by a faint whimper that rises from somewhere in the house, a tiny, frantic sound stifled before it can fully escape. I freeze, glancing around—the open doorway, the vacant bed, the dusty rocking chair in the corner. Could it be an animal outside? But then I hear it again, except this time it doesn't stop. The whimpers roll into hushed whispers, the sound twisting my gut. I feel a prick of fear that tells me I've gone too far, crossed a line I shouldn't have. Why do I keep doing this to myself—these reckless moves and impulsive decisions aren't like me.

I back toward the window, trying to stay calm, to keep from bolting in panic. Then, just as I'm about to exit the same way I came, I see a face staring at me from under the bed.

Penny Lark's face.

The shock of it nearly stops my heart. Her black hair is drenched, dripping and clinging to her face. She turns her head slightly, one eye peering at me through a parted curtain of hair.

I jolt backward, missing the window altogether and landing hard on the floor with my spine jammed against the wall. Before I can scramble to my feet, Penny lunges, scuttling out from under the bed and onto my lap in one unnervingly fast move.

I open my mouth to scream, but her cold, slick hand seals over my lips, silencing me. In the dim light, I see how wild her eyes look. "You need to leave," she whispers, almost humming the words. "They're... watch-ing." She draws out the final syllables in a sing-song, twisted lullaby that sets my nerves on edge. "They're always watching. If you keep asking questions, you'll disappear, too."

My chest heaves, blood roaring in my ears. "Who's they?" I whisper against her clammy palm. "Who is watching, Penny?" She shoots a frantic glance around the room. "They. Their. Her. Him. His. They. Their. Her. Him. His. Him. My him. My Michael. *My Michael!*" She shrieks his name and hurls her head forward, slamming it into the floor just inches from my leg.

Blood seeps across the floorboards, pooling near my thigh. I catch only glimpses of Penny's twisted features as the light slices through the window, shining across her face. I'm too stunned to move until I feel the warm trickle of blood spatter hit my face. With a strangled cry, I push her away and lunge for the window.

I hurl myself out and land in an awkward sprawl, scrambling to get on my feet. I don't look back. No one chases me, but my heart pounds so fiercely I can't hear anything else. I burst into a sprint.

Only when I'm behind the wheel of my car do I realize how badly I'm shaking. I stare at my own reflection in the rearview mirror, splatters of crimson line my jawbone. In my mind, I can still see Penny's wide, frenzied eyes and smell the coppery tang of her blood in that tiny bedroom.

I jam the key into the ignition, throw the car in drive, and peel away from the Lark house as though the devil himself is on my tail.

Fear clings to me like an oily residue, refusing to slip away. My mind reels, trying to process Penny's horrifying behavior, her cryptic words—"They're always watching." As the road stretches on, I realize I'm now running from something far more sinister than I could have ever imagined. Now I know—deep in my bones—that whatever haunted Penny Lark is now coming for me.

16

I keep my eyes locked on the road as fresh rains begins to fall, hammering the windshield. The glare of headlights and the smear of yellow lines blend into a blur. A faint streak of Penny Lark's blood stains my jeans—a sickening reminder of the nightmare I just fled. Over and over, I see her bashing her head against the floor, hear that gruesome thud echoing in my mind, merging with the roar of rain and thunder outside.

My fingers ache from gripping the steering wheel so hard. I try to clear my head, slow my racing thoughts. I start going through questions I need answered, almost like a checklist:

Who are "they"? The person responsible for the skulls in the chest? Why would Penny lie about her son? Is she being coerced? Threatened? Is she delusional, sick? I can't shake the memory of her wild, terrified eyes and the panic that seeped into my own soul.

I think about going to the police. My foot hovers over the gas, and more than once, I almost flick the blinker to turn back into town. But something deep in my gut warns me that might be dangerous—especially if Penny's right and there are people out there watching. I need someone I can trust implicitly.

I approach the highway on-ramp, frustration knotting my stomach, and fumble around the cup holder for my phone. I need a steady voice on the other end of the line. I need home. With Nate gone, only one name bounces through my head: Shannon.

Shannon Morgan has been my best friend since we were twelve—always the pragmatic one, always with a plan. She graduated from the University of Maryland School of Law with a 4.0 GPA and a desire to make a difference in the world. When my life spun out, when CPS questioned my ethics after Lila's death, Shannon stood by my side, both in court and out. She dismantled the prosecution's arguments until I was cleared, bolstered my courage, and refused to let me give up. She's the only person I can think of who can keep me grounded right now.

My hand trembles as I dial her number. It only rings twice before she answers, her voice playful and light.

"Please tell me you finally listened to Chromatica, and it's changed your life?" she teases, voice airy. "BLACKPINK, Ariana, and the rocket man himself? I mean, come on, what a record."

But she notices my silence. "Margot? What's going on? Are you okay?"

I swallow, the steering wheel creaking under my tight grip. "No, I'm not okay," I manage. "I... I need help. I don't know where else to turn."

She doesn't miss a beat. "I'm here. Talk to me."

I take a shuddering breath. "I've been doing some investigating into a missing-person case. It's about a boy named Michael, stolen from his home fifteen years ago. I... found his mother, Penny Lark, she's not far from the new house in Mount Dora. When I probed her for information regarding her son, she told me that she didn't have a son. And not in like a "my son is gone" kind of way, but in a "I never had a son" kind of way.

"Okay, sure, that's tragic, but Margot, trauma like that can–"

"I wasn't finished", I interject.

"I knew something was wrong. The exchange didn't feel right. The way her eyes changed when I mentioned Michael's name; I knew I couldn't just leave. I went around to the side of her house. And Shannon, I found the boy's room. It looked untouched with his bed and toys still there. Above the bed was Michael's name in colorful, wooden letters."

I let the story spill out, in excruciating detail, which I hoped would help me make sense of what I just experienced, but no luck. "Right as I was ready to leave, I heard this awful whispering sound. Shannon, the woman was hiding under the bed, her son's bed. She was already in the room when I broke in."

"Jesus Christ, Margot, you're going to get arrested!" Shannon exclaims.

"No, listen Shan! She scared the shit out of me, I tripped and when I did, the woman *crawled into my lap*. She told me as clear as day that someone was watching her and if I didn't stop asking questions, they'd make me disappear too. And then... and then she started slamming her head into the floor, Shannon. There was blood–I just freaked out, I ran." Tears start flowing now.

"Okay, okay. This is nuts. Margot, you broke into a woman's house after stirring up memories that are probably extremely triggering. I'm not surprised the poor woman was self-harming!" I can hear the disappointment in Shannon's voice. I screwed up and it's really hitting me now.

My voice begins to shake with pent-up fear, the intensity of the day's events still thrumming in my veins. "Yes, okay. You're right. I didn't choose the most ethically sound pathway, but I'm not calling for you to absolve me of my sins, Shannon. There's something going on in this town. It wasn't just the fear in her eyes," I say, running a hand through my damp hair. "It was like a whole history she didn't dare mention. Like if she even breathed the truth, something horrible would happen." My stomach twists. "What could be so scary, that you'd rather deny your only child ever existed versus tell the truth?" I inquire.

I hear Shannon sigh, and I can practically see her sitting on her back deck in Maryland, red wine in her hand after a long day at the office. "I don't mean to pry," Shannon says softly, "but... where's Nate in all this?"

My heart squeezes. Shannon has never liked Nate, and for good reason—as my best friend, she hears all the worst parts of our relationship.

"He's in DC," I say. "His company sent him there for a customer meeting."

She hesitates. "So... you went to this woman's house by yourself?"

I can almost hear the continued disapproval in her voice. "He doesn't know about any of this. He's been busy," I mumble.

A moment of silence. "Margot, your move was supposed to help you put distance between your past CPS work and a new life. Sun, beaches, bikinis, lots and lots of fruity alcohol; those were your assignments when leaving Maryland, *not* missing persons cases. Why? Why are you doing this?"

"Shannon, come on. I was going stir crazy in that house all alone. I needed something to do. I needed some reason to get out of bed in the morning." I say with more shame in my voice than I intended.

"I'm sorry, but I think you just proved my point. You're

digging up cold cases, all alone, in a big creepy house, far away from home because you're bored? That's it. I'm getting on a plane."

"No!" My voice comes out sharper than I intend. "I'm okay, it's okay, everything's okay, really. It's been... intense, with the move, the fallout after... the trial, but I've been doing well. The depression has eased up. No new nightmares, and I'm continuing my therapy. I'm healthy. I just... I missed it. I needed to be helpful." God, I'm such a liar. None of the things I just said are true. Who am I?

She sighs, and I hear her rustling around. "If you say so. But there hasn't been that much time since you moved, since everything that happened... I love you, Margot. You know that. I'm just worried."

A tear slips down my cheek, surprising me. "I know you are. I just don't want to drag you into this mess. It's probably a giant nothing-burger. The Lark thing was just... it really freaked me out."

Shannon's voice softens. "Uh, hell yeah it did. That sounded fucking terrifying! But listen, I'd always rather be there for you than sit on the sidelines imagining the worst. So, if you need backup, or if you just need someone to talk to— anything—you call me, and I'll show up."

I grip the phone tighter with my left hand. "Thank you. I just needed to hear a friendly voice. I'm already feeling better. I promise I'll make good decisions from here on out."

"I believe you... twenty-five percent, with the other seventy-five leaning towards absolute bullshit, but alas, what is a girl to do..."

I laugh, a genuine, strong belly laugh which feels so good. Although the guilt of withholding information from her, such as the chest of skulls I've recently discovered, minimizes the laughter and leaves me questioning who I am again.

"Would you be willing to help me with this missing persons case from afar if you have some time?" I ask.

I hear her crack her knuckles, which has always been an awful habit of hers. "Oh, hell yes. I'll do some digging from my end. I still have contacts in law enforcement, people who owe me favors. Let me see what I can find on Mount Dora—missing persons, sealed records, anything juicy or interesting. We'll get to the bottom of whatever is happening down there. But Margot—promise me you'll stay safe. No more solo investigations without a plan."

I exhale, the tension easing just a bit. "I promise. No more breaking and entering."

"Good," Shannon says firmly. "I'm here for you, always."

A wave of relief washes over me, and I'm blinking back tears when I end the call. I let my head fall against the headrest, exhaustion flooding every muscle in my body.

Before I know it, I'm parked in front of Hawthorn Manor. The rain is thicker now, beating a furious staccato on the car roof. Through the windshield, the house rises up in dark shapes and angles, looming and secretive. The shadows seem to move with the storm's flickering light, like the house is breathing, alive.

I suck in a shaky breath, gathering the courage to push open the car door. I dash through the downpour and up the porch steps, finally stepping into the stale warmth of the foyer. Water pools around my ankles, and my heart thuds with leftover adrenaline. My mind is a cacophony of half-formed thoughts, questions, and fears, but I'm too drained to pursue any of them tonight.

At the same moment I close the door behind me, approximately one and a half miles away, a heavy droplet of rain strikes an old roof. It slides beneath a loosened slate tile, slipping silently through the ceiling and landing on the cold, swollen face of a man I love very much. He lay on a cold, dirty floor, fear in his eyes, waiting for the monster to fulfill its promise—to add Nate Bennett to the pile of skulls waiting in the center of the room.

17

I walk into the kitchen, the gentle hum of the old refrigerator blending with the crisp click of my shoes on the tile. I set the kettle on the stove, waiting for that soft whistle I find oddly comforting, even in the midst of Hawthorn Manor's creeping unease. Morning light seeps through the curtains, painting the walls in warm, golden hues—like the sunrises back home. For one fleeting moment, it reminds me that there's still beauty in this world, despite the dark shadows closing in.

The kettle's call snaps me out of my thoughts. I pour hot water into the French press, steam fogging my view of the citrus trees outside. In this moment, I can almost believe this is the peaceful retreat Nate and I imagined when we first moved in—something simple, far from the nightmares that took over after Lila's death.

As the steam clears, I look out at the yard. Part of me wonders if Cecilia Hawthorn ever stood here, at this exact time, gazing out at the same trees. Did she sense the secrets buried within these walls? The hidden room behind the bookshelf, the floorboards, that chest, and the key I found? Could she have known?

I stare past the glass, thinking how Cecilia's story intertwines with mine. From what I've learned, she struggled to conceive, just like me. Even though times have changed, that deep-rooted expectation that a woman should be able to bring life into the world still lingers. The pain of wanting something so natural and being denied never goes away. The ache ties me to her, transcending decades. I picture her in this kitchen, grappling with the same doubts and fears I do now. Was she ever convinced she wasn't enough?

A flutter of wings catches my eye. A bird settles on the spindly branches of a once-thriving citrus tree, now merely a skeleton. I imagine how bountiful this grove must have been before a blight took hold: bright oranges dangling from branches, workers laughing and gathering fruit under the Florida sun. Echoes of those joyful days seem to hover out there in the overgrown yard, but stop short of entering the manor itself.

I feel a tug at the back of my mind to immerse myself further in what it must have felt like back then, so I step outside. As I wander the property, I take in the remnants of the old groves—stumps, rotting and hollow, quietly consumed by time. I follow row after row of unkempt grass, imagining how it must once have been flattened by the steady tread of work boots. I close my eyes and let the birdsong and the soft, warm breeze wash over me. In my mind, I hear the growl of diesel trucks, the steady hum of machinery cleaning oranges as they dropped from the trees, and the distant echoes of music and laughter threading through the air. But when I open my eyes, all of that disappears, and I'm left staring at Hawthorn Manor once again. My heart aches for the promise of what might have been, for the life Nate and I thought we could rebuild here. But it's hard to cling to hope when so much has happened in such a short period of time.

I reach the remnants of a massive tree, its warped branches stretching toward the sky like stiff, arthritic fingers. I try to recapture the optimism we had when we bought this place, that idea that we could mend what was broken, but the memory feels so far away; time is cruel like that. George Hawthorn, so famed for his generosity and sense of whimsy, now seems tangled in something much darker—those skulls, that hidden chest, the panic and fear seen in Paula and Penny. None of it aligns with the image I had of him.

My thoughts remain on Penny Lark. That entire experience only confused me more. Even talking to Shannon for some guidance hasn't exactly eased the knot in my chest. It appears there are so many secrets hidden within the walls of my own home; it almost makes me feel like a vagabond, like someone without a true home at all.

My mind then falls to the map and key. How do I connect them to George, to this place, to everything I've seen? I pause at the edge of the neglected garden, my gaze roaming the horizon as I try to anchor myself. There's no straightforward next step. Penny was my best lead, and now I'm left with nothing but bigger questions.

When I return to the kitchen, my coffee has gone cold. My mind drifts toward the police again—whether it's foolish or not, it's the only option left. Maybe I'm naive, but I want to believe there's still a semblance of justice out there, that not every officer is corrupt or dismissive. I rinse my mug in the sink, then snatch up my keys, deciding once and for all: I'll go to the police station. If anyone can find out what 's really going on at the Lark residence, it's them.

I drive through the quiet streets of Mount Dora, the morning sun spilling across the pavement. When I reach the station, there's chaos—a swirl of uniforms, sirens reflecting off the white building. Chief Miller is leading a group of officers into the parking lot. He's just climbing into his cruiser when he notices me pulling up.

"Margot?" he calls. "What are you doing here?"

His voice sounds worn-out, like he's been awake for far too long. "I need a favor," I begin, my nerves jangling. "But... what's going on?"

He sighs, looking deflated. "We found a body."

My chest tightens. "A body? Oh my god. My thing can wait. Please go do what you need to do."

His gaze sharpens, and I feel him measuring my reaction. "Awkwardly enough, Margot, I was heading to Hawthorn Manor right now."

I can feel my face betraying my surprise. "Hawthorn– but I was just there? There are no bodies. None that I know of."

"The body wasn't found at Hawthorn Manor, but the last person to see the victim alive lives there."

For a moment, I have no idea what he's talking about, but the instant he takes in another breath, I know what words are going to come out of his mouth. "Penny Lark," he says. "Widow, lived off Hilton Avenue. We found her face down in Lake Dora."

Shock widens my eyes. Just yesterday I saw Penny smashing her head against the floor in her missing son's bedroom—unhinged, but alive.

"I—" I can't find the words.

Miller continues, "She had water in her lungs, so she definitely drowned. But she also had defensive wounds, clumps of hair missing... her face was beaten nearly beyond recognition. And here's the strangest part: Penny used to teach swimming lessons at the local summer camp. Just about every kid in town learned to swim from her. So how does a swim instructor drown in a lake the day after you visit her home?"

My stomach twists as his words sink in.

"You were seen at her house," he says carefully. "And we have witnesses placing you by the lake, multiple times; some even reporting suspicious behavior on your part. Those are some odd coincidences, Margot. I was on my way to speak with you so that we could make some sense of this."

My knees feel weak. "You think I... had something to do with her death?" I manage, my voice almost breaking.

He runs a hand over his hair, looking uncertain. "I think you should tread lightly. We don't know each other well, but your name keeps showing up on my desk—first with this missing skulls event, now with a drowning victim. Either you have terrible luck or something is going on with you that appears to put this town's citizens at risk."

I know I need to say something, but my lips are frozen in place. I have no idea where to even begin.

"Why don't you come inside? I also need to speak with your husband. Can you have him to come down as well, please?"

I stare at the pavement. "Nate's in DC. He has been for days."

Chief Miller gives me that same pitying look I got from the police after Lila died, the one that sets my nerves on edge. I feel the old panic creeping over me—facing accusations, seeing suspicion in the eyes of those I hoped would help. My mind reels, replaying the fiasco from years ago when everyone turned on me over Lila's case, whispering that I'd failed to protect her; which... was true.

It's happening again, I realize, that feeling of the world closing in. Fear locks my legs in place. If they suspect me, it could ruin my life. After everything I've worked for, fought for —could I lose it all again?

"Am I under arrest, Chief?"

He looks uncomfortable, pausing for a moment too long.

"No, you're not under arrest. I'd simply like to get to the bottom of what happened to Ms. Lark. I believe, based on information we've gathered, that you may have pertinent information to piece together the truth. We're just talking."

The phrase is like a gun that jolts me out of my state of inaction. I know those words, I've heard them before– two years ago, from the Anne Arundel County Police Department, when Lila was found dead. The words fall out of my mouth before I can fully comprehend what wheels they'll likely set in motion.

"I'll need to speak to my lawyer first."

The change in the Chief's eyes from pity to fury is instantaneous and it catches me by surprise. "Call who you need to, I'll be waiting inside." He turns away from me slamming the cruiser's door, hard.

Now shaking and numb, I pull out my phone and begin dialing one of the two phone numbers I still know by heart. It rings once, twice, and then her familiar voice fills the line.

"Margot, this better be good. I was about to deep-condition my hair."

My voice trembles. "Shannon? You remember how I told you not to come to Mount Dora? I need you to ignore that. I need you right now... I need my best friend. But more importantly, I need my lawyer."

18

I sit in the Mount Dora police station, my senses assaulted by the stale odor of old coffee mixing with the tang of sweat. The building is old—like much of this town—and the low ceilings seem determined to press me down into the scuffed linoleum. Every scrape, every chipped corner, tells a story of decades of use. Officers buzz around with paperwork, their usual banter smothered by the grim tension following Penny Lark's death. I catch the quick, sidelong glances they throw my way, as if I'm some foreign object in their midst.

A moment later, they lead me to a small interrogation room. No cheer in here—just exposed brick that might once have been charming, now only claustrophobic. Memories of the Lila case slam into me. Back then, I spent hours in a frigid, windowless room, too scared and too ignorant of my rights to stand up for myself. I know better now, but I also don't want to look uncooperative. At least this room is warmer, which is something; I've always hated the cold.

Eventually, Chief Miller and Deputy Jenkins walk in. Jenkins has an unsettling smirk, with narrow, darting eyes and a stooped posture that reminds me of a rat creeping through the shadows. I've decided I don't like him. Miller, on the other hand, offers me a sympathetic look.

"Margot, are you comfortable? Need anything? Water, maybe a blanket?" he asks gently, but I'm not fooled. His voice might be kind, but his eyes are a little too focused, a little too eager. This is a tactic: act friendly, get me talking. I shake my head, throat dry. They hover, offering coffee, a phone call, anything to loosen my guard.

Miller clears his throat. "Margot, can you tell us why you went to Penny Lark's home yesterday?"

My stomach twists. I'm not supposed to talk without Shannon here. I know exactly how this works: they hope I'll slip up and say too much. My pulse drums in my ears, but I force myself to look calm. The fear from earlier pushes back into my chest, and I realize how badly I misread this situation when I came here for help. Now I'm the one under scrutiny, ensnared in a web of suspicion.

I swallow hard and speak, careful with my words. "I've been researching Hawthorn Manor," I say. "I heard Penny might have information on its history, so I wanted to ask her a few questions. That's all. I was curious."

Jenkins leans forward, that nasty smirk deepening. "You just happened to drop by her place the day before she drowns in the Lake? Sounds like more than plain curiosity."

My palms sweat against the armrests, and I can feel how flimsy my story sounds out loud. Jenkins opens his mouth again, but before he can spew more accusations, the door swings open with a sharp creak.

Shannon strides in, posture straight and eyes blazing. She's in a sleek outfit—skirt suit, crisp blouse—and she radiates a confidence that seizes the whole room. "All right," she snaps, "that's enough. You boys have had your fun. You know you can't question my client without me present. Out. Now."

Jenkins looks ready to argue, but Miller holds up a hand, sighing wearily. He leads Jenkins out, leaving the door to click shut behind them. All the tension in my body rushes out in a wave of relief.

"Shannon," I whisper, fighting tears. "How in the world did you–"

She crosses the space in a heartbeat, pulling me into a firm hug. I bury my face against her shoulder, and for the first time in what feels like forever, I feel the crushing weight on my chest lift, even if just a little. She's here. Maybe this nightmare is finally going to end.

"I may or may not have immediately gotten on a plane when you called me last night. The fear in your voice just didn't sit right with me. I couldn't leave you alone to manage whatever is happening here." She pulls back, looking me squarely in the eyes before motioning to the room we're currently in. "And it seems like I made the right decision."

We both giggle and then she refocuses, her gaze intense. "Listen, before we get into anything that's happening here, I need to share some information with you." She puts her brief-case on the table and pops it open revealing a trove of loose papers and folders, featuring handwritten notes on almost every surface.

"After we talked yesterday, I started digging into every-thing I could find about this town. And to be quite honest, I've even impressed myself. There is *a lot* of information here. And while a lot of it is interesting, there are a few items you must know."

I frown. "Okay, I may be more nervous now than when I was being interrogated by the cops a second ago. What is it? What did you find?"

She takes out a thick folder, her expression both excited and scared. "George Hawthorn had a sister—Amelia. She died when she was six, back in 1976. Their father, Normand, appeared to have one priority, and one priority only, which was his citrus business. This often left both kids alone with their mother, Dot, who allegedly was an alcoholic. There were rumors of domestic abuse, some of them even reported, but nothing ever came of them."

My heart skips. I think back to the photo I discovered in that hidden desk compartment—"A.H. 1976." That must have been her. The little girl in the photograph was George's sister, and she died that year.

Shannon flips open the folder, revealing what looks like a newspaper clipping. "Check this out. It's Amelia's obituary photo—she's with a group of other kids. The caption reads, 'The Bugs: (left to right) Andrew Miller, George Hawthorn, Amelia Hawthorn, Cecilia Doyle, Marty Hughes.'"

I blink at the grainy picture, not recognizing the majority of the names or faces. Shannon leans close, her tone dropping to a hushed whisper. "Andrew Miller. As in Chief Miller—the guy I just asked to leave this room."

My jaw falls open. "They were childhood friends?"

She nods, a sly smile spreading across her face. "Even better, they were a ragtag group of treasure hunters inspired by some short story by Edgar Allan Poe. And look at who else is there. Cecilia. George's future wife. They were all friends at one point, getting into mischief, hunting for treasure, and clearly falling in love."

I stare at the photo, my mind racing. Chief Miller, Cecilia, and George had all been photographed together. They had all known each other when Amelia had died.

This changed everything. Or maybe it changed nothing. But one thing was certain—bad things were happening in this town. Amelia, Cecilia, and Penny were dead. George was missing. And it looks like the police chief was right in the middle of it all.

Shannon and I sat in the dim, warm room, the air dense with anticipation. For the first time since this nightmare had begun, I feel a glimmer of hope. I have something now—something that finally connected the many pieces of what was going on in Mount Dora, Florida.

The problem is, he wears a gun and badge.

19

I watch the door swing open, and Chief Miller strides back in with Jenkins on his heels. Their expressions are startlingly casual, almost smug, like they're convinced they already have the upper hand. My pulse quickens at the sight of their self-assured grins, and I see Shannon straighten, ready for a fight. The tension crackles through the small room like static electricity.

"Chief. Deputy." Shannon's tone is razor-sharp, bristling with authority. "Before we proceed any further, I'd like to gain some clarity on this situation: Is my client under arrest? Because if she is not, this entire line of questioning lacks any legal basis. I see no probable cause or articulable suspicion here—merely the fact that Margot visited Penny Lark, like she has many Mount Dora residents. That is insufficient to transform a perfectly lawful visit into grounds for custodial interrogation. If you intend to charge her, cite the specific statute and present your evidence that ties her—beyond mere conjecture —to this alleged crime. You and I both know coincidence does not constitute probable cause, and holding her without substantive proof is a flagrant violation of her Fourth Amendment rights. So please, Chief, enlighten us: exactly what compelling, admissible evidence do you possess that justifies keeping her here in the first place, let alone asking her questions, alone, after she's made it clear she wants legal representation in the room."

Jenkins glances at Miller, clearly uncomfortable with Shannon's relentless questioning. Miller, who was so confident a moment ago, can't hide the way his mouth tightens. For a few beats, he looks like he might explode.

Shannon isn't about to give him a reprieve. "Also, since Penny's body was discovered under suspicious circumstances, I'd like clarification on exactly what you found. It sounds like you divulged information regarding her state to my client earlier today, though I'm sure you wouldn't do such a thing due to the glaringly obvious unethical and illegal implications of sharing information with a potential suspect before making them aware they *are* a suspect, right?"

I sit there, my heart pounding, trying not to show how incredible it is to watch Shannon work in her element. This is the same feeling I had during Lila's trial—Shannon's as fierce as I remember. She leans forward, then drops the bomb I didn't see coming. "And one last thing, Chief. Why is it that the people around you always seem to wind up dead? Amelia, George, Cecilia, and now Penny Lark. That's quite suspicious, wouldn't you say?"

Miller's face darkens, and his jaw sets like stone. "George Hawthorn isn't dead," he snarls, voice low and shaking with pent-up anger. "He's missing. And if you're suggesting I had a hand in any of those deaths, you're out of your mind. Yes, I was their friend, just like I am to the majority of this town. I am also a police officer. Amelia's death was a tragedy. All of it— every horrible thing that happened in that house—was Normand Hawthorn's fault. He abandoned those kids with a drunk and never looked back."

His voice rises, spittle flying as he jabs a finger inches from Shannon's face. "He cared more about those damn orange trees than his own children."

Shannon just fixes him with a cool, measured stare. "Thank you for clarifying that, Chief. So, you've essentially admitted you have no evidence and are holding my client here under false pretenses. Which means you have nothing to charge her with. We came seeking answers—you gave us nothing but wasted time."

Miller's shoulders lift, like he's gearing up to yell again, but no words escape. Jenkins shifts in his seat, refusing to meet my eyes.

Shannon stands, and I scramble to my feet as she motions for me to join her. "That's what I thought," she says, voice icy. "We're done here."

We make it to the door when Miller's furious growl echoes behind us. "Don't leave town, Margot." He practically spits my name. "This is still an active investigation."

Jenkins blocks our path for a moment, flashing a sinister little grin. "We don't appreciate outsiders meddling in our town's affairs. Especially when someone ends up dead."

Shannon glares back, her tone loaded with contempt. "Noted, Deputy. Now, move."

Jenkins mutters something under his breath and steps aside, letting us exit. The hallway beyond feels stifling, and my pulse is still racing. It's only once we pass through the station's double doors that I exhale a shaky breath, the humid night air washing over my clammy face.

Shannon and I slip into my car, slamming the doors with more force than necessary. As I pull out of the lot, I look back at the building, the station's parking lot lights flickering behind us. The shapes of the patrol cars and the looming figure of the station seem to shift ominously under those sputtering lamps, like shadows are reaching out for us.

For a while, neither of us speaks, the silence broken only by the hum of the engine and the occasional slap of tires against asphalt. Finally, Shannon glances at me. Concern and determination blend in her eyes. "So. Now what?" she asks, her voice gentler than it was inside.

I can still feel the leftover adrenaline buzzing in my veins. The image of Chief Miller's furious face looms in my mind. "Thanks to that brilliant brain of yours," I say quietly, "we already know our next clue."

She frowns, looking puzzled. "We do?"

"It's time to find Marty Hughes."

20

I keep casting sidelong glances at Shannon as she scrolls through her phone, tapping rapidly on the screen. We're cruising down the interstate, headlights illuminating the dark road ahead. I can't help noticing how she's already lost in research—digging into whatever she can about Mount Dora and Penny Lark. And it makes my stomach churn, knowing I've barely scratched the surface of what's really going on.

She must sense me staring because she suddenly stops typing and looks up. "Something on your mind?" she asks, her tone gentle, but her eyes razor-sharp.

I tighten my grip on the wheel. "I... I need to tell you something. Well, I need to tell you a lot of somethings. The real reason I was at Penny Lark's in the first place. The real reason I'm in this mess."

Shannon's brow furrows, and she sets her phone on her lap. "Margot, you know you can tell me anything."

"Yeah, I know, it's just—" I swallow past the knot in my throat. "Look, I never wanted to drag you into all this. I'm scared about how you'll react—and more importantly, I'm scared of getting you mixed up in something dangerous."

She crosses her arms, waiting. "Welp, I'm already here, so you might as well start spilling."

I grip the steering wheel so hard my knuckles whiten. "Okay. So... a few nights ago, when Hurricane Barbara came through, our main floor flooded. Nate had already left for DC. Water was everywhere. I was inspecting the floor trying to figure out where the leak was coming from when I found a floorboard that wasn't nailed down like the rest."

She stares at me, waiting for me to continue.

"When I pulled up the board, I found this black plastic film canister, like the kind we used to take to have developed. Inside that canister was a piece of paper–with a treasure map drawn on it."

She blinks, obviously caught off guard. "A treasure map."

I let out a weak laugh. "I know, it sounds insane, but it's true. It was hand-drawn and had a stereotypical X near this body of water, with streets that looked a lot like Mount Dora. So I poked around a little, and I found it. I found the chest. I dug it up myself and everything. Then I paid a guy who runs a boat touring company to help me take it across the lake so I could get it into my car and bring it back to the house."

Her face shifts from confusion to alarm. "Margot, wait–you *dug up* a chest–"

I push on, wanting to get it all out before I lose my train of thought. "Once I had it inside, I had to find the key; the chest had this big, thick lock on it. Long story short, I uncovered a hidden room behind a bookcase in the house and inside that room, I found the key that opened the lock. When I finally got it open..." I pause, feeling nauseous just thinking about it. "I found sixteen human skulls."

Shannon's mouth falls open, but she doesn't speak, so I keep going. "I freaked out and went to the police. I told them what I had found, but when we got there, the skulls were gone.

Not the chest; that was still there. But the skulls themselves, they had been removed."

I feel a tear run down my face. "The cops didn't believe me, of course, and I can't fault them for that. But instead of considering the possibility that I *could* be telling the truth, they basically chalked it up to a hallucination. But I *know* it wasn't a hallucination, I know what I saw, what I... smelled. And so, I figured if there were sixteen skulls, maybe there were sixteen missing people. That's why I went hunting for missing-persons cases in Mount Dora. That's how I found Michael Lark and ended up at Penny's house."

At first, she's silent. Then the anger surfaces. "Are you— Margot, do you realize how dangerous this all is? You've been playing detective with potential serial murders, for God's sake! You call me out here for a 'missing persons case' and then spring this on me?" Her voice rises, and she's half-shouting. "What if something happened to you? Have you even thought about that? Nate would return and have no clue where you were or why you were in this mess at all!"

My chest tightens. "I know, I know. But Shannon, I didn't go looking for this! I didn't ask to find that map. But once I did, it felt like fate... like some sort of opportunity to... to do something with my life, to be valuable again. Even if for nothing but a silly treasure hunt. What else was I going to do in that house all alone? Ever since Lila, I–"

"Stop," Shannon snaps, cutting me off. "You found actual human remains, Margot. You know approximately *zero* people in this fucking town, drawing all sorts of attention to yourself, have had multiple interactions with police already, and are a potential suspect in a murder case. And now I'm here, representing you, *just* learning about this right now!"

Tears prick my eyes. It had been a long time since Shannon yelled at me like this. "I'm sorry. I never meant to keep you in the dark. I wasn't sure how to tell you. Once Chief Miller sprung the Penny Lark death on me, I knew I was officially in over my head. I'm so sorry."

She presses a trembling hand against her forehead, exhaling hard. "Jesus, Margot."

The car grows quiet except for the hum of the tires. My vision blurs with tears, and I blink them away. I know I screwed up. I know how badly I messed things up by not telling her.

After several heartbeats, Shannon's voice softens. "Look, I'm furious and terrified and so worried for you. But I believe you. And I'm going to help you figure this out." She shifts, turning to face me more directly. "But once we do, you're coming back to Maryland with me. You hear me? I don't care what's going on with Nate or Hawthorn Manor or anyone else. You're walking away from this town."

A shaky laugh escapes me. "Really? Just… pack up and leave? But I only just got here."

She flicks me off. "Don't test me. I'm more stubborn than you, and I'll physically haul you out if I have to."

Relief mingles with lingering fear, but at least I don't feel alone anymore. Shannon's always been the fiercest protector I've ever known. "All right," I whisper. "Let's get out of this mess. Then I'll go with you."

"Damn straight, you will" she replies.

I manage a small smile. "So, we need a plan. We don't know what Marty knows—or if he's involved—but he did leave Mount Dora. That's got to mean something. Maybe he's distant enough from it all that he'll talk."

Shannon nods, her gaze distant as if she's mentally composing a strategy. "We start slow. Mention Hawthorn Manor, watch his reaction. If he's out of the loop, he might still know stories about George Hawthorn from back then. And if he does know something big, we definitely don't want him to clam up. We can't spook him."

I sigh, my grip tightening on the wheel. "Right. So, no immediate talk of... you know. The skulls." My stomach flutters at the thought. "You think he's part of it?"

She shakes her head, her expression conflicted. "Hard to say. If he left town, maybe it's because he wanted no part in whatever's happening. Or he might've seen something he shouldn't have. Either way, we need to approach carefully."

I nod, forcing myself to focus on the road. Despite the tension, having Shannon here steadies me. She always has a plan.

We finally spot the big box store, "Optimum Office Super Store," looming right in the middle of a strip mall. It's a huge, nondescript building with bright fluorescent letters on the sign hugged on either side by a discount furniture store and a fabric store.

After parking near the entrance, I take a moment to collect myself. "We can do this," I whisper under my breath, more to convince myself than anything.

Inside, the buzz of overhead lights mixes with the sound of scanning registers. A young greeter offers a halfhearted welcome, which I barely register. Shannon and I head straight for the customer service desk, where a woman with vibrant red hair looks up from her computer.

"Can I help you?" she asks, smiling politely.

I nod, trying to keep my voice steady. "We're looking for Marty Hughes. I believe he's the manager?"

She picks up a phone and pages him over the intercom. A few moments later, a tall man with graying hair steps out from the back. His name tag confirms he's Marty. He flashes a warm smile, coming over to greet us.

"Hi there, I'm Marty. What can I do for you ladies?"

My heart pounds. I remind myself to breathe. "Hi, Marty, I'm Margot, and this is Shannon. We're hoping you may be willing to chat with us for a few minutes. My husband and I just recently moved to Florida from Maryland. We, uh—we bought Hawthorn Manor in Mount Dora."

Marty's friendly expression crumbles the moment I say "Hawthorn Manor." His shoulders go rigid, eyes darting around like he's worried someone might overhear. "Listen, I don't know you," he says in a tense whisper. "And I don't want anything to do with Mount Dora or that house. You need to leave."

I feel Shannon stiffen at my side. I take a tentative step forward, making my voice as gentle as possible. "Please, Marty... if you know something, anything, please. We're not here to cause trouble."

He shakes his head firmly. "No. I've been done with that place for years. I want nothing to do with it. I'm sorry, but you need to go."

He steps out from behind the counter, guiding us toward the doors. My heart sinks, but desperation flares up inside me. Just before reaching the exit, I whirl around and pull out the old newspaper clipping Shannon found—the one with Amelia, George, Chief Miller, and Marty as kids, labeled "The Bugs."

"Marty, please." My voice trembles. "I know you were one of them. We don't know who else to trust, but we do know something's horribly wrong in Mount Dora."

Marty's eyes lock on the yellowed photograph. The color drains from his face, and his gaze turns glassy with tears. Slowly, he takes it from me, his hand shaking. "It's been years since I've seen these faces," he murmurs. He brushes a fingertip over the grainy images. I catch a glimpse of a wistful smile, quickly replaced by haunted worry.

Shannon edges closer. "We're just looking for answers. We don't want to drag you into any danger."

Marty looks up, scanning the store once more. After a shaky breath, he mutters, "Follow me."

He leads us down aisles of office chairs, folders, and printers. Eventually, he unlocks a door marked "Manager's Office." We slip inside, leaving the store's bustle behind. The room is cramped, stacked with paperwork and cardboard boxes. Photos on the desk show a smiling family—a woman with warm eyes, two college-aged daughters, and a teen boy standing in front of a sailboat.

A flicker of pride and sadness passes over Marty's face. "That's my wife, Josie. My kids: Emma, Rachel, and Tyler. Emma's at Florida State, Rachel's at UF, and Tyler's in med school at UCF. Everything I do– it's for them."

He glances at Shannon and me, his posture stiffening. "Which is why I'm telling you now: if I share anything with you, you keep my name out of it. My wife's battling breast cancer, and my kids need me. I can't afford to get pulled back into... whatever happens there."

I nod, my voice hushed. "We understand. We won't bring trouble to your door. I promise. Please, we need to know what's really happening in Mount Dora."

Marty seems to sag as if the weight on his shoulders is too heavy to carry. He lowers himself into the chair behind the desk and drags a hand over his face. Taking a deep breath, he begins to speak, his voice low and filled with a heavy sadness. "What you have to understand is, everything the Bugs did back then, it was all because of Dorothy Hawthorn."

21

The air in Marty's cramped back-office feels thick and stale. I can't shake the sensation that everything is about to change in this room—that the final pieces of this puzzle are about to click together. Shannon sits beside me, and I feel her tension prickling the air. Across the small desk, Marty exhales, looking like he's bracing for a storm.

"George's favorite book," he begins, "was Poe's *The Gold-Bug*—he was obsessed with it. Everything we did as kids tied back to that story somehow."

I exchange a quick glance with Shannon. She looks as puzzled as I am.

"The Gold-Bug," Marty explains, "is a classic treasure hunt story that incorporates cryptography and hidden messages—one of the first popular stories to really showcase how coded clues can lead to buried treasure. That concept fascinated George. He saw it as proof that sometimes, what's hidden can change the world. William Friedman—founder of the NSA—credited *The Gold-Bug* for inspiring him to become a cryptographer."

Shannon leans forward, arms resting on her knees. "So,

George wanted to make an impact on the world... using cryptography?"

Marty nods, a faint, sad smile tugging at his mouth. "Yes. In his own way, that was George's dream. He was forever crafting puzzles, building secret contraptions. Anything he could do to challenge the rest of us. Andrew Miller—yes, your very own Chief Miller—Cecilia Doyle, Amelia Hawthorn, and me... we were inseparable back then. Called ourselves 'the Bugs' because of Poe's story. George made it up, said we were just like William Legrand, the main character in the book. Amelia was George's kid sister, so she tagged along. He grumbled about it sometimes, but because Cecilia doted on Amelia, that was enough for him to put up with it."

I notice Marty's voice soften when he says Amelia's name, and for a brief moment, an almost wistful expression warms his face. But it fades just as quickly, replaced by a shadow.

"We grew up the way most kids did in the seventies," he says, running a hand through his graying hair. "Riding bikes, exploring, solving silly mysteries around town—like who kept stealing candy from McMyers, or why Farmer Jackson's cows kept breaking loose at night. We were known around Mount Dora as a rowdy group of junior detectives." He glances away, eyes flickering with memories. "Those days felt magical. But, like everything else, they came to an end."

Silence settles for a moment. Shannon shifts in her seat, clearly sensing there's more—something darker. I sit very still, my heart hammering in my chest.

Marty sighs. "Cecilia was originally from Ocala. Her parents, Margie and Thomas Doyle, moved to Mount Dora when she was a baby. Margie taught at our school, took a special liking to George from the start. And Cecilia, well, she was big into history, loved the architecture of old churches.

Hawthorn Manor was built in that gothic style mostly because she wanted it that way."

He rubs his hands together, the skin dry and pale. "George was different. Born here in '62, he had deep roots in Mount Dora—especially through his father, Normand, who ran a large citrus grove business. It made the family well-off, and the town respected him." Marty's voice wavers. "Normand was hardly ever home, and when he was, he seemed more invested in refining the town's image of him, rather than being a father to his own kids. That left George and Amelia in the care of their mother, Dorothy— 'Dot' to most."

Marty pauses, running his tongue over his lips as though his mouth has gone dry. "Dot gave birth to Amelia in 1970, and after that... she went to a dark place. Postpartum depression, we'd call it now, but back then no one talked about it much. She started drinking heavily. Everyone knew, but nobody intervened. Normand's influence, small-town silence... it was easier to look the other way."

A chill skitters up my spine. Shannon inhales sharply, and I reach over to gently squeeze her arm.

Marty closes his eyes for a second before continuing, voice low. "One day, George and Amelia started turning up with bruises. We Bugs saw it, but we were just kids ourselves. We had no idea how to help. By winter of '75, things escalated. Dot passed out drunk one night holding a lit cigarette, and she nearly burned down half the house. Destroyed their Christmas tree and the gifts underneath it. I still remember seeing George afterward—he looked hollow. The curiosity and joy in him just... vanished."

He steeples his fingers, staring down at the cluttered desk. "George spent that Christmas at my house. He told me that Dot was a ticking time bomb. He begged his father for help, but Normand wouldn't even acknowledge there *was* a problem, let alone intervene. George said he feared something terrible would happen if no one intervened. We tried to reassure him, but... in the spring of '76, it all came crashing down."

My heart thuds heavier, bracing for what's next. I notice Shannon's breathing is as uneven as mine.

Marty meets our gaze, his own eyes glistening. "Amelia died that year. The official story was that she accidentally fell down the stairs. But George, Andrew, and I—we knew. Dot's temper was explosive. We'd seen it, even felt it. George didn't tell us the details outright, but we understood that night changed him forever. Amelia was gone, and everything about him hardened."

A wave of grief seems to pass through the small office, like the air itself is slowing down to listen to Marty's words. I feel myself leaning in, almost forgetting to breathe.

"After Amelia's death, George clung to Cecilia," Marty says. "She was his anchor, and her mom tried to give him some semblance of a family. Andrew and I drifted to the sidelines. George and Cecilia were always whispering, hiding things from everyone. There was a period there when the "Bugs" didn't really exist at all. Amelia was gone, George and Cece rarely spent time with us; so it was just Andrew and me. Then, that Fall, Dot died too—same cause, supposedly. Fell down the stairs just like Amelia. People whispered about curses, ghosts, or just bad luck. But Andrew and I suspected it wasn't so inno-cent. George hated his mother. And if he felt like she caused Amelia's death..."

He trails off, voice trembling. I realize he's on the verge of revealing something monstrous. Shannon shifts next to me, and I grab her hand to steady myself.

Marty licks his lips. "But we were best friends. We stuck together, even when we knew something wasn't right." He looks up, his eyes haunted. "One night, George called us back to Hawthorn House. We hadn't all been there since Amelia's funeral. The place was dark and neglected. He took us upstairs to see Normand, who was frail and dying from lung cancer by that time. And then we sat down in the parlor, and George told us the truth about Amelia—that Dot had killed her in a drunk rage. Threw her down the stairs over something as trivial as a misplaced lighter. George was there, saw it happen—and Dot just walked away. Like it was nothing."

Shannon's hand goes stiff in mine, and I realize I'm practically crushing her fingers in my grip. I force myself to let go a bit.

Marty's voice shakes as he speaks. "Cecilia tried to keep George from doing anything rash. But he told us he dreamed of killing Dot every night, that he couldn't stop picturing Amelia's broken body. The only thing he wanted was revenge. Eventually, that rage... it won."

A hush falls over the room. I feel an almost tangible coldness, like the secrets of Hawthorn Manor are leeching into the air around us. Marty looks spent, drained by recounting these horrors. My mind swirls with questions: Did George actually kill Dot? Was there a cover-up? And how do those tragedies lead to the nightmares unfolding in the manor now?

A glance at Shannon shows me she's pale, her jaw set in grim determination. I know she's already forming a plan, but her eyes mirror my own fear.

Finally, I manage to speak, my voice wavering. "So... you think George...?"

Marty nods, pain etched across his face. "And from that day on, nothing in Mount Dora was ever the same."

22

I t was night when everything changed in Hawthorn House. George returned home, his father's absence providing the opportunity.

The house lay cloaked in darkness, the only sound the creaking of old floorboards under his careful steps. George moved with purpose, his eyes fixed on the dim hallway. Dot's room was at the end, on the second floor. He ascended the stairs, the old wood groaning beneath his weight, each step deliberate and heavy. He reached her room and peered in to find her sprawled on the bed with a bottle of gin tipped over, soaking her nightgown. The acid smell of alcohol filled the room.

George called her name, voice echoing down the narrow hall, loud enough to break her drunken stupor.

Dot rose slowly, her eyes unfocused, and staggered toward the staircase, her limbs moving like those of a marionette with cut strings. George slipped away into Amelia's old room, hidden in the shadows, as Dot stumbled closer. She moved like an apparition, her face hollow and devoid of expression, her clothes clinging damply to her body. She reached the stairs, taking her first faltering step downward.

George emerged from the darkened room, his voice cutting

through the heavy silence. "Amelia was the only good thing to come from this family, and you took her from this world." His words echoed, hard and final. Dot turned, her glazed eyes meeting his, recognition flickering for a split second.

There was no time for more. George lunged, and his foot met her chest. Dot fell, tumbling down the staircase, her body colliding with the wooden steps, each impact punctuated by the sharp crack of breaking bones. Her screams were fleeting, swallowed by the viciousness of the descent, until she finally lay motionless at the bottom.

George stood at the top of the stairs, expression unreadable, waiting. Below, Dot's body shuddered, her breaths wet and labored. Blood pooled around her head, and she mumbled, her words a jumble of sounds that never entirely formed. He walked down the stairs and watched unflinchingly as her movements slowed and her eyes lost focus.

When the last flicker of life had faded, he turned away, stepping over her crumpled form without another glance. The door swung open, the night air spilling in as George walked out, leaving only silence behind him.

23

I can sense the tension in the cramped office the moment Marty utters those words: "And from that day on, nothing in Mount Dora was ever the same." It's like a dense weight settles over the room, pressing in from all sides. Shannon is beside me, pale and silent, her eyes locked on Marty. He doesn't look at either of us; he just keeps staring down at his hands, as if speaking these memories aloud might tear him apart.

"Cecilia knew the truth," he says, voice low and weary. "And she carried it with George. They shut me and Andrew out after that. We were never fully part of their secret, only pieces on the periphery. But we knew George had changed—his warmth replaced by something colder, darker. Almost like he believed he had to become the monster he once feared his mother was."

My stomach churns. George Hawthorn, the philanthropic figure who once charmed this entire town, has been revealed as something else entirely—a killer. I glance over at Shannon. She's staring at the floor, jaw clenched. Her knuckles are white where she's gripping her notebook.

Marty rubs his temples, like recounting all of this is taking every bit of strength he has left. "Once George told us what really happened, I felt this awful mix of horror and relief. On one hand, our friend was confiding in us again—like we were the original Bugs, all together. But on the other hand, he'd just admitted to murder." He exhales a shaky breath. "I'd be lying if I said I never thought about turning him in. But how could I betray my best friend after everything he'd endured? So the four of us made a pact, right there in that living room. We vowed never to reveal Amelia's or Dorothy's real cause of death. We thought George deserved peace after all he'd gone through."

I swallow hard. The notion of that silent agreement sends a chill through me. "So why break it now?" I ask quietly, trying to steady my voice. "Why tell us all this?"

Marty sighs. "Because George once promised he could control his darkness. After Dot was gone, he swore there'd be no more violence. I believed him—he was my friend and he'd already lost so much. Then Cecilia died on the lake, and everything spun out of control."

A prickle of dread courses through me. I can't help wondering if, somewhere deep down, I already suspected George was capable of this. Part of me feels a twisted kind of vindication at having those suspicions confirmed. Yet I'm also horrified—what if that single murder wasn't the end?

Marty leans forward, elbows on his knees. "We Bugs grew up. We drifted apart, but we still lived in the same town. George, Andrew, Cecilia, and me—we were all woven into Mount Dora's tapestry. George took over his father's citrus business; Cecilia poured her heart into Hawthorn Manor, dreaming of kids they never managed to have. Andrew joined the police department, rose through the ranks fast as lightning. And me... well, I eventually inherited McMyers Corner Candy Store, turned it into a general shop with a pharmacy. The four of us essentially provided for the town in different ways—food, medicine, safety, hope. For a long while, it felt... good."

He hesitates, and there's a flicker of sorrow in his eyes. "But then Cecilia died, and it shook everyone. The funeral was closed-casket; her body was in no condition for viewing. George was devastated, but it was different from the heart-break I'd seen him bear as a kid. He wasn't angry this time, he was empty. He cut himself off from the community. Stopped tending the grove, stopped showing up for meetings. His business started crumbling, and the town felt the blow."

Shannon leans in, her brow creased in concern. "What happened next?"

Marty's gaze shifts, like he's peering into a distant memory. "Mount Dora was quiet, hardly any crime. Sometimes we had minor theft, mostly from Freddy Bahn—a guy a few years behind us in school, fell into addiction. But, two months after Cecilia's passing, Freddy disappeared. At first, no one even noticed. But eventually people asked questions. No leads surfaced, and it became this hushed mystery."

A heaviness settles in my chest. I know where this is going—I can feel it, and every nerve in my body bristles at the implication.

"Andrew and I started to worry," Marty continues, rubbing a hand across his mouth. "We knew George's history, knew what he was capable of when grief and anger mixed. We decided to visit him at Hawthorn Manor. Strangely, we found him in high spirits—warm, almost nostalgic. He looked different, had grown his hair and beard out. He hugged us, poured us whiskeys in front of the fireplace. We laughed about old times."

His voice drops, and I see the pain in his eyes. "It was the best night we'd had in years. Then, as we were leaving, Andrew spotted a wallet on the entry table—that wasn't George's.

George always carried a worn leather wallet with a tiny orange stitched into it, a gift from his father. This one was different. Andrew distracted George, and I peeked inside. The ID belonged to Freddy Bahn."

Shannon sucks in a sharp breath. My own heart thunders so loud I think they might hear it. Marty draws a deep breath and lets it out slowly.

"That's why I left town," he says, voice thick with regret. "I'd kept George's secret because I understood what he'd gone through. I loved him like a brother. But a second murder? I couldn't handle that. It broke something inside me. So, I packed up my family and moved to Winter Haven in 2009, and I've steered clear of Mount Dora ever since."

He looks up at me, eyes drained, and continues quietly. "My gut says Andrew had something to do with George's disappearance after that. Maybe he confronted George about Freddy, and things went south. Andrew was always the type to protect the community, even from his best friend if it came to that. And George... after the deaths of Amelia, Dot, then Cecilia... I can't imagine what was left of his sanity. I think they had it out—maybe Andrew killed him, or maybe he instructed George to vanish. Either way, Andy is still there in Mount Dora, and George is gone."

An uneasy hush stretches between us. My thoughts whirl around Marty's theory: if George is truly dead, who's behind the events in Mount Dora?

Marty must read the turmoil on my face because he murmurs, "I don't have all the answers. I only know that once, my friend killed someone to avenge his sister. And it might not have ended there."

He leans back in his chair, exhaustion carving lines into his features. I glance at Shannon, who's scribbling frantic notes in her legal pad. She lifts her eyes to me, and I can see they're shining with a mix of fear and resolve.

She turns to face Marty again, and voices the same exact thought I just had: "If George really is gone... then who's causing all this chaos now?"

Marty rubs his palms on his thighs as if he can't get them clean. "I wish I knew," he says softly. "Or maybe I don't. All I know is, whatever's happening in Mount Dora, it's bigger than all of us."

I nod, trying to steady myself. *Bigger than all of us*, I think. The phrase bounces in my mind, echoing with a hollow ring. Because if George Hawthorn isn't the monster lurking in the shadows of the manor anymore, then someone—or something—else is.

24

I grip the steering wheel as Shannon and I drive home, both of us reeling from everything we just heard. My thoughts tumble in a clash of disbelief and excitement: George is a killer—there's no escaping that fact. But did he continue killing? Is he responsible for Michael and Penny Lark? Those questions feel substantial and unanswered.

Marty's theory keeps echoing in my head: George might have died after killing Freddy Bahn. If that's true, there's a second murderer in Mount Dora, and yet the idea of multiple serial killers operating in a quiet little town feels improbable. The more we dissect the situation, the more Shannon and I realize how little we actually know.

One certainty grips me: Andrew Miller, the Chief of Police, is corrupt. Maybe not to a diabolical degree, but he clearly knew about several murders and disregarded the law because the murderer had been his friend. If he killed George, for whatever reason, he qualifies as a dirty cop. Plus, he never left Mount Dora, unlike Marty, which seems even more suspicious.

This means the Mount Dora police force can't be trusted. If Andrew is dirty, that rot might run through the department. Our earlier instinct to avoid law enforcement was on point.

The local police aren't only incompetent when it comes to solving these murders—they also pose a threat to us. I don't trust them, and I don't feel safe with them.

My gaze drifts out the window, and my thoughts keep racing. I replay every word Marty said, the tightness in my chest still there. I recall the way his face crumpled when he remembered his friends.

Suddenly, something clicks in my mind, and I blurt out, "Holy shit, Shannon!" I sit bolt upright, practically throwing my hands in the air.

Shannon, focused on her phone, jerks in her seat. "You can't do that to someone, ya nut job!"

I'm too excited to care. "There are two houses, Shan. Two. Houses." I stare at her, waiting for the realization to dawn.

"Yes... but Marty said one burned down during that Christmas fire, didn't he?" she asks, sounding skeptical.

"He said there was a fire, yes. But he never said the house burned down. How could it have, if George returned there and killed Dot?"

Shannon's frown deepens, and she glances at me, her eyes going wide as the implication sinks in. "Wait... Are you saying there's another house still standing?"

"That is *exactly* what I'm saying."

By the time we pull into Hawthorn Manor's driveway, the sun is sliding below the horizon, casting deep shadows across the property. I kill the engine, and we hurry inside, straight to the study. I lead the way, my heart pounding with anticipation.

She takes in the massive room, the dusty bookshelves, the large windows. "You know," Shannon quips, trying to lighten the mood, "this place is huge and creepy as hell. Couldn't you have picked a smaller haunted house?"

I manage a half-hearted smile and focus on shifting the books in the correct order. When the bookcase juts open,

Shannon jumps back, raising her hands in a mock karate stance. "What in the actual Scooby-Doo shit is this, Margot?"

I ignore her dramatic reaction and step inside the hidden room, heading straight for the wall where I saw something earlier—a faded, frayed plot map. "Look," I whisper, touching the fragile paper. "Here's Hawthorn Manor on the southwest side of the grove."

Shannon leans in, scanning the map. "And here," she says, pointing to a spot on the northeast side, "is another house."

We stare at that outline together, the same realization hitting us at once. Another house. On the same property. Hawthorn *House.*

We knock knuckles, adrenaline igniting our determination, and dash outside. The sky has deepened into purples and pinks, the sun nearly gone. We trudge through rows of dead citrus trees, the air turning chillier by the minute. The grove seems to go on forever, the twisted branches snagging at our clothes, as if trying to hold us back.

The flashlight on Shannon's phone bobs over uneven ground, and our feet crunch over dry leaves that crackle in the silence. The chill bites at my skin, making the trek feel even longer. Then, just as darkness fully settles, I spot it.

An old house rises in the distance, nearly swallowed by a row of overgrown cypress trees. It's much smaller than Hawthorn Manor, the roof sagging with several windows broken. The front porch tilts precariously, as though the entire building is slowly sinking into the earth. It looks forgotten, an echo of the past waiting for someone to notice it again.

Shannon and I exchange a single look—fear and determination swirling between us. We've found the old Hawthorn House. Whatever secrets this house is hiding, we're about to uncover them.

25

I reach for the heavy handle first, but quickly realize the door itself isn't fully shut. Surprised the wind hasn't forced it open yet, I gently push the door inward. The hinges groan so loudly it makes my spine prickle, the echo rippling through every dark corner inside. A suffocating, stale smell pours out—a nauseating cocktail of wood rot, mildew, and something sharp and metallic that sets my nerves on high alert.

Shannon crinkles her nose, covering it with her hand. I grope along the wall and find a switch. With a reluctant click, dusty overhead bulbs flicker awake, throwing a jaundiced light across the room. I narrow my eyes, struggling to see in the weak glow. The bulbs buzz, fighting to stay lit, but they reveal just enough for us to take in the drapes of spiderwebs and the shadows lurking in every corner. Curtains, thick with dust, weigh down the windows, soaking up what little light there is.

"This place is giving me the creeps," Shannon whispers, her voice barely above a breath. "It feels like the Tower of Terror at Disney—minus, ya know, the whole fun ride part."

I give a small nod, my throat too dry to speak. A thick, oppressive energy throbs all around us, like the walls themselves are sneaking closer to us whenever we look away. We walk deeper in, each footstep echoing unnaturally loud. Every room we pass seems haunted by the same story—drapes of darkness, forgotten furniture, and crooked family photos. There's a silence so deep it rings in my ears.

I pause at a line of photos along the hallway. Faces stare back from behind the glass: George, his little sister Amelia, and their parents, Normand and Dorothy. Their smiles are so forced it almost hurts to look at them. The nerve endings on my head start to prickle.

"Margot...look." Shannon's voice quivers behind me.

She stands at the base of the stairs, gaze pinned to a dark stain pooled across the worn floorboards. Even in this dim light, it's unmistakable, the color and shape telling a bleak story.

"Is that..." Her voice cracks before she can finish the last word.

I nod. "Blood. This is definitely where Amelia and Dorothy both died."

My stomach twists. Every step I take sends a new wave of fear shuddering through my body. My eyes dart around, half-expecting some ghastly figure to lunge from the shadows.

We stop at the basement door. I feel cold air seeping through the gap beneath it, like a warning. My hand hovers over the doorknob, and a strange pulse in my temples makes the door look like it's breathing. Shannon rests a hand on my shoulder, silently reminding me we're in this together. I grit my teeth and push the door open. It groans on its hinges, revealing a steep descent into darkness.

A surge of frigid air smacks me square in the face, laced with an overpowering coppery stench that makes my eyes water. The smell clings to my tongue, thick and nauseating. I gag, swallowing the bitter tang of fear. Shannon tries for a shaky joke. "Silver lining: if this is how I die, at least I won't have to pay off my student loans."

I force a weak snort. "Your parents paid for your college, you idiot," I mutter, but my voice trembles, betraying my terror.

"Shhh!" she hisses, flashing me a taut grin as she starts down the steps.

Each step groans an ominous welcome, and a wet sloshing noise grows louder with every footfall, like we're closing in on something vile and alive. The darkness presses in, crawling over my skin, setting every nerve aflame. With three steps left to go, I freeze.

There, against the far wall, something shifts. A shadow. And it's not ours.

"Shannon," I whisper, the word barely making it past the dryness in my throat, "do you see that?"

She squints into the gloom, eyes wide, and nods. My chest constricts so tightly I can hardly breathe. Someone else is down here. The thought ricochets through my head, turning every heartbeat into a thunderclap.

Forcing myself to move, I edge onto the next stair. The shape along the wall jerks, then stops cold, like it senses me. My lungs burn, but I'm terrified to breathe, as though even the slightest sound might trigger something unspeakable.

Click. The basement plunges into absolute blackness, so intense that for a moment I'm not sure I still exist. My ears ring with silence. My hands grope blindly in front of me.

"Shannon?" I rasp, my voice cracks in fear.

"I'm here," she calls, shaky but audible.

Then I hear it—the ragged, heavy breaths of a stranger, prowling along the wall, inching closer. My stomach lurches violently. Every hair on my body stands on end. It's the primal fear of being hunted, of prey cornered in a predator's den.

I shuffle urgently toward Shannon, but the darkness feels alive, twisting us apart. My arms wave through emptiness. We're both off the stairs now, but I can't tell how far into the room we actually are.

"Shannon?" I call again, more desperate this time.

"Margot, stay close!" she says, voice barely above a hiss.

Suddenly, someone—something—charges up the stairs. The thunder of footsteps explodes above us, and the door slams shut, leaving an even deeper hush behind. I'm suffocating in this void, my heart hammering so violently I think it might burst out of my chest.

I swallow, forcing my dry throat to speak. "Shannon?"

"I'm here." Her voice is nearer, a thin lifeline in the dark. "Hold on."

I hear her fumbling, the clink of her phone. Then, a flash of light explodes from the phone's screen, illuminating her pale, terrified face for a heartbeat. Her eyes are wild, sweat carving tracks through the dust on her cheeks. Before either of us can speak, the phone slips from her fingers, smashing screen-first onto the floor. Everything goes black once more.

"Fuck!" Shannon curses. "Hold on, I'll find it."

I shuffle forward, feeling the walls closing in. My foot strikes against something and I stumble. My knee collides with cold porcelain, sending a jarring shock up my leg. Biting back a yelp, I reach down and trace my fingers along a curved edge— an antique claw-foot bathtub.

A wave of dread slams into me. In the darkness, my fingertips graze something wet and viscous, smearing across my skin. Blood, I know it without even needing to see the liquid. My stomach turns inside out. I jerk my hand away, struggling not to vomit as my mind whirls with awful possibilities. The stench intensifies—a sickly mixture of rust and decomposition that clogs my lungs.

Just when I'm sure I can't take another second, Shannon manages to flip the breaker on the wall. Dim, flickering light floods the basement, and in that moment, I see the tub for what it is: a horror show splashed with crimson. My breath falters, and my vision swims.

"Margot, don't look!" Shannon cries, her voice trembling with pure panic.

But it's already too late. My eyes latch onto the figure slumped in the bathtub. An adult man—headless. Smeared trails of blood snake from the jagged stump at his neck, winding up the stairs like a grotesque path leading out of this dungeon. My gaze drifts to his limp left arm draped over the tub's edge only inches from my face. And resting exactly where it should be—between his pinky and middle fingers—sits my husband's wedding ring.

26

I barely register Shannon's frantic voice, her words warping and muffling as though they're coming from somewhere underwater. Everything slows to a dreadful crawl. Nate's left hand lies only inches away—his wedding ring catching the faint light. I can't reconcile what I'm seeing with reality. The air around me thickens, colors blur into each other, and the world wavers at the edges. My focus tunnels, collapsing inward, darkness nibbling at my vision. I keep telling myself: It can't be Nate. It can't be him in that bathtub.

Yet, here he is—or what's left of him. My Nate. My mind reels at the impossibility, the horror. I reach out, my fingers trembling like leaves in a storm, and touch his palm. It's still warm. Tears spill unchecked down my cheeks, each drop splattering on the dingy floor.

Somewhere behind me, Shannon's voice slices through the haze, snapping against my consciousness like a whip. "Margot! We have to go. They could come back. Margot, please—get up!"

Her urgency barely penetrates the thick grief that has crashed over me, heavy and unrelenting. My knees feel fused to the floor. How can I possibly leave him here? None of this was

supposed to happen. Nate should be in DC, miles away, doing...
anything besides lying here, soaked in blood. We were
supposed to fight and scream and then reconcile. We were
supposed to grow old together.

Shannon latches onto my arm, desperation fueling her
strength. She tugs, shakes, pleads—each pull yanking me back
from the black pit threatening to consume me. My body
responds automatically, though I feel hollow inside. My legs
lock and unlock, stumbling in a mechanical march up the
stairs as Shannon sobs, half-leading, half-dragging me
forward.

"We have to go," she begs, her voice raw, cracking on every
word. "Please, Margot. I know you're in shock, but we have to
move. Now!"

My brain is stuck on a loop, replaying images that layer
over each step. Nate smiling on our wedding day, his arm
around my waist, whispering, "I've got you," against my ear as
we danced. My foot lifts onto a stair. I remember the first night
in our new home, the comforting weight of his hand on my
back, his fingertips making soothing circles. Another step.
Then the promise we made: no matter how bad life got, we'd
stand by each other.

Somehow, Shannon gets me through the hallway, guiding
me with single-syllable commands. "Door. There. Go. Keep
walking." Her voice wavers, on the edge of panic. "Just a little
further, Margot. Come on."

We burst outside into the grove, the tree silhouettes
twisting in the darkness. My vision swims in and out, but I feel
Shannon pause beside me, panting, tears streaking the grime
on her face.

"I don't know if I can leave you here," she whispers, voice
trembling. "Should I run ahead, get the car? But I can't just—"

She's looking at me, expecting something, some response,

but I've got nothing. The world has drained of meaning. I'm a shell, sleepwalking through a nightmare.

Shannon steels herself and loops an arm around my waist, half-carrying me through the blackness. Branches whip at our legs, and my foot catches on tree roots, but she keeps going, one dogged step after another. There's a fierceness in her grip —a raw determination that feels like it's the only thing keeping me upright.

Finally, we break free from the grove and stumble toward Hawthorn Manor. Its dark shape looms, a silent witness to everything that's happened. I can't bring myself to speak. I can't bring myself to feel anything at all.

Shannon pushes open the door, guiding me inside. The overhead lights glare down, brutally ordinary against the horror we've just left behind. She guides me into the living room, to the sofa. I sink onto the cushions, noticing Nate's blood smeared across my palms. My stomach twists; I want to scream, but no sound escapes.

All I can think is: Nate is dead. He was supposed to be safe, far away, alive. Now there's blood on my hands—his blood. My eyes flick to Shannon. She's trembling, her shirt soaked with tears, and guilt crashes down on me. Why am I still breathing? Why do I get to exist while he's—?

A surge of hatred for this house grips me. This goddamn place that's seen so much violence, so much pain. I hate it for bearing witness, for standing here unchanged when everything else is ruined.

My head feels like it's splitting open. I shut my eyes tight, trying to slow time, to shrink the crushing tide of grief. Nate's face flips to another memory: a battered young girl huddled in the corner of a locked bedroom. Bruises, scratches, helpless tears. Lila is another one of the many victims of my inability to protect anyone I love.

It's too much. My chest constricts; my vision darkens. I let out a ragged exhale and feel myself slip off the couch, my legs giving way beneath me. Shannon's voice warps, fading to a distant hum.

And the last coherent thought crashing through my mind is one simple, harrowing truth: They would all be better off if I had never existed.

27

I wake with a jolt, disoriented and drenched in sweat. Nightmares mixing with memories seem to blur at the edges of my vision, and I struggle to piece together which is which. I blink, forcing my gaze to focus. I'm on the living room couch, and across the room, Shannon is curled in an armchair, legs tucked in tight, head leaning back. A faint gleam catches my eye—a knife, resting on the side table beside her, reflecting the dim morning light.

My pulse hammers as last night's horrors throb at the back of my mind. I feel suddenly untethered from time. Hours, minutes, days—I can't tell how long I've been lying here. My phone... Where is my phone? I pat at my pockets, search the cushions, no luck. Staring around the room, I see Shannon's bulging bag of police documents and the plot map scattered on a side table, the edges crinkled from being carried around. It all looks so out of place, like a bizarre staging of my own panic.

I swallow the dryness in my throat and rise slowly, not wanting to wake Shannon. My body aches. Each step toward the kitchen feels deliberate, each board creaking like a siren in this quiet house. The click of ice hitting a glass, the hiss of the faucet, the low hum of the fridge's water dispenser—every noise is jarringly loud.

I take a cold sip, lifting my chin and my arm overhead to stretch the knot out of my lower back. My hand brushes something small and familiar on the counter—a dead iPhone. It must have been tossed aside when we made it home last night.

I have no energy, no idea what to do next. All I want is to curl up and vanish. Instead, I shuffle toward the staircase, haunted by a sickly ache pounding at the base of my skull. The first step up triggers a flash: Nate's headless body, that brutal slash of red against sterile white porcelain. My stomach roils, and I cling to the banister, knuckles whitening.

Another step. I see Shannon's face, terrified, transfixed by the gruesome scene. I press my lips together, trying to swallow the surge of nausea.

Next step. The grueling walk back in total darkness, the twisted branches of dead citrus trees scraping at my sleeves.

When I reach the landing, my heartbeat is a wild staccato inside my ribs, yet I feel oddly numb. I walk into the bedroom, setting the phone on its charger with a kind of distant detachment. My reflection in the dresser mirror stops me; I barely recognize myself—pale, eyes sunken, like the essence of who I was has seeped out through the night. Maybe a shower will help. Maybe I can scrub away the scent of blood and terror from both my body and subconscious.

I pull off my stained sweatshirt, goosebumps raising on my arms as the cool air hits my skin. My bra strap slips down one shoulder. I reach for the button on my jeans, but a prick of alarm cuts through my haze. Something is off.

The chest.

I glance to the corner of the room. It's empty. Yesterday, that battered old chest was there—I'm sure of it. My heart stutters, and adrenaline flares in my veins. How could it be gone? My mind scrambles to retrace every step—police station, Marty Hughes' store, Hawthorn House—but I can't shake the looming, gut-twisting realization: someone took it.

I hurry to the top of the stairs and crouch, inspecting the wood for fresh scratches or dirt. Nothing. It's impossible that someone alone carried that massive chest down these steps without leaving a mark. Had there been a group of people creeping around her home? Or what if they used another way —what does that mean? My pulse is a drumbeat in my ears.

I grab hold of the banister again as my world spins. It feels like my feet have been pulled out from under me and are now floating in the air, high above my head. George Hawthorn was obsessed with hidden rooms, secret compartments. What if there is another one up here–a way for someone to take the chest without using the stairs?

I move through the upstairs hallway, rummaging desperately. I shove aside chairs, test the walls, check every seam for a disguised door. A surge of adrenaline propels me. Whoever did this stole not just the chest, but likely the skulls as well. They might be the one responsible for the horror in that basement. And if I catch them here, that would put me face to face with a killer.

Another realization hits me like a freight train, pulling the wind from my lungs. If someone else has access to this house, this floor; if someone else intentionally took the skulls that day, but left the chest, they did it for a reason–to humiliate me in front of the police, in front of Walter. Someone wants to paint me as crazy. *What the fuck is happening?*

I search and search and come up with nothing. No hidden door, no secret panel. My frustration reaches a boiling point. Nate's voice echoes in my mind—his warmth, his laughter— and then the image of his headless body crashes in. Rage and grief sear my chest.

I yank books off a shelf, flipping them aside and screaming at the silence. I'm not thinking clearly. I slam my fists on the bathroom door so hard my arms shake. Tears blur my vision, but I refuse to stop.

A bottle of shampoo meets my hand, and I hurl it at the mirror. The glass shatters like ice, shards catching the light as they scatter across the sink.

"Why?" I scream, voice cracking against the tile. My knees buckle; I collapse onto the cold floor. My sobs tear out of me, raw and ugly. It's all too much—fear, helplessness, guilt— piling up until there's nothing left of me to fight back.

"Margot!"

I hear Shannon's voice ring out, a burst of alarm in the hallway. She rushes in, kneeling by my side, clutching my shoulders with urgent care. "What's going on? Are you hurt?"

I shake my head, tears blurring my words. "The chest... It's gone. It was here, and now it's just...gone. Someone took it."

Shannon wraps her arms around me, and I fold into her, trembling with sobs that rack my whole body. She holds me like a lifeline, letting me weep until my chest starts to burn. When my cries subside, she pulls back, pressing her forehead gently to mine.

"Margot, we have to go to the police," she says, voice careful but firm. "There's a body at Hawthorn House, and now a robbery here. Please, this is beyond us right now. We have to let them handle this. We need help."

I look up, eyes swollen, throat raw. She continues, voice soft yet resolute. "I'll be there every step. Then we'll go home. We'll figure things out and rebuild—together. You and me."

Her words land, but something in me snaps. The terror that held me hostage twists into something darker, hotter, filling the void. My grief morphs into fury so potent it makes my hands shake. I clench my teeth, push myself upright, and stare at Shannon.

"Shannon. Someone's been kidnapping and murdering people in this town for years. They took Michael Lark, destroyed Penny's sanity. They took Nate—my husband, my anchor, my hope for a future. And the police in Mount Dora have done nothing. Chief Miller's lived here his entire life, and it's only gotten worse."

My anger flares, each new thought like a lit match in a pool of gasoline. "They've had every chance to act, but they failed. Maybe they're corrupt, or maybe they're just incompetent. Either way, I refuse to rely on them."

I'm pacing now, arms stiff at my sides. My voice climbs, fueled by raw anguish. "I let Lila down. I let you down. Nate, Penny—so many people, hurt. But Shannon, this isn't some twisted scavenger hunt. It's not a game, to me. This is my legacy, my opportunity to be who I've never been able to be. Those skulls belonged to victims who have no voice, no chance at justice. But I can speak for them, act for them. I'll end this, no matter what it takes, so nobody else ends up in that chest."

Shannon stands, meeting my frantic energy with a wary calm. "You're not alone, Margot. I'm with you. We'll find whoever did this together. But please"—she rests a hand on my arm—"you have to let other people help you. I'm scared."

I shudder, the anger still pulsing in my veins. But her concern slices through my rage. She's right. I glance at her and realize I'm still crying; tears blur my sight. I brush them away, inhaling a shaky breath.

"You're right, you're right. I love you," I whisper. "I'm so sorry I brought you into this mess. Thank you for always being here."

She holds out her arms, and I crash into her hug. Whatever comes next, I won't face it alone.

Shannon pulls back, assessing me and then herself. "Let's get cleaned up, organize our documentation, and then figure out the best way to share this with the police."

I look down and then at her. She's right; there's still blood on my arms and chest. We're both filthy. A hot shower, some clean clothes, my best friend, and the truth; together will find whoever murdered Nate. And when we do, I'll make sure they never get another chance to hurt anyone else.

28

The rhythmic drumming of the shower lulls me as I sit on the edge of the bed, listening to Shannon rinse off the grime of everything that has happened. It feels like an eternity has passed in just one day—like I've stepped into a different life altogether. Every time my thoughts drift, they circle back to the image of Nate in that bathtub. His blood, that dirty floor, and the glint of his wedding ring still on his finger. My throat tightens just thinking about it, a fresh wave of tears threatening to overwhelm me.

I breathe unsteadily, trying to keep myself from collapsing into another spiral. I grab my phone, unlock it, and stare at my voicemail inbox. I hover my thumb over the play button of the last message Nate sent me. Even the thought of hearing his voice shakes me, but I can't help myself. My body craves the comfort of that familiar sound.

I press play. Again and again, I listen to his words.

"Good morning! I don't know about you, but I slept like a baby last night. Being with you always helps me rest easy... I love you, Margot."

The words feel like a knife in my chest. I press my knees to my body, curling in on myself, tears slipping quietly down my cheeks. Even if it's just a recording, it carries echoes of the man I love—reminders that tear at my soul.

Click.

I freeze, my eyes snapping open. There's a tiny sound right at the end of his message, so subtle I've always missed it. I replay the voicemail, leaning in closer, my heartbeat picking up speed.

On the next replay, I hold my breath, focusing on those final moments. It's soft—like a tiny tap. My mind skitters through possibilities, but it's too subtle for me to pin down. I loop it once more, but my chest aches from hearing Nate's words over and over, so I pause to gather myself. I close my eyes, massaging my temples. Maybe it's just background static —or the phone glitching.

I frown at the screen. Maybe it's the beep of a voicemail ending? Or the sound of Nate setting his phone on a table? My mind runs through half-formed theories, but none of them feel quite right. My gut is telling me it's something else. For a few minutes, I just sit here, toying with the phone, replaying the last few seconds until I'm sure I'll never un-hear that click.

Finally, I force myself to stop. I take a deep breath, letting my focus fall around the room aimlessly until my gaze lands on the laptop lying nearby. Curiosity piques my interest. I stand and cross to it, pressing random keys several times, listening to the muted click. My heart picks up, but I'm not yet convinced. I pause the voicemail, start it from the beginning, and focus. The warmth in Nate's tone twists my insides, but I power through, determined to compare the sounds side by side.

In my weary haze, I try matching the timing. When Nate says, "I love you, Margot," I hit my space bar just before the voicemail ends. That's when I hear it, a perfect echo: that subtle, soft click from my own MacBook. I repeat the test a few more times, each successful match driving a spike of dread into my stomach.

It's identical. I look at the external hard drive on the desk, a coil of nausea building as I realize what this might mean. My hands are shaking as I connect the drive. I find the file name, "Honeymoon_Morning_Diaries_4.mov," and click on it. My heart thunders in my chest so hard I think I might faint.

A video fills the screen: Nate's familiar smile reflected in the hotel mirror, camera in hand. He creeps toward the bed, throwing open the curtains and crowing like a rooster. I'm half-asleep in the footage, begging for a few more minutes of rest, until Nate laughs and climbs in beside me, holding the camera out in selfie mode. Then comes his line: "Good morning! I don't know about you, but I slept like a baby last night. Being with you always helps me rest easy... I love you, Margot."

It's the exact recording. I can't breathe. My knees give out, and I crumple onto the floor. A cold stone of truth settles in my gut, heavy and absolute. Nate never left me that voicemail. The killer has been inside my room—rooting through my computer, my personal files, and then used them to exploit me.

My tears threaten to choke me. Nate probably never even made it to DC. He might have been imprisoned for days. He was likely alive, somewhere dark and terrifying, while I sat here, berating him for ignoring me. And by the time I found him in that basement, his body was still warm. He died alone, scared, and I wasn't there. A violent wave of sickness rises, and I stagger to my feet, sprinting to the bathroom.

I barely make it to the sink before retching, stomach acid burning my throat. The vomit splashes onto the fragments of broken mirror, the shards reflecting my face in jagged, distorted pieces. That's how I feel—shattered into irreparable fragments. The killer stood right where I stood, rummaging through my life. They took Nate, then the skulls, the chest, and now this final invasion.

I slump down, my back sliding along the vanity. I feel hollow, emptied of everything that made me who I am. A maniac lurks somewhere within reach, but I have no fight left. Let the police pin Penny Lark's mysterious death on me for all I care. Let them cart me away. Everything good in my life is gone, and I can't even summon the strength to scream anymore.

The treasure map in my jeans pocket pokes at my thigh, and I pull it out, preparing to tear it to pieces. How can this flimsy paper have unraveled my entire world?

Behind me, the shower handle squeaks. A moment later, Shannon steps out, a towel clutched around her body. She sees me on the floor, eyes red and raw, but no tears left.

I look up at her, voice raspy. "Shannon, I'm done. Just...get dressed. We should finally go—"

My words freeze as I catch sight of the map. Something is happening to the paper. Words appear in a deep, inky black, creeping across the tattered surface: "Aureus Scarabaeus." Below it, Roman numerals form in precise rows:

XXIII-V-VII
XLII-II-IV
XV-III-VI
LXVII-VII-VIII
XXXII - IX - II

A tremor runs through me, cold as death. It feels like the house itself is watching, playing with me—laughing at my constant rollercoaster of emotions. Fear prickles along my scalp, and my heart pounds so wildly I can't imagine it staying in my chest.

I don't know what these codes mean, but the knowledge they exist—that this map can shift and show new secrets—rips through the last threads of sanity I have left. I look up at Shannon, body quaking, unsure if these words spell salvation or damnation.

29

C obalt chloride—that's the key phrase glowing on my phone screen. It's a chemical compound used as a humidity-activated ink, changing from a colorless to colored ink when exposed to moisture. I close the web browser and exhale, thoughts whirling. It explains how the hidden writing on the map slowly appeared: George Hawthorn must have brushed the paper with cobalt chloride, which allowed the shower's humidity to do the rest.

I set my phone aside and refocus on the map spread across the coffee table, my heartbeat thrumming at this very tangible clue. For the first time in...forever, there's a real lead, something that might pull me out of this black hole. If Shannon and I can decode this cryptic message, maybe we can end this nightmare and get back to Maryland, leaving behind this horrible attempt at a newer, happier life.

I can't lie to myself. Part of me wants to rip this map into shreds—its pretentious hidden clues and veiled promises to reveal something *actually* worthwhile. The thought of playing into whatever twisted game is unfolding here, of being a pawn in George Hawthorn's puzzle, makes me feel sick. We still don't know enough about him to say with any certainty that he's actually tied to these skulls—or to the feeling of terror and silence permeating through this town. But the idea of him tugging at our strings from beyond the grave infuriates me.

And yet, I can't deny how enticing it is. Ever since the night this house flooded, I've been starving for answers, and after everything I've lost, I feel entitled to them. I need to know what the fuck is really happening in Mount Dora. So, I swallow my pride, forcing aside the nauseating thought that some dead man, who once sat in this very house, is now smirking from beyond the grave at the idea of someone picking up the bread-crumbs he left. And here I am, sifting through those details, piece by piece, desperate for the truth.

I narrow my eyes at the newly formed letters and numbers: *Aureus Scarabaeus,* followed by lines of Roman numerals. Shannon sits on the floor, leaning against the armchair, stifling a yawn while wrestling with her laptop. Her hair is a mess, her cheeks tear-streaked, but her posture radiates a new sense of purpose.

"'Aureus Scarabaeus,'" she says, reading from her screen. "Translated from Latin: Gold Scarab."

My stomach jolts. "Shannon, Marty already gave us what we needed. A scarab is..." I pause waiting for it to click.

"A bug! The Gold Bug! Holy shit!" She exclaims, pumping a fist into the air.

"Bingo. George was obsessed," I say. "It was his favorite book, right? So, this makes total sense. Whatever these numbers are, they have to be tied to that story. Problem is, I've never read it. Have you?"

Shannon hums thoughtfully, then nods at the Roman numerals. "Negative. Could be coordinates?"

"It crossed my mind." I let out a tense breath. "But they look too short for longitude and latitude coordinates, right?"

Let's just convert them to standard digits first and see if anything pops out at us?"

Working side by side, we list each set:

$$XXIII - V - VII \rightarrow 23 - 5 - 7$$
$$XLII - II - IV \rightarrow 42 - 2 - 4$$
$$XV - III - VI \rightarrow 15 - 3 - 6$$
$$LXVII - VII - VIII \rightarrow 67 - 7 - 8$$
$$XXXII - IX - II \rightarrow 32 - 9 - 2$$

We stare at the results, trying to see if the sequences match any pattern. Shannon plugs them into Google, checking if they map to GPS. Nothing. Meanwhile, I try scrolling through cryptography sites, my eyes glossing over with terms and concepts I haven't the faintest clue about. Atbash. Rail Fence. Affine. Autokey. Who knew there were so many types of ciphers in the world?

My eyes continue to lazily fall on the Google page until it hits me like lightning. I begin to read out loud - *"A book cipher is a cipher in which each word or letter in the plaintext of a message is replaced by some code that locates it in another text, the key."*

It made perfect sense. *The Gold Bug* famously used a book cipher—a secret message hidden within the pages of a book. It was one of literature's earliest and most celebrated examples of cryptography, inspiring countless generations of puzzle-solvers and treasure-hunters. George had taken that inspiration and implemented it here. These numbers were not coordinates. They were a book cipher left behind by a man obsessed with secrets hiding in plain sight.

But to decode it, we needed the story itself. Another quick Google search tells me that the original short story was published in 1843, but countless versions have existed since. I scroll through listings online, my heart sinking as I realize how many editions are out there. *The Gold Bug* had been published in newspapers, turned into anthologies, and republished in numerous formats. If George had based his cipher on a particular version, we would need that exact one to unlock it.

My heart pounds faster as I say, "Shannon, I think these numbers might be referencing a specific edition of The Gold Bug. Poe wrote that story in 1843, but it's been reprinted a million times. If George used a book cipher, we need the same edition he used."

She nods, pushing off the chair. "Okay, that makes sense. But if he hid these clues all over the house, it would make sense for him to leave the needed copy here as well, right? Maybe it's still here in the house somewhere."

I jump up, heading to the bedroom shelves where I once spent hours adding my many books to the shelves already populated by so many volumes left behind by the Hawthorns.

We run our hands along the rows, scanning spines. My pulse leaps when I see a battered, time-worn copy: The Gold Bug, Dodd, Mead & Co., 1923.

"This has to be it," I whisper.

We clear space on the writing desk. With the map and notepad ready, I flip to page 23, and Shannon leans over my shoulder, counting lines out loud. Then I count words:

Page 23, line 5, word 7: "Deep"

I jot that down, and we repeat the process:

Page 42, line 2, word 4: "Scarab"
Page 15, line 3, word 6: "Cipher"
Page 67, line 7, word 8: "Door"

Page 32, line 9, word 2: "Turn"

Putting them together yields: Deep scarab cipher door turn.

I read it aloud, frowning. "It's not exactly a sentence. More like...five words that maybe sort of could be another clue. The last part—door turn—makes me think of physically turning a door, or a doorknob. But deep scarab cipher?"

Shannon's brow creases as she taps her pen anxiously against the desk. "Deep scarab makes me think deep bug again, maybe it has to do with the chest? That was buried. There are bugs in the soil, right?"

I shake my head. "That doesn't feel right. Whatever remains of this puzzle, I think it's here in the house; everything else has been."

The initial hit of adrenaline from finding the book cipher was diminishing, and I could feel sleep tugging at me. The past twenty-four hours had been exhausting, and my body begged for rest, true, uninterrupted rest.

Shannon paced the room, her hair tied up in a ponytail, flapping around behind her as she muttered potential leads under her breath. I watch her and smile. She's my best friend in the world, the smartest person I've ever known. If anyone can help me figure this out, it's her.

My focus shifts back to the task at hand. If I am going to figure this out, I need to think like George—step into his logic, his obsession with cryptography, his love for intricate puzzles. Hidden clues. Treasures. *The Gold Bug.*

I turn the phrase repeatedly in my mind, each iteration leading me down another blind alley. The words feel like they're mocking me, yet I can't shake the feeling that the answer is right there, just waiting for me to connect the pieces.

Determined not to waste any more time, I stood up. "Let's

split up. Look around the house for anything that could relate to digging, soil, a bug, anything like that. George has used all kinds of gimmicks up to this point, so nothing is off limits."

Shannon nodded. "I'll take this floor, you take the main. Yell if you find anything."

I drift from room to room, my fingers brushing the edges of furniture, gliding along carved doorframes with my senses heightened, searching for anything that might break the mystery wide open.

It's well past midnight, or maybe even later—time is a blur.

I flick on a lamp in the living room, and its sickly glow chases away the shadows from the fireplace. My gaze falls onto the intricate woodwork, the elaborate carvings that framed the hearth with an almost reverent beauty. There, amidst the shadows, is something I missed before.

A carved shape, barely discernible in the dim light, is set into the right side of the fireplace frame. It is subtle, almost invisible, but as I lean in, the details emerge: a bug, its six legs spread out, with pincers like a beetle, carefully etched into the wood. My heart begins to pound as my eyes shift to the left side of the fireplace, where I find an identical carving. This can't be a coincidence. It has to mean something. I scream for Shannon, and she arrives within moments.

"Look– they have to be connected to this, right?" I trail a fingertip over the carving on the right. Each leg is individually carved, unlike the left carving, which is just a solid shape. Shannon's excitement ratchets up a notch. "Can we just acknowledge how nuts this is? Out of all the houses in America, you had to buy the national treasure house of secrets?"

I press one of the tiny legs, and it gives way with a barely audible click, staying depressed. My heart leaps into my throat. I press another, then a third, until finally, after the fourth leg, we hear a strange sound—a mechanical whirring deep inside the wall. The legs reset, jutting back out, and I realize that we're dealing with a combination.

A four-digit code. What could it be? I try to recall everything we had learned about George, his past, and what mattered to him. The years that had defined his life float around in my mind—Amelia's birth year or perhaps Cecilia and George's anniversary?

I skip the second option because I don't know the year the couple was married. But I do remember our conversation with Marty that Amelia was born in 1970. My heart sinks: there are only six legs, plus the creature's pincers, and the second digit required a 9.

"What about the book itself, Margot? When was The Gold Bug first published?" Shannon asks.

I almost jump out of my skin. I hug Shannon and litter her face with kisses. Of course, that sequence didn't require a 9 because the year *The Gold Bug* was published– 1843.

Assuming the legs were ordered as North Americans read, I press the bug's first pincer from top left to bottom right, then the eighth, the fourth, and finally the third. Each tiny carved appendage clicked into place...

Silence.

Shannon and I stand perfectly still, waiting. Several moments pass and I turn to speak when I hear a soft metallic creak, as though gears were shifting behind the wall. The bug's carved body slowly pushes outward, protruding from the frame, leaving its legs behind. It looked like an old-fashioned dial waiting to be turned.

"Ho-ly... shit." whispers Shannon.

I swallow hard, glancing at my best friend. With my heart pounding, I grasp the bug's body and twist it clockwise. The turn was almost too easy, the mechanism smooth and deliberate. A deep, resonant click echoed through the room, followed by the unmistakable sound of something unlocking.

I push the bug back into place, holding my breath as I listen. A muffled noise comes from somewhere deeper within the house. My pulse quickens as we both turn our heads, straining to locate the source of the sound. Nothing seems different. There were no sliding panels, no secret doors swinging open. But I know something, somewhere had moved.

"Something definitely unlocked," Shannon whispers.

"I agree. Whatever we just did moved something." I whisper in return, wondering why we're whispering at all.

We search the corners, the underside of the mantel, behind the sofa. Nothing.

"Let's split up," Shannon says. "It might be in another room. You check the ground floor. I'll go upstairs. If you find anything—shout. Although maybe a little less than before, you scared me half to death."

I don't love the idea, but it's logical that time could be critical with a timer counting down until whatever we opened, closes again. "Be careful," I say softly, catching her anxious expression. She nods, jogging up the steps while I methodically sweep the foyer, the kitchen, the hall closet. Each minute that passes without discovery makes my nerves jangle harder.

When I've checked every crevice, I hurry to the staircase, a knot of worry in my chest. "Shannon? Did you find anything?" I call, heading up. No reply. The second-floor hallway is silent but for the faint hum of electricity.

I poke my head into the spare bedroom—no Shannon, no changes. Then I approach our bedroom, the one I once shared with Nate. My hand hovers over the doorknob, bracing myself against a flood of painful memories. Summoning courage, I push it open.

"Shannon, you in—?" My voice dies. The desk in the corner

is swung away from the wall, like it's mounted on a hidden hinge. There's a narrow gap of blackness behind it, the wood paneling parted.

My pulse spikes. I swallow hard, stepping closer. The gap is just wide enough for a person to slip through. A draft of cold air wafts out, carrying a stale, musty smell. My hands tremble as I grip the desk edge and shift it farther aside, peering into the darkness beyond.

"Shannon?" I whisper. My voice echoes faintly, but no answer comes.

Fear prickles the back of my neck. My friend wouldn't just vanish. The only explanation is she entered this secret passage. But why didn't she call for me? Why go without me?

Steeling myself, I slip through the opening. Shadows swallow me whole, the air thick and suffocating. "Shannon, can you hear me?"

Silence.

30

I bend down, my shoulders wedging through the tight threshold behind my bedroom wall. My phone's flashlight slices jagged beams through the oppressive darkness, and every time the light grazes a shape, my imagination warps it into something menacing. My pulse hammers in my throat as I step inside, each footfall swallowed by an eerie hush.

I call Shannon's name over and over as I push deeper into the darkness, my fear increasing with each moment of silence.

At the center of this cramped, hidden space stands a drafting desk. Scattered papers lie across its surface like fallen leaves in a forgotten storm—worn, crumpled, dust-ridden.

Cautiously, I move closer to the drafting desk and switch on a small lamp. A jolt of yellow light flares, flickering once before steadying. It sends our shadows dancing across the walls, turning the cluttered contents of the room even more sinister. I realize now that this space is larger than I expected, the corners fading into gloom. Shelves line the walls, cluttered with tattered books, rusted tin boxes, and glass jars filled with things I can't begin to identify. A stale, musty smell clings to the air, thick with the weight of secrets that never saw the light.

My eyes drift to a solitary, narrow bed in the far corner, its thin blanket half-pulled off, as if whoever used it left in a rush. A small dresser sits nearby, piled with more tools, scattered papers, and books. It's as if some frantic force was at work here before everything froze in time.

I turn, glancing back at the wall I just passed through, trying to picture how all this might look from the other side. That's when I notice the small pinholes puncturing the wood, each letting in a thread of light. My heart rate spikes with fresh alarm—I realize *what* these must be.

Peepholes.

I lower my face to one of them, dread pooling in my stomach. On the other side is my bedroom—the entire view, right down to the comforter Nate and I picked out together. Bile rises in my throat as it sinks in: Someone was *watching* me. Watching me sleep, undress, share my most private moments with Nate. Every detail was on display for a voyeur hidden in these walls.

A nauseating wave of violation churns inside me, but I grit my teeth against the urge to bolt. I remind myself I'm alone here —whoever used this room doesn't appear to be here now. I can't let fear hijack me; I came too far to turn back empty-handed. For all my hopes, though, the chest is nowhere to be seen. A crushing disappointment gnaws at my insides. *I was so sure it would be here.*

I let my flashlight wander across the walls and corners, searching for any sign that I've missed something. Then, in the far edge of the lamplight, I see a narrow passageway extending into the darkness, like a tunnel leading deeper into the house's bones. A chill brushes my skin, as though some cold, unseen current flows out of that opening.

My throat tightens, but I force myself forward. The passage twists in cramped, suffocating turns, the walls pressing in on me until my shoulders almost graze the wood. More peepholes appear in random intervals, each revealing another slice of my home. One overlooks the bathroom, and I catch my reflection in the mirror. A flash of memory—myself stepping out of the shower, vulnerable, oblivious—rips through me. My guts knot in horror.

But I keep going, swallowing the bitter taste of revulsion. I'm here for answers, and I won't leave without them. With every cramped step, I start to see how extensive these secret corridors are, winding through the structure like hidden arteries. My mind reels at the realization that none of us were ever alone in Hawthorn Manor. Not truly.

Suddenly, the walls feel even tighter. My breath comes in ragged bursts. I glance at my phone, noticing it was only able to charge to nine percent battery. A new spike of fear grips me. If it dies, so does my only source of light and any chance of calling for help. I break into a clumsy, urgent jog. The passage twists, disorienting me, and I fight to keep calm.

I turn a corner, heart hammering in anticipation of escape —but I'm met with yet another room. It's laid out almost identically to the first: the same creeping shadows, the same stifling air. On one wall, more peepholes allow dim glints of light to seep in. My breath catches when I recognize the room on the other side.

The nursery.

The one Nate and I once dreamed of filling with life, of hearing a baby's laughter, but which remained agonizingly vacant. Raw grief twists inside me as I step back, swallowing the ache. Then, in the center of this hidden space, my phone's failing beam settles on something I've been searching for all along—the wooden chest, yawning open, its lid propped as if in silent invitation.

And even in the faint light, I see them: the faint outline of skulls waiting to be found for a second time.

31

I stand motionless, my gaze locked on the chest. For so long, I've needed to see these skulls—to prove I'm not unraveling and to silence the echo of that humiliating encounter with the police who dismissed me like some delusional, hysterical woman. Yet now that I'm here, the chest only radiates dread. My mind reels with the possibility of finding Nate among its grisly contents. I wonder if I'd even recognize him.

What makes a face *recognizable* once it's stripped of muscle and skin—when it's reduced to a raw, bare skull? I can't stop imagining the macabre difference between old bones, yellowed and brittle, and those newly stripped, the surface still smooth and pale. The thought of some killer meticulously scraping and cleaning flesh sets my stomach roiling, but it stays fixed in my mind all the same, refusing to leave.

Before I can stop myself, I'm on my knees, the chest looming over me. It summons me forward with cruel inevitability, my legs moving as if directed by someone else's will. And then I take them in: sixteen skulls, each one old and discolored, and a seventeenth that's fresh enough to be unmistakably *new*. I don't need a closer look to know. My heart cracks, and I crumple, my forehead hitting the edge of the chest as tears spill hot and fast. A sick part of me was waiting for proof, but now that I have it, none of it matters. Nate is gone.

I sit there, staring blindly at those hollow sockets, letting numbness wash through me. Everything I've worked toward, everything I cared about—destroyed. I should stand up, but my body sags under the weight of loss. At last, with agonizing slowness, I haul myself upright and swipe the back of my hand across my damp cheeks, fighting for breath. I yank out my phone and take picture after picture with trembling fingers, capturing every angle of these gruesome remains until my phone finally dies. But now, at least, I have evidence—something real to bring forward.

But as I flip through the images, a hollow truth punches into me: I no longer care about the house, about making a fresh start, or about the redemption I once hoped for. All I want is to go home—to Maryland. I close my eyes, conjuring the smell of Old Bay on freshly steamed crabs, the vivid reds and oranges of fall, the muted crunch of snow underfoot in winter. That's my home, my safe haven. *Not this.* Not a place of death and betrayal, where I've lost everything.

I open my eyes, voice cracking in the dim, suffocating passageway. "I'm sorry, Nate," I whisper, tears coming again. "This was all my idea—this house, this move. I thought I could fix...everything after Lila. Fix us. Fix me. But I was wrong. So wrong."

A vivid ache hits me at the memory of Lila's tiny face, that old regret flaring up like a bruise I can't help pressing. I'd convinced myself this house would bring closure, that it would forgive me for not saving Lila. Instead, I dragged Nate here with me, and now he's gone, another causality in my attempt to have the picture-perfect white picket fence life.

A cold emptiness settles over me. I turn from the chest, fueled by determination rather than panic. I start retracing my steps through the maze of passageways, using the peepholes as my map. One shows me the guestroom, so I pivot east. Another looks out on the living room, where Shannon and I sat hours ago working out how to open this cursed passageway. My stomach clenches at the thought of Shannon– if she came in here, she's likely just as lost as I am.

At last, I emerge in the first hidden room, the one with the drafting desk and unmade bed. Relief floods me—I'm finally close to escaping. I have my proof, and now I just need to find Shannon and get this phone to the police.

But as I stoop through the entrance, something catches my eye—a shape on the dresser near the bed. My heart jumps into my throat. Reaching for my phone, I remember too late that its battery is dead. The only illumination is the flicker of the old lamp and the sliver of weak light from a peephole.

I move closer, adrenaline spiking. My fingers curl around the object, and I drag it into the trembling lamplight. It's a Yankees baseball cap, frayed along the edges with a cracked brim. My hands shake worse as I turn it over, tears blurring my sight, until I make out a single word scrawled in fading ink on the inside:

"Bambino."

32

I stare at the Yankees cap clenched in my trembling hands, and the world around me seems to spin in slow motion. My lungs constrict as the realization slams into me again and again, like relentless waves against a cliff. *Walter's hat.* It's here, hidden away in this secret room behind my own bedroom walls.

I squeeze my eyes shut, trying to force my brain to conjure some benign explanation. But the truth claws at me from every angle—I can't escape it. Walter was here, not just once, not by accident, but over and over. He lived in these walls, kept that chest of skulls, and meticulously planned every horror I've just uncovered. My mind screams in protest, but there's no denying the obvious: Walter, the gentle, dependable man who always showed up at my lowest moments, is the very monster who's been tormenting me all along.

My thoughts are a frenzied mess, tumbling and colliding in my head. How could I have never asked where he lived? How did I not realize he was living *here,* behind the walls, hiding all evidence of his crimes? Scenes of our conversations flicker through my memory—the warmth in his voice, the calm way he'd say, "I'm here to help," every time I felt alone. Now I see each moment for the lie it was, a twisted manipulation. Walter, the groundskeeper, the boy raised near this property, the one who claimed to protect me when Nate was gone—he's been the threat all along. The darkness I feared was never distant; it was right here, watching from the shadows.

My knees threaten to buckle, my stomach knotting itself tight. Every nerve in my body screams that I have to *go*—right now, before I can't move at all. The hat slips from my hands, landing on the floor with a soft thud.

I stagger backward, clambering through the cramped opening into my bedroom. My vision blurs with panic, tears, and disbelief. Every inch of this room now feels like a stranger's domain, its comforting familiarity stripped away in an instant.

Dawn light leaks through the curtains, painting everything in a gentle glow that mocks the horror lurking beneath. I force myself to stand straight, air rasping in my lungs as I try to calm the frantic pounding of my heart.

That's when I see him. Walter is perched on the edge of my bed, shoulders sagging, face caught between sorrow and a kind of weary acceptance. His eyes lock onto mine, and I feel the entire room contract until it's only the two of us. His hands and boots are both covered in mud, leaving marks all over the floor and bedspread. My breath leaves me in a rush, cold dread crawling across my skin.

"Margot..." he says softly, his voice threaded with regret, like he pities me for finally understanding.

I want to scream, to unleash all my fury and terror, but my throat closes up. My eyes burn, and a dozen memories collide: every conversation, every moment of trust, now coated in blood and deceit. I feel my knees give, my body threatening to collapse. And Walter just sits there, motionless, waiting. Watching. His familiar face distorts with each ragged heartbeat, as the mask finally slips away, revealing the monster I never realized lurked underneath.

33

I stare at Walter, my heart banging against my ribs as I try to reconcile this ordinary-looking man with the horror he's unleashed into my life. His face is unremarkable—almost serene—and that fact alone is deeply unsettling. Because I know now: behind those calm eyes lurks a murderer.

He's perched on the edge of my bed, fingers drumming lightly on the mattress. He doesn't look upset or panicked, only mildly interested, as though assessing my next move. And that eerie composure makes my skin crawl.

"Margot," he says, voice low and coaxing, as if speaking to a startled animal. "I know what you're thinking. This all looks...bad."

His words almost break me. *Bad* doesn't begin to cover it. But I don't wait for his next lie.

I bolt, spinning on my heel and sprinting down the hallway. All I can think about is getting out, finding Shannon—and then ending this nightmare. I feel Walter behind me, not rushing but following with deliberate steps.

"Don't run, Margot," he calls down the corridor. "We have to talk eventually."

His voice is like a slow, mocking echo. My lungs burn by the time I hit the stairs, my bare feet slapping the steps in a blur. *Where is Shannon?*

I reach the front door, heart leaping with relief. If I can just get outside, I can scream for help, flag down a passerby, *something*. I grab the knob, twist, and yank. It moves, but not enough—the deadbolt is locked. Usually, the key dangles on the inside, but now the ring is empty, the key gone.

Walter must have taken it.

"You're not going anywhere," he says softly from behind me.

My stomach lurches; panic flares. I whirl around, half expecting to see Shannon standing there—but it's only him. *Where is she?* A pained gasp escapes me. "What did you do to Shannon?"

He tilts his head, wearing that same damn near-smile that makes me want to sob with rage. "Haven't seen her," he says casually.

"Stop lying!"

He shrugs, as if my accusation barely registers. "She might be lost... this house can be tricky. You of all people should know that."

My anger ignites. I'm aware this is a stalling tactic, and I don't have time for it. I race away from the front door, veering into the kitchen. If I can slip around, maybe I can catch Walter off guard or find some other way out. Behind me, his footsteps remain infuriatingly measured, as though he's certain I can't escape.

"Margot," he calls in a lilting tone that makes my skin crawl. "This is pointless. I know every corner of this house— inside and out. You won't find a hiding place I can't reach."

I push into the kitchen, scanning for something—anything —I can use to defend myself or break a window. A heavy skillet? A knife? I circle the island, but Walter's silhouette appears at the threshold, blocking the path.

My stomach flips. I pivot and bolt back toward the hall, praying I can dodge him on the stairs. Maybe I can find Shannon before it's too late. He doesn't lunge—just steps aside, letting me pass, which feels even more unnerving than if he'd grabbed me.

I bound upstairs, two steps at a time, ignoring my burning calves. If Shannon is anywhere in this house, I have to find her. I reach the landing, eyes darting to the bathroom door—no, too flimsy. The guest room? Too obvious. Under the bed? He'd find me in seconds.

No. There's only one option left: the hidden passageways behind the walls. The same claustrophobic tunnels where I uncovered that horrifying chest, the same place Shannon vanished into. Fear knots my insides, but I press on.

Tears sting my eyes as I slip into my bedroom, crossing straight to the small panel behind my dresser. This is how I got in last time. With shaking hands, I tug the panel open, revealing the tight corridor beyond. Walter's voice drifts closer, calm and cold.

"Margot, be sensible. I'm not the villain you think I am. Just let me explain," he coaxes, as though we're discussing a mild disagreement and not a string of murders.

My heartbeat clangs in my ears, and I force myself to breathe quietly. Walter's in my bedroom now—I can hear him stepping around, muttering to himself in a twisted, sing-song voice.

"Is Margot under the bed?" he taunts, like he's playing hide-and-seek. "Not there. Behind the door?" A theatrical sigh. "Nope."

The floorboards creak as he moves across the room. I press

myself deeper into the darkness, stomach churning at how close he is. My heart thrashes so hard I'm sure he can hear it.

"Is Margot in my room?" he murmurs, voice turning almost reverent.

Terror seizes me. A moment of breathless silence stretches, and then his fist slams against the wall. A thunderous crack reverberates through the wood, sending a shockwave that rattles me. I gasp, stumbling backward and smacking my spine on the edge of the drafting desk. A cry lodges in my throat.

"Shannon, Shannon..." he mutters, switching tactics. "She's such a sweet friend, isn't she? Isn't that why you're so desperate to find her?"

Tears leak down my cheeks. *Focus.* I let my hands explore the cramped passage, feeling for the path. If Shannon got lost in here, maybe I can pick up on something—footprints in the dust, or an echo of movement. The memory of how she once teased me about being too stubborn to give up sparks a flicker of determination. She might still be alive. She *has* to be.

Walter's footsteps shift, moving across the floor. I force myself deeper, ignoring the tightness in my chest. The corridor is black as tar. I can't see an inch in front of my face, so I press one hand against the wall, letting it guide me. The air is dense, smelling of dust and stale secrets.

Behind me, I hear Walter leave my room, his voice fading. Maybe he assumes I'll come out eventually. Maybe he's searching for a quicker route to corner me. *He knows these passages*, a dreadful voice in my head reminds me, *maybe better than I ever will.*

Still, I keep going, step by slow step. The space twists, branching off in corners that feel impossible to navigate blind. *I have to find Shannon.* If I can't, I'll at least look for an exit—a loose board, a gap to the outside, some way to get out and call for help.

Behind my eyes, I see Nate's face, recalling the violent discovery of him in the bathtub. I think of Lila, Penny—so many names swirling in the darkness. Walter took them all from me. Not Shannon. Not again.

My hand meets a solid wooden panel. No latch, no door-knob—just more wall. I curse under my breath, leaning my forehead against it, swallowing the anger and grief. On the other side of this panel, Walter could be waiting, or Shannon might be unconscious, or...

I inhale slowly, pressing on. Darkness or not, I refuse to stop searching. Walter might own these walls, but he doesn't own my will. I won't give him the satisfaction of submission.

Somewhere up ahead, the tunnel splits. My fingertips graze a corner. I pick one direction at random, hoping it leads me closer to where Shannon might be. Behind me, faint echoes of Walter's methodical steps filter through the old timbers.

I take another trembling breath, gather what courage I have left, and plunge deeper into the blackness, determined to find Shannon—or an escape—and to bring this entire night-mare to an end, one way or another.

34

I stumble through the cramped, suffocating darkness of these hidden passageways, straining to stay just out of Walter's reach. Hawthorn Manor has turned into a twisted labyrinth, the very walls seemingly conspiring to trap me. Each time I think I've found a path, it veers into another dead end. My breath comes in ragged bursts, and the only relief I find is through the tiny peepholes carved into the walls —brief, taunting windows into a home I once thought was mine.

I press my eye against one of those openings, my heart racing. Beyond it, I see the kitchen, still achingly familiar yet warped by all that's happened. It feels like years ago now, since Nate and I first stepped foot into this kitchen, imagining the Thanksgivings we'd spend here together, cooking and baking our favorite foods. The memory slams into me, nearly overwhelming me with grief. Then, before I can process the pain, a giant, bloodshot eye fills the peephole from the other side.

Walter.

"Peek-a-boo, Margot," he says in a singsong murmur. "I see you."

I jolt backward, stifling a yelp, hand clamped over my

mouth. My back hits the rough wall, reminding me just how cornered I am. The echo of Walter's footsteps drifts along the corridors, sometimes seeming to come from right beside me, as though he's walking parallel on the other side of these panels, waiting to snatch me if I slip. Other times, I swear he's in here with me, only steps behind, his breath just inches from my neck.

The pathways twist left, then right, then left again, a demented puzzle with no obvious solution. I'm losing track of how long I've been trapped in this claustrophobic warren. Each second drips into the next, exhaustion gnawing at my bones. I can't stop, or he'll catch me. So, I push on, adrenaline fueling my every shaky step.

I pause to press my face against another peephole, desperate for some idea of where I am. This time, the living room slides into focus—and my heart wrenches. Shannon and I were just in this room together, looking for an answer to a puzzle I wish we had never found.

An old memory grips me: Shannon, defiant and protective, arms crossed as she argued on my behalf back home—when the courts pinned me with partial responsibility for Lila's death. Shannon was my shield back then, unwavering. She saved me from sinking beneath all that guilt, stood between me and the world's pointed fingers. And now I had dragged her into whatever *this* was.

Tears fill my eyes, shock warring with disbelief, grief curdling into anger. In my heart I know he's done something to her. I just can't admit it out loud to myself. My rage burns through my tears: Walter will pay. I clench my fists, pressing them against the wall.

Movement flickers in the living room. Walter steps into view, and I hold my breath. He doesn't look so calm anymore— his motions are jittery, his expression coiled. He paces, mumbling to himself, glancing at some unseen presence beyond my narrow line of sight. Is there...someone else in the house?

My pulse spikes. Walter is flailing, gesturing around the room like he's trying to explain something. He looks desperate —terrified, even. I lean closer, ear against the wall, struggling to catch a word or name, but I only hear the low rumble of his voice, one-sided and agitated.

Then Walter steps to the very center of the room. He sighs, hanging his head, and for a moment, he looks sad—until he lifts his gaze and locks eyes directly on the spot where I'm hiding.

My blood goes cold. He stares at the wall that conceals me, eyes narrowed, a small smile curling his lips, like he *knows* I'm watching. Then, silent as a predator, he slips out of sight.

I suck in a shaky breath, heart pounding. I realize in a flash: these passageways have more than one entrance. He's going to hunt me down from some other route. I can't stay here; I have to move.

Turning away from the peephole, I edge forward, hands ghosting along the rough wood. Every muscle tenses, ready to bolt at the slightest sound. My mind spins with the question of how large this hidden network is, how many corridors criss-cross the house's foundation. Suddenly, the ground drops beneath my feet. I lurch forward, nearly pitching headlong into empty space.

A series of steps descends into darkness—leading downward, and I know for a fact Hawthorn Manor doesn't have a basement. Not one I've ever seen, anyway. Fear collides with a raw, urgent need to escape, and that need wins. I scoot onto the top step, lowering myself carefully. The air grows damp, carrying a rank odor that sets my nerves on edge.

My feet dip into frigid water, and a gasp hitches in my

throat. It's so cold it practically numbs my ankles, and each step sends a ripple through the dark, stagnant pool. The ceiling here is barely high enough for me to stand upright, forcing me to hunch. The walls tighten around me, muddy and slick, studded with uneven stone. Tiny scratching sounds tell me I'm not alone—rats, insects, or who knows what else. I shiver, refusing to let my imagination run wild. *Walter* is the real danger.

I feel around in the darkness and recognize there are two pathways in front of me. I take a breath, step to the left, and begin moving forward. Within a few steps, my world starts to tilt and I realize I'm descending. The odd feeling of water rising is the only real proof that what I'm sensing is actually true. A brief flash of panic surges through me as I imagine continuing down this path, only to find the water moving up further until I drowned.

No, instead I turn back, retracing my steps. This time, I take the right path, which does not feel like it's descending. Step by step, I push on. The tunnel twists left, then right, random water droplets falling on my head and neck, chilling me to the bone. A suffocating panic tries to claw its way up my throat, but I clamp it down. *I will not die here.* Not in some watery crypt with Shannon still out there, somewhere. I steady myself with each shallow breath, inching deeper into the gloom.

Then I see it—a wavering, pale light dancing on the surface of the water so faint I think I might be imagining it at first. Hope flares inside me like a match in the dark. I press forward, the water splashing louder against my legs. I can hear something, too—a voice?

Not Walter's. This voice is gruffer, urgent, but muffled by the tunnel's constant dripping. The corridor opens abruptly into a small cellar, water draining through a grated floor. Candlelight—or some other flickering glow—bobs against the damp walls. I pause, heart in my throat, fighting the urge to turn and flee. But I can't. Whoever's beyond this tunnel has to be safer than what I left behind.

Swallowing hard, I push forward, stepping into the dimly lit space. Water sloshes around my shins, draining toward the grate. My eyes adjust slowly to the change in light as I look around. The drips echo off the stone, forming a steady back-drop of white noise that nearly drowns out the voice. But it's definitely there—closer now, distinct from the rasp of my own breath.

I take a deep breath, forcing myself to calm down. Then, slowly, I step forward, emerging from the tunnel's darkness and into the flickering light of the basement—a basement I knew all too well.

35

I blink against the flicker of the dim overhead bulb, my vision struggling to adjust after what feels like an eternity in those pitch-dark tunnels. The faint light sways, casting jerking shadows across the scene. My heart drops like a stone the instant I recognize where I've emerged: Hawthorn House's basement. The white metal tub sits there, still stained red from Nate's blood, his headless body sprawled as if in grim parody. The tiles are slick with mud and gore, forming a monstrous mosaic that wrenches my stomach.

But I'm not alone. Standing over Nate's body is Chief Miller.

He whirls at the sound of my footsteps, and I catch the confusion blazing in his eyes. Without hesitation, he draws his sidearm, leveling the barrel at my chest.

"Freeze!" he barks, voice clipped and shaking with tension. I see panic and distrust etched across his face as he locks onto me.

I throw my hands up, a shiver raking my spine. "Chief, listen to me," I plead, trying to steady my breath. "I'm Margot Bennett. Walter—he—"

"Turn around!" he roars, taking a measured step closer, gun unwavering.

A crack of raw fear tears through me. He's not hearing me. To him, I'm a suspect. Maybe an accomplice to this nightmare. My eyes flick to the tub, where Nate lies motionless, and a sob tears from my throat. As someone I had initially pegged as dirty, in this moment, Chief Miller is the only one who may be able to help me. My last chance.

"Please," I say, my voice cracking. "He's the one who did this—Walter, he killed my husband, he took Shannon, and—"

"Shut up!" Chief Miller snaps, grabbing my shoulder and spinning me so hard I gasp. The grimy, blood-smeared wall slams into my cheek. "You think I'm an idiot?" he snarls close to my ear, wrenching my arms behind my back. My shoulders scream in protest as the handcuffs bite into my wrists.

"That...that body, it's—" My breath hitches, trying to get the words out. "It's Nate. My husband. Walter did it."

Chief Miller grimaces, glancing at the tub. "He doesn't even have a head. How the hell would you know it's your husband?" His suspicion practically drips off him.

I want to collapse. The weight of the day's horrors crushes me, and I can't find any words that might break through his anger. The silence is broken by the sound of a phone ringing. I watch as he picks it up, glaring at me. "Don't move," he growls.

I slump against the wall, my wrists screaming, tears slipping down my cheeks. I've never felt so helpless. Footsteps thunder overhead, and I can hear him placing a call from the top of the stairs. His voice is ragged, furious, but I can't make out every word—only the anger:

"...body here... yes, Hawthorn House... I have Margot Bennett in custody... I want to do this by the book... No... Fine."

The chief comes back down, jaw tense, eyes dark with

something that might be fear or loathing. He grips my cuffed arm, forcing me to stand. "Get up."

I stumble, nearly tripping on the blood-smeared tiles. My brain roils with shock, unable to shake the image of Nate's lifeless body in that tub. The chief half-drags me up the basement steps and through Hawthorn House's hallway. Everything tilts, spinning in a sickening blur. I expected to be leaving this place behind forever—not locked in cuffs, not under suspicion of murder. Outside, the night air hits me like a slap, cold and unforgiving. He shoves me into the back of his police cruiser and slams the door.

We pull away, the engine's growl blending with the pounding of my heart. I gather my courage, leaning forward as much as the cuffs allow. "Chief, please," I manage, voice trembling. "Walter is dangerous—he'll—"

"I don't want to hear it," he snaps, eyes forward, knuckles white on the wheel.

Terror clamps around my chest. I'm losing precious time. Shannon is missing, Walter is still out there, and nobody's listening. "He'll kill you, too!" I choke out, desperation flooding me. "You have no idea what he's capable of—"

The car screeches to a halt, pitching me against the front seat. Luckily, there was no metal barrier between the front and back seats, or I would've likely broken my nose against it. "I said shut the fuck up!" he snarls, slamming his hand against the ceiling.

He slams on the gas, and the cruiser lurches forward again. Rain spatters the windshield, quickly growing into a furious downpour. The world becomes a murky kaleidoscope of shifting shadows. I press my forehead to the glass, peering through rivulets of water, feeling like I'm drowning on land.

Time slips by. My heart thuds faster as we wind along a curving road, the scenery half-drowned in darkness. Something about this route nags at me. It feels *familiar*. A horrifying certainty creeps up my spine.

"Chief...where are we going?" I whisper, my throat bone-dry.

He doesn't answer. I see a flash of pointed peaks and glowing windows. My lungs seize. *No.* We're returning to my house. My blood runs cold, an icy dread rooting me to the seat. I can't tear my gaze away from the looming shape rising out of the darkness.

"Please," I croak, hysteria thundering in my veins. "Don't. You *can't*—"

The cruiser bumps to a stop on the gravel. Lightning forks across the sky, illuminating the porch—and on it, Walter paces like a caged animal, muttering frantically to himself. He whips around, catching sight of me in the car. His eyes blaze, his mouth twisting into a grin I feel in my gut.

A scream rips out of me, raw and wild. I flex every muscle in my body as if I can melt into the seat and vanish. The rain pelts the roof with deafening force, matching the manic pulse in my ears. Beyond the window, Walter stands, arms tense, beckoning with a silent invitation.

I'm trapped, cuffed in the back of a patrol car, with no idea why Chief Miller brought me *back*. My mind reels, and I realize once more how little control I have over my own fate. I scream, raw with terror, and my body curls into itself, drawing my knees up to my chest.

There is nothing I can do.

Nothing that will stop what is coming.

36

Rain soaks the air, washing everything in a dull roar, and lightning flashes in the black sky, exposing the familiar outline of my home. I'm trapped in the back of the police cruiser when Chief Miller slams his door shut. The sound of metal on metal is swallowed by the howling wind, but I can still feel its finality thud in my chest. Through the rain-splattered windshield, I watch him approach the porch, his uniform clinging to him, weighed down by the downpour. My breath is shallow; I can't look away.

Walter stands there, a dark shape pacing in circles across the battered porch. He looks positively manic, his body tense, his head swiveling with each flicker of lightning. Even from inside the car, I can sense his anger radiating into the night. Rain hammers the roof, blending with the wild thrashing of my heart.

I fumble for the door, trying to escape, but the handle doesn't budge. Child locks. I'm stuck. A jolt of raw panic drives me to the window instead. I brace my feet and slam my shoulders into it, but the glass doesn't give. I scream in frustration, tears spill now. The wind tears the sound from my lips, devouring it instantly.

Outside, Chief Miller and Walter are shouting at each other, their words lost in the relentless storm. Their anger is unmistakable: arms flailing, fingers stabbing at one another, at the cruiser, at the house. I swallow hard, seeing something truly vicious in the sharp, rigid lines of Walter's face.

Summoning courage, I launch my body sideways, kicking with every ounce of strength. The window cracks but doesn't break. Lightning stutters overhead, illuminating the yard in haunting flashes: shattered branches, water-logged debris, the once-proud porch turned into a battered stage for this showdown.

Another kick. My legs are weak, numb from fear. Still, I see tiny fractures webbing across the glass, teasing me with the chance of escape. I grit my teeth, gather what's left of my energy, and slam my foot out one more time, perfectly timed with a thunderclap. The window shatters, bulletproof film peeling away in a single piece.

An instant later, the door on the opposite side is wrenched open. I jerk my head around, a flash of lightning reveals the familiar damp, furious features of Chief Miller.

"Get out," he snaps, voice lost in the wind. I barely have time to react before he lunges in, grabs a fistful of my hair, and yanks me from the cruiser. I slam into the muddy ground with a sickening splat, water and silt drenching my clothes. Pain ricochets through me; my lungs forget how to breathe.

Walter looms just behind Miller, like a demon. The moment he releases me, Walter snatches my arm with a bruising grip. Rain pours off his brow, and for a heartbeat, I see the reflection of lightning in his eyes—wild and unhinged.

I let out a shaky breath and try to twist free. "Where is Shannon?" I scream, my voice tearing from my throat. "She went upstairs after we opened the hidden door, and now she's gone! You took her, you sick bastard. Where is she?"

His lips curl into a mirthless grin, ignoring my thrashing. He says nothing, just hurls me toward the house. The front door yawns open, swallowing me in darkness. A flicker of lightning reveals the dim hallway, the grand old furniture now battered, askew.

I stagger, snapping my head around to see if Shannon might be here—any sign of her, some clue. "Shannon!" I shout, voice echoing off the walls. No response. God, if he hurts her...

Walter pushes me to the empty chair and turns to Chief Miller who is following us into the living room, my living room.

"You know, I've always appreciated the things you've done, Andy. Even—"

"Shut the fuck up, George," Chief Miller snapped, his voice cold. It cut through the noise, through the rain and the wind pushing into the room. I lift my head, blinking against the water that had run into my eyes, trying to understand what I just heard. *George?* He just called Walter, *George.*

The realization hits me like a jolt—a final, sickening piece of the puzzle snapping into place. Walter is George Hawthorn? So, he hadn't disappeared, hadn't abandoned this house. He had simply become someone else. But why? Why would a man go from being the owner of the grandest estate in town to its caretaker? The questions buzzed in my mind.

"I understand you're upset," George began, his voice soothing.

"No," said the chief. "I am done with this... horror show you've let yourself become, George. I'm done. I let it go too far. I should have stopped you years ago, but now it's gone beyond anything I can fix. I won't be part of it anymore. Your hold on this town, on me, ends here. I'll cover this one up, just like the others. But after this, I'm finished. If you harm another soul, I will make sure everyone knows what you are. I will take you down, even if it means going down with you."

George stands there, the rain dripping from his clothes, his face a picture of something almost serene, as if he was expecting this. "I understand," he says, his voice quiet, nearly soothing. You've always been my most loyal friend. My only loyal friend, really. Ever since Cece died—"

"Don't," Chief Miller hisses, his finger raised, trembling. "Don't you dare."

George raises his hands, palms out, a gesture of innocence. "I'm done," he promises.

The Chief looks towards me, his eyes meeting mine. I see something in them—something raw and broken. Regret. "I'm sorry," he whispers, his voice barely audible over the storm. "I'm sorry for what I've done, for what I couldn't stop. I should have protected you." He steps forward, removes the handcuffs from my raw, red wrists, and steps back toward the door.

"At least tell me where Shannon is," I plead, trembling with rage and grief. "Tell me she's alive!"

Walter just smirks, rain dripping from his hair onto the hardwood. "Haven't seen your friend," he says softly. "She must've left. Maybe she's had enough of you, Margot."

My vision blurs with hot tears. "Liar!" I shriek. I lunge for him, fists swinging, but Chief Miller grabs me by the shoulders and hauls me back, guiding me carefully behind him.

Miller's next breath rumbles in his chest like the distant thunder. "God damn it, George! he growls. "You said you were finished with this madness, that you'd keep your darkness tucked away. You told me no more bodies. 'One last time,' you said, but now there's a body just waiting around to be found in Hawthorn House. You're going to kill Margot here, and now someone else is missing?" he's shaking now, his voice growing louder with each word.

"I can't keep burying your sins. I won't. The fact I have for so long..." He shakes his head, voice ragged. "That's on me, but it's over. I'm done."

George lets out a low, bitter laugh. He stands there, rain plastering his hair to his skull, that same half-smile on his lips. "Oh boy, Andy finally grows a pair!" he applauds patronizingly, "but you forget, you were part of this, too; always have been."

Lightning cracks outside, throwing their faces into sharp relief: Miller's trembling anger, George's cold detachment. With a snarl, Chief Miller draws his gun, pointing it at George's chest. Adrenaline explodes inside me. For a crazed second, I'm convinced they'll kill each other.

Instead, Miller grips the weapon with purpose. "George Hawthorn," he says, voice breaking with suppressed emotion, "you're under arrest. For the murder of Nate Bennett, along with many, many others." He squares his shoulders, the gun unwavering in his hand. "Put your hands behind your back."

I stare, hardly daring to breathe. For months, I've felt hopeless, trapped in a never-ending nightmare. But seeing Walter, George, whatever his name was, forced to comply, arms raised and eyes dull with resignation, I feel a spark of relief. I let out a strangled sob, almost laughing with disbelief. "Oh my God," I whisper to myself.

Walter moves slowly, whispering something under his breath, so low I can't catch it. He's... smiling? The subdued grin on his face is chilling. He looks almost proud, or possessed. I glance at Miller, who sets his jaw and snaps the cuffs around George's wrists.

Within minutes, George is marched back outside, the storm's fury lashing at us all. Miller pushes him into the back of his cruiser, where I was stranded only minutes ago. I dash forward, ignoring the rain slicing across my skin.

"Miller," I gasp, adrenaline spiking all over again. "Please.

Make him tell us where Shannon is—he took her! He must've. You have to force him—"

"No," Miller cuts me off, voice tired. "I'm done abusing my power. Everything's official from here. I'll bring him in, process him by the book. We'll get the truth legally, not by intimidation. I've... done too much of that already."

My heart writhes like a caged animal. "But that's not good enough! After everything you've done, allowed to happen, *now* is when you want to be the good guy?" I stare in disbelief.

"I'm sorry," he says, stepping away, eyes brimming with regret. "We'll find your friend. We'll find Shannon. I promise."

I stand there, drenched, wanting to scream. The door to the cruiser shuts with a heavy thunk, and Walter's eyes, just visible through the rain-streaked window, lock on me. There's a terror in them, an insanity that makes my blood run cold.

With trembling hands, I grip the cruiser's door handle, yanking it open. Miller shouts behind me, but I barely hear him. I need to try, even if it's insane. The moment I crack the door, the smell of stale sweat mixes with wet leather. George turns his head, and the sharp overhead light makes his eyes disappear, black holes existing where pupils should exist.

"Where's Shannon?" I shout, voice cracking. "What have you done with her?"

George says nothing for a long moment, eyes drifting shut. Then, in a sing-song hush, he murmurs, "Do you really want to know, Margot? Would you do anything for the answer?"

I recoil at his tone. "Name it," I whisper, hateful tears blurring my vision. "Just tell me she's alive."

He half-laughs, the cuffs rattling as he shifts his hands behind him. "I want a hug," he says, voice dropping to a child-like hush that crawls up my spine.

My stomach revolts. "You're sick. Absolutely insane—"

Behind me, Miller's footsteps splash through the mud. "Don't do it, Margot. Don't get close to him. You're not safe—"

But I can't fight the guilt, the desperation. Shannon is all I have, all I trust. If there's even a shred of hope she's alive... I push aside reason, ignoring the frantic pounding of my heart, and nod.

I lean into the cruiser. Walter's eyes widen, a slick grin crossing his face. The wind tears at us both, rain streaming onto the seat. I inch closer, feeling his breath warm against my cheek. The feeling is vile, invasive, a thousand times worse than I imagined. My mind screams at me to pull away, but I force my arms around him, feeling the cold bite of the cuffs pressing into my chest. My stomach heaves; I can smell the stale blood on him–does it belong to Nate, to Shannon?

George lets out a ragged sigh, and in my ear, he whispers one word that sends my heart crashing: "Pier."

My entire body goes rigid. "What...?" I manage.

"The pier," he clarifies, a ghost of amusement coating each syllable. "That's where you'll find Shannon."

I recoil, stumbling out of the cruiser, nearly falling into the storm again. Miller lunges, grabbing me, steadying me as I pitch sideways. "Margot!" he yells over the wind. "What did he say?"

I'm shaking so hard my teeth chatter. My voice emerges in a hoarse croak. "He said she's at the pier."

My mind spins back to when I found Walter in my room, right after seeing the muddy footprints from the hidden passage. Realization slams into me: he must've taken Shannon —dragged her to the pier—and circled back to intercept me. She hasn't been at the house for hours now.

Lightning stabs across the sky, revealing Miller's stunned expression. "We'll get a team," he mutters, "comb the pier—"

I'm already sprinting, my legs burning, water up to my

ankles in the flooded grass. Shannon is out there, alone. I refuse to let her be the next victim claimed by this cursed town.

As I race away, the thunder cracks with deafening force. Rain lashes my face, blinding me, but it doesn't matter. Chief Miller's shouts fade behind me as I tear across the yard, to the road that'll lead me to the water's edge. Deep in my chest, I plead with God for the first time in my life.

Please let her be there.

Please let her be alive.

37

A raw, desperate breath tears at my lungs as I tear down the road, the rain drilling into me with near-hurricane force. Every muscle in my body howls for oxygen, but I can't stop. I keep running, the muddy asphalt slick beneath my shoes, lightning splitting the sky like it wants to claw the earth in half. I can just make out the faint glow of the dock lights in the distance, and the flickering promise of them propels me forward. My hope says Shannon is there, she has to be.

I burst onto the pier, my ribs a screaming vise around my heart, the wooden planks slippery under my feet. This isn't just any thunderstorm; it's a monster. I momentarily think about how fitting it all is, my story here started during a raging storm and it may end during one as well.

"Shannon!" I choke out her name, voice ragged. The wind snaps it away, burying my plea in sheets of pounding rain. Lightning erupts, illuminating the pier with a silver glow, and I sprint its full length, water spraying off my heels. No one. Not even a shadow. Just ragged gusts of wind hurling water against my face like needles. My voice tears from me in a wail, "Shannon, where are you?"

Silence. Rain. Darkness.

My hope cracks. Walter lied. He said she'd be at the pier, but there's not a single soul out here. No movement, no sound. Only my breathing, strangled and panicked, and the scream of the wind.

Headlights crest the hill behind me. They blind me at first, my eyes burning as I whip around. The beams shine so bright that my vision whites out; I can't see which car it is until the floodlights bounce upward at the railroad crossing. For an instant, the silhouette is unmistakable: Chief Miller's cruiser. He's come after all.

I lunge toward the pier entrance, a surge of relief tangling with my fear—maybe he can help me find Shannon. But I'm torn in two. My body whips around again, wrestling with the dark stretch of the dock. She must be out there. And yet... there's nothing. Where is she? I'm frozen in place with no direction.

An agonized sob rips from my throat. "God, please," I beg, voice breaking under the roaring sky. "Don't take her too. I can't lose her." Tears mingle with the rain, the sting of it all choking me. I'm paralyzed, fists clenched, staring in wild confusion between the bright headlights at the road's end and the blackness at the far edge of the pier. It's too dark, too wet. The sky flickers with lightning, but it shows me nothing except the shaking outline of the boards stretching into emptiness.

Chief Miller's cruiser is close now. I'm about to sprint to him when, in the brief silence after a thunderclap, I hear it:

My name.

It's faint, nearly swallowed by the wind, but I freeze, every nerve on high alert. Another roar of wind drowns all else, but then... again. "Margot!"

"Shannon?!" I scream, spinning in circles, pulse crashing in my ears. I don't see anyone on the dock. No movement in the water. Panic slams into me; I'm certain I heard her, but where is she?

A lightning bolt detonates across the sky, painting everything in stark brightness for an instant—and that's when I see it. Off to the side, near the cattails lashing violently in the storm, one of those run-off tunnels I remember Donny explaining. The big concrete tubes that funnel rainwater downhill into Lake Dora.

Her voice echoes again, so close it feels like it's inside my skull. Shannon. My best friend. I plunge off the dock, sloshing through the flooded marsh, the thick plants whipping my arms. The bank drops off sooner than I expect; suddenly I'm chest-deep in murky water, mud tangling around my ankles. Adrenaline rockets through me. I can't touch the bottom. Gasping, I half-swim, half-scramble to the tunnel's mouth. The concrete rim is slick with algae, and my chest seizes, starved for air. But I cling to the rough edge, panting, ignoring the sting of the wind-driven rain.

"Shannon!" I shout, voice cracking. She calls back, her tone raw, as if she's screamed a thousand times already. I haul myself forward, into the tunnel, pushing past the thick cattails and the tangle of some rusted metal piping. Inside, it's pitch-black, and water laps at my chin. A wave of claustrophobia clamps around my heart. I have no phone, no light. The ceiling is so low it nearly grazes my hair, moss and grime brushing my scalp. I can't see a damned thing.

I force myself to move deeper, each step a battle as the current from the storm runoff surges around me. Her voice draws closer. My foot slips; I plunge under for a terrifying second, sputtering back up in time to hear her again, just ahead. "Margot—help me—!"

I surge forward, arms outstretched, until my fingertips brush flesh—Shannon's fingers knot through mine in a desperate grip. Lightning flashes outside, and for a heartbeat, we're both lit in ghostly white. I catch a glimpse of metal bars, thick and corroded, slicing across my line of sight. A grate. It's blocking the tunnel's exit into the lake, and Shannon's on the other side. She's soaked, shaking violently.

"Shannon!" I gasp, nearly choking on the filthy water. "I found you."

She says something, her words drowned by a crash of thunder. I cling to the bars and feel something else—hard metal binding her wrist. I trace the length, heart pounding, until my hand finds a chain looped around the grate. My stomach drops.

I meet her eyes, only inches away through the bars. The water is already up to her chest, swirling around her chin. Every gust of wind outside pushes in more water, flooding the tunnel. Her lips quiver, tears mixing with the relentless torrent.

"You're handcuffed?!" I manage, voice ripping from me. "Oh God, Shannon..."

She coughs, voice hoarse. "Key—there has to be a key... I don't know... I can't—" Another wave crashes in, forcing her to tilt her head to keep from swallowing water.

I'm spitting curses at the darkness, scrabbling for any solution. The water's climbing. Soon, we'll both be forced underwater entirely. I rest my forehead against the bars, the cold metal biting my skin. If I had any tears left, I'd sob them all out right here. Shannon's alive—but not for long if I can't save her. The knowledge of that is a gnawing terror far deeper than any fear I've ever known.

I grab her face between the bars, pressing my forehead to hers. "I'll get you out," I vow, my voice trembling. "I promise. Just hold on!"

I'm nearly out of breath, but I force my body back out of the tunnel, water sloshing around my chest. Shannon's voice hits me like a physical blow—she's begging me not to leave her behind—but the storm rages too loudly, swallowing her cries as soon as they form. I hate myself for turning away, but I have no choice. I need something to free her from the handcuffs keeping her anchored to the tunnel.

Rain whips across my face as I swim and thrash, desperate to reach the embankment. My heart lurches when I realize it's too high, the concrete lip slick with algae and water. There's nothing to grip, no ledge to leverage. I push at the wall, sobbing with frustration, then shift toward the dock instead, but it's also too high for me to hook my elbows over. My muscles spasm, halfway giving up. Lightning stabs the sky, illuminating the battered pier as waves threaten to pull me under.

A surge of panic electrifies every cell in my body: I can't get out. Water floods my mouth as my head slips beneath the surface. I'm going to die right here—both Shannon and I lost to this violent, swirling night. Then a hand plunges through the dark water, gripping my arm hard. Before I can register what's happening, I'm dragged upward in a rush of air and thunder, landing on the soaked dock with a painful thud.

I choke and sputter, water gushing from my nose and mouth. My eyes sting from the salt of my own tears. A flash of lightning reveals Chief Miller's face hovering above me, lines of worry carved into his features.

"Breathe," he shouts, voice raw against the wind. "You're okay, Margot. Breathe!"

My lungs claw for oxygen, each breath a victory over the suffocating fear that was closing in. He hovers there, repeating himself—telling me I'm safe, to inhale, to calm down. It feels like an eternity before I manage a full breath that doesn't tear at my throat.

"Shannon," I croak, voice cracking over the rain's roar.

"She's in the tunnel—handcuffed, the water—" I can't form the words fast enough. My entire body quakes with desperation as I scramble upright. "We need bolt cutters—she's trapped—"

I stop dead. A thick shadow rises behind Miller, like an apparition swelling out of the night. Lightning flares and illuminates him: George Hawthorn, still wearing the cuffs that Chief Miller locked around his wrists. His eyes are wild, teeth bared in a hateful grin.

"Miller!" I cry, lunging forward. But I'm too slow; George slams his chained arms over the chief's head, hooking his wrists around Miller's throat in a vicious chokehold. Miller's feet leave the dock for a split second, his arms flailing, and then both men crash down onto the boards. The storm devours every sound except the primal struggle of them thrashing for control.

Chief Miller claws at George's arms, legs kicking wildly, but George's grip only tightens. Horror grips me, but I force my legs to move. My wet sneakers squeak against the wood as I stumble over, reaching out to pry George's arms off Miller. The darkness is crushing, the pounding rain blinding. Just as I get close, another burst of lightning shows me George's face twisted in savage triumph. He smashes a kick into my ankle— pain flares bright and hot, jolting up my leg like fire.

My vision washes and I teeter backward, arms windmilling, bracing for the splash that will seal my fate. Summoning every scrap of strength, I fling out a hand, my fingers catching on a dock pylon. The momentum nearly wrenches my shoulder from its socket, but I hold on. My foot dangles over the storm-tossed water.

Shannon. My mind howls her name. I can't see the tunnel, but I know the water is only climbing, possibly seconds away from submerging her. Yet Miller is choking, eyes bugging in terror as George tightens the chain around his windpipe. Lightning flares again, revealing Miller's face, veins bulging.

He releases a final, choked whisper—"Margot...help..."—but I can't. I have to choose. My chest burns with guilt as I hobble across the slick dock, ignoring Miller's strangled pleas. My best friend is drowning in that tunnel. I lurch off the platform, stumbling through the mud toward the police cruiser, the door still hanging open.

My fingers claw frantically at the interior, throwing aside the radio, pushing papers, searching every compartment. My lungs can't keep pace with my pounding heart. Finally, I spot a latch under the steering column. I yank it, hearing a faint pop behind me. The trunk.

I slip on the soaked ground but manage to fling myself upward, grabbing the trunk lid. Inside is a chaotic collage of police gear: extra cuffs, flashlights, evidence bags, road flares, a battered shotgun, a set of maps. No bolt cutters. My stomach wrenches, cold dread hollowing me out.

"No," I whisper, voice almost lost in the deluge. "No, no..."

Shannon's going to drown if I don't free her. I spin in a dazed circle, searching for something, anything, but all I see is that shotgun. My heart seizes at the idea. I've never fired a gun, never even held one. But if I can't cut the chain, maybe I can blow it off.

I grab the shotgun with trembling hands. It's heavier than I expected. I pump it once, the solid thunk making me flinch. I crash the trunk door down and turn—only to find George standing right in front of me.

Lightning reveals his face, soaked hair matted to his skull, blood trickling from where the cuffs had dug into his wrists, one now dangling freely. He's breathing hard, but his eyes are wild with purpose. If he's here, I know that Chief Miller is dead. The guilt soaks into me and I wonder if I did the right thing.

I raise the shotgun, voice high with fear. "Back up!"

He just smiles, water streaming down his jaw. "You're too late. She's already gone." He points toward the tunnel as thunder shakes the sky. "It's full now. She's drowned, Margot. It's over."

"Shut up!" My voice cracks. "Get away from me."

I shuffle back a step; he takes one forward. "We were meant to be here," he screams, voice raw in the downpour. "Right now. This moment. It's fate, can't you see?!"

Lightning ignites his face again, madness carved in every line. My stomach flips, tears stinging my eyes. The storm saturates every breath, my hair plastered to my neck, heart thundering in my ears. I take another step back, shotgun shaking in my grip. He laughs, closing the distance to a mere three feet.

"You won't shoot me," he growls, voice low and certain.

I tighten my jaw, adrenaline roaring through my veins. My finger curls around the trigger. "Wanna bet?"

I pull it.

The world explodes into thunder and light.

38

I squeeze the trigger, but all I get is a hollow click. Shock slams through my body so hard it feels like I've been kicked in the chest. My frantic finger pumps the trigger again, and again that sickening click mocks me.

George's laugh rips across the night. It starts low, almost playful, then rises into a manic howl that drowns even the hammering rain. My stomach twists in a way I've never felt before. And then, as if he's flipped a switch inside himself, he cuts off the laugh. His eyes lock onto mine through the curtain of rain. He inhales sharply through his teeth, drawing saliva back into his mouth, and scowls.

"You were actually going to shoot me," he says flatly. It's not a question, and it's not an accusation. It's like he's marveling at the idea. There's hurt and fury shimmering behind his gaze, and I can't decide which side of him is more terrifying. Suddenly, I want to bolt, to fling the useless shotgun at him and run. But my limbs refuse to cooperate.

He leans in a fraction, reading the panic flaring in my eyes. "You're scared," he murmurs. "You should be. Everyone is dead. The storm's too loud, the town's shut inside. And you?"

His grin returns, twisted and hungry. "You want to run. I can taste it. But listen to me—she always gets what she wants. I'll do anything she asks of me. And tonight"—he dips close enough for me to catch the stench of his breath—"she wants you."

His final word is breathed against my ear. It jolts me like a shock of electricity, blasting through the paralysis in my muscles. I spin on my heel, fumbling the shotgun and letting it crash to the mud as I take off toward the woods. Rain stabs at my cheeks, wind roars in my ears, but I keep screaming for help, for anyone, even knowing I'm probably wasting air. The storm devours everything.

My ankle is on fire, swollen and unsteady. Every third step sends a fresh stab of agony right up my leg. Branches whip my face, leaving tiny cuts. I zigzag blindly among the trunks, trying to stay hidden. Finally, I glance back, heart in my throat, expecting George's silhouette right on my heels. But I see nothing. He's not behind me. Despite the throbbing in my foot, I push on faster.

A break in the canopy reveals the faint lights of Hawthorn Manor. My eyes hone in on the front door. If I can just get inside, lock or barricade it... Even if George finds another way, I can slow him. My phone is inside. All I have to do is call for backup, get help.

Headlights flicker through the trees in front of me. I freeze, dropping instinctively into a crouch. My throat seizes as Chief Miller's cruiser prowls slowly up the winding road—except I know it's not Miller at the wheel. The side spotlight flares white through the rain, searching the underbrush. And George's voice floats on the storm, singsong and mocking, "Margot... where are you?"

My heart scrambles in my chest. He's still having fun,

playing his cat-and-mouse game. But I'm hardly able to walk at this point, let alone outrun a car. My ankle throbs and the swelling's creeping above the top of my shoe. Another block or two and I'll be limping too badly to move. I look down the hill back towards the center of Mount Dora. Racing all the way back to the police station or a random house, hoping their hurricane shutters and doors aren't already drawn seems like an impossibility in my condition.

Hawthorn Manor is the only real chance I have.

Clamping a hand over my mouth to stifle a cry of frustration, I push away from the road, hobbling through the last stretch of trees that stand between me and the house. My lungs burn from the humidity and fear, my ankle throbs with every uneven footstep. But I refuse to stop. The storm scythes at me with wind and water, and I'm half-blind with rain, but finally—finally—I see the driveway. My house is right there, looming in the gloom.

The front door is wide open, light from the hallway casting a dull glow into the night. I pause, breath stuttering. I scan the darkness for any sign of movement but see none. It's been several minutes since I saw the police cruiser or spotted any light combing through the trees. He may have doubled back.

Summoning my last scrap of courage, I sprint out of the tree line. My ankle feels like it's splitting in two with each step, but adrenaline blasts me forward.

I'm panting, nearly delirious, as I cross the open gravel. I swear something moves at the corner of my vision—a dark silhouette racing toward the house as well. My heart nearly bursts. George. He's found me, I know it. Desperation rips through every cell, and I throw myself up the porch steps. One, two, three, in a blur. I hit the threshold, chest heaving, and stagger inside. Relief surges through me—I made it. I'm inside.

I spin to slam the door shut—and never see the fist that slams into the side of my head. White-hot agony explodes across my skull, and a shriek dies on my lips. I'm weightless, falling. My brain registers the impact of the floor before everything descends into black.

39

A clap of thunder jolts me awake. I sit on the sofa in my living room, my breath shallow and uneven. I scan the room until my eyes lock on the man I once believed was Walter, standing by the fireplace that now roars with flames. Outside, the storm rages, thunder rattling the windows.

My hands clench at my sides, knuckles stretched pale as fury and sorrow ignite within me. Every muscle trembles with the need to both run and confront him. I can't stop thinking of Shannon—her cries echoing through the water runoff tunnel, the way I hear her voice call out to me one last time. My best friend is gone.

"Why?" I manage, trying to sound strong despite the cold dread pooling inside me. Rain hammers against the windows, perfectly in step with the pounding of my heart. "Why pretend all this time? Why take my best friend? Why kill her?" I choke over the lump in my throat, my voice rising to be heard over a jarring thunderclap. "You murdered my fucking husband. You murdered my best friend. Michael and Penny Lark. All those skulls were people with lives, with dreams and families. For what? To feed your own sick desires? Why?! Tell me, George. Why?"

I'm shouting now, tears flooding my vision, my chest heaving with sobs I can't afford to show him. But I can't stop; I have to say it all, the betrayal and agony clawing for release.

When I'm finally spent, breathless and trembling, George —no, not Walter, but George Hawthorn—slowly exhales, letting my cries fade to the storm's roar. Lightning flashes across his face, revealing a steady, almost gentle expression, as though he pities me.

"Are you done?" he asks softly.

I let out a strangled laugh. "No!" My voice cracks, but I press forward, shouting all the fury and grief I have left—the people I lost, the nightmares he's forced on me, the shattered hope. I hurl accusations like spears, every word a desperate attempt to wound him the way he's torn me apart. He listens without flinching. Even the thunder outside feels dim compared to the blood pounding in my ears.

Eventually, I collapse back against the sofa, panting. My head throbs, and my entire body is tight with tension. It's like my soul has been scoured raw.

George's gaze drifts to the window before returning to me. His voice, when he speaks, is unsettlingly calm. "I wasn't always a monster," he begins. "As a boy, I was just like any other child. I had anger, sure, but so does everyone. Then there was my mother, Dorothy..."

He keeps his eyes on mine, letting the words linger. 'You see," George continues, his voice softening, "Dorothy had a way of instilling darkness in our home. She was always there with her best friend. Gin. They were inseparable. The alcohol brought out a side of her that was pure evil." He rolls up his left sleeve, pushing his arm forward. Tiny, organized lines of scars ran up and down his arm—too many for me to count. "I was her ashtray," he says. "And Amelia was her punching bag." He speaks without emotion—a hollow recounting of events. "One day, she pushed Amelia from the top of the stairs, straight down to the bottom. She didn't touch a single step on the way down. She died right there in front of me. When her neck snapped, something inside of me did too."

I can barely breathe, the horror of his words twist my insides.

George meets my gaze, his eyes cold and detached. "I confided in Cecilia after that. Cece made it her life's mission to save me, to keep that darkness at bay. And it worked for a while. She loved me. Truly loved me. And I loved her more than anything. But the darkness never left. It haunted me, buried too deep, festering." He shakes his head slowly. "One night, I had a nightmare. Amelia's face. Her broken body at the foot of the stairs. It felt as though the only way to escape it was to finally do something. I left Cecilia asleep in bed, snuck out, and I killed my mother. I pushed her, just like she pushed Amelia. I watched her fall. It was vindication. And for a moment, it tasted sweet."

My mind is reeling.

George looks outside and then back to me; his eyes almost soft. "When I returned to Cecilia's, sneaking through the window, she was waiting for me. She knew what I'd done before I even spoke a word. She saw it in my eyes and felt it in my touch when she pulled me close. But she didn't turn me away. She held me. She believed she could save me." His gaze drops to the floor now, his voice barely a whisper, almost lost to the roaring storm. "But killing my mother didn't end the darkness. It quieted it for a time, but the shadows were always there, lurking, biding their time. Cecilia and I fought against it, convinced we could hold it back. We built this house because I couldn't bear the old one. Not after seeing my family destroyed there. I wanted a new start. A sanctuary. A place where we could finally have the life we dreamed of." George gestures around the room's grandeur, contrasting with the anguish in his voice. "But..." He hesitates, his expression hollow, as if the words could crush him.

"We couldn't have children. No matter what we tried, it was hopeless. The medicine available back then offered no answers and no hope. We had to accept our new roles. Cecilia, the matriarch of a town that adored her, and me, the man who would do anything for her, including suffocating my deepest desires. And when Cecilia died, it shattered me. She was every-thing. The love of my life. The only light in the darkness. And suddenly, she was gone. I remember her laughter filling this house, her touch that could chase away even my worst thoughts. Without her, there was nothing but emptiness. There was no one to blame, no one to direct my fury at. I was lost. The rage stayed, bubbling, filling every corner of my mind, and that's when the hauntings started."

George's voice drops to a ragged whisper, his words trem-bling. "She haunted me, Margot. I could hear her laughter. Empty, hollow. Her crying in the dead of night, her voice calling out to me from the darkened halls, always whispering something that I couldn't quite catch. One night, I woke up, and she was lying next to me, as real as you are now, tears streaming down her cheeks, her skin cold, one eye missing. She just stared at the bottom of the bed, never turned to me, never spoke a word. And when I got out of bed and came around to meet her gaze, her single eye refocused on me, and she screamed. No words. Just a blood-curdling, heart-stopping scream. She was gone when I opened my eyes again, but the indent and the chill she had brought were still there. And Margot, she would leave signs. Cryptic, chilling messages that clawed at my sanity. I remember stepping out of the shower once, and there it was. Her handprint on the fogged mirror, perfectly clear, fingers splayed as though she'd been standing right behind me, her presence lingering just beyond my reach. Another night, I woke to see her silhouette waiting in the darkest corner of the room, just a shadow barely distinct from the blackness, her quiet sobs threading through the silence. It was a sound so fragile and desperate it made my blood run cold. She never spoke. Not a single word. Her contact was always begging, pleading. Her sorrow was too deep and consuming for words."

George's eyes glaze over, lost in the memories, and his voice breaks. "So, I went to Lake Dora, stood at the water's edge, and begged her to find peace. And you know what happened? She finally spoke to me. She answered. My darling, Cecilia. I couldn't see her, but I could feel her. I could smell her. She whispered to me. Pleaded for me to bring her company. She told me she was lonely, Margot! And how could I refuse her? She was the love of my life and of course she was lonely. My poor Cece, forced to exist on that god awful lake all alone." George drifts in and out of focus, the moments between words growing longer and longer as he recalls the memory.

"I would do anything to give her what she wanted. And so, I did. At first, I considered killing myself, Margot. I thought about simply ending it all. Throwing myself into Lake Dora to join Cecilia in the afterlife. But I knew better. I had promised Cece, long ago, that I would never take my own life, even if she went before me. She made me swear, and I kept that promise. Deep down, I knew that killing myself wouldn't bring her peace. Cecilia needed company, but not me, not before it was my time. It had to be someone else. The very next day, I walked the streets of Mount Dora, searching. Freddy Bahn was a nobody. The town drug addict who no one would miss. And so, I took him. I strangled him and buried him by the lake, at the exact spot Cece spoke to me the night before. And for a while, Margot, it worked to both quiet Cecilia's spirit as well as my own darkness."

My stomach twists as George's voice softens, becoming almost affectionate.

"For one year, I had peace. But then Cecilia returned. It started just as before. The wails that tore through the house in the middle of the night, the whispered words that twisted around in my brain. Her silent screams from passing reflections in the windows until I couldn't sleep, couldn't think, couldn't breathe. It was all happening again, and I knew what she needed this time. I had to give her someone she knew, someone she would recognize, someone who might bring her comfort. So, I brought her Mary Alcott. She had been Cecilia's friend for years. Her laughter had filled our home when things were still bright and hopeful. I thought that maybe Cecilia's spirit would finally rest if she had a familiar face in the afterlife. I was right. I strangled Mary, just as I had Freddy. But after that, I faced a problem. Someone would eventually find the bodies. The freshly turned soil and marks of my work would attract suspicion. I needed to find another way to get them to Cecilia. A way that would leave no trace, no footprint for others to see. That's when I started to question where someone's spirit truly resides. Most people believe it's in the heart. But not me. No, the heart is just flesh. An organ that rots away like any other. The actual vessel for a person's spirit, the seat of their essence, is the skull. Bone is eternal, bound intrinsically to the spirit world. That's why many cultures and ancient religions have revered it for centuries."

"So, I severed the skulls of Freddy and Mary. I took their skulls and discarded the rest of their bodies into Lake Dora. And when it came to disposal, I learned a thing or two. Did you know that female alligators are particularly vicious when guarding their nests? They're ravenous, relentless. Almost as if they're driven by a primal fury. I knew they'd handle the rest. So, I tossed what remained of their bodies into the murky depths of Lake Dora, and in moments, the water came alive. The thrashing, the bubbles, and then... stillness. They were gone. Devoured. It was as if they had never existed. Just whispers swallowed by the lake, destined to remain forever, playing the role of Cecilia's ghostly community."

I sit in stunned disbelief, struggling to comprehend the casual way in which George was recounting his murders. There is no trace of guilt, no hint of remorse. Only a chilling detachment that revealed the true horror of the man before me.

George continued. "After Mary, everything grew more complicated. As I feared, the next year, right on cue, the hauntings began again. My dear Cecilia, restless even in death, had grown impatient. A year passed, and the friends I had offered were no longer enough to satisfy her. Most men might have found it too much to bear. Perhaps they would have fled, torn down the house, and left Mount Dora far behind. But I am not like most men. Instead, I craved her return. I missed her. Even in her terrifying form, with her sadness and rage, every moment of contact filled the void in me. To feel her presence, even fleetingly, was like warm sun on my skin after an endless winter. And so, I set out to bring her a third offering."

George's eyes grew distant, his voice almost playful as he continued. "Douglas Lane, if I remember correctly. But something was different. She wasn't pleased with Doug. I could feel it. Mere moments after watching the life leave his eyes, I felt her spirit overwhelm me in a way it never had before. It was almost like possession. She never spoke aloud, but her presence filled me, reaching in and controlling my soul. I felt her emotions twisting through mine, forcing my hands away from his throat. This was not the one she wanted. I was baffled. I looked into Douglas' terrified eyes, trying to decipher what Cecilia was asking of me. And then, in a flash, it became clear. She desired the one thing she could never have while she was alive. A child. For a brief, fleeting moment, even my blackened heart hesitated at the thought of sacrificing a child. But that hesitation was simply a moment, nothing more. It passed, and my resolve solidified. My love deserved this. She deserved everything she had been denied. And so, I transformed. I became not just a hunter of men and women but of children, too."

40

GEORGE, 13 YEARS AGO

I slip in through the open window, the cold rain lashing at my face, soaking my clothes. The nightlight's weak glow paints the bedroom in shifting blues, the corners lost to darkness. The storm outside rumbles with a low, constant anger, but the boy—Michael Lark—sleeps on, oblivious to the danger creeping into his world.

My heart thrums against my ribcage, a quiet drumbeat of anticipation. My breath comes shallow and quick, fogging in the damp chill of the room. I take careful steps over the scattered toys on the floor—bits of plastic, a small truck, a stuffed bear. Each step must be silent. The old floorboards are treacherous, always eager to give me away with a creak or groan.

There he is. Michael. His lashes flutter slightly as he dreams, a gentle sigh escaping his parted lips. A worn, floppy-eared rabbit lies tucked under his arm, and a thin dinosaur-patterned blanket wraps him in a fragile cocoon. For a moment, I pause, my chest tightening at the innocence of it all. But I clench my jaw, forcing that useless sentiment away. I'm here for a purpose.

I hover over him, wincing at how loud my own breathing sounds in the hush of the storm-lulled house. Thunder growls from the clouds above, drawing closer, as if the night itself has been building toward this moment. I reach out, pressing my fingertips gently to his shoulder. He stirs, eyelids flickering. I can't afford to let him cry out—my hand clamps down over his mouth before he has the chance.

His eyes snap open, shock flooding them. He tries to move, tries to scream, but all that emerges is a muffled whimper. The swirl of confusion and terror on his face sets my pulse racing. I twist my other arm beneath him, pulling him against me as he thrashes, the blanket tangling around his legs. His small hands paw at my wrist, nails scratching at my skin. It won't help him.

Outside in the hallway, a door creaks. My gut twists. His mother– Penny. She's nearby, maybe already rousing. I can't let her see me. Michael wriggles in my arms, panic giving him strength, but I shove down any pity that tries to surface. I made my decision long ago. I move toward the window as fast as I dare, stumbling through the scattered toys.

One of Michael's feet catches the edge of a plastic tractor— his toy skitters across the floor, and the noise makes my heart stutter. I jerk him tighter to my chest, forcing him to still. He bites down on my hand, but I barely feel it. Adrenaline coats everything in numb urgency.

I get one knee on the windowsill, using my shoulder to push it open wider. The storm air slaps us, driving rain stinging my cheeks. Thunder cracks overhead. I swing my leg out and lower us carefully, dropping down into the yard in a crouch. The wet grass soaks my knees.

Behind us, I hear her. Penny's footsteps moving over the worn floorboards in the hallway. Then her voice, uncertain at first: "Michael?" She's half-asleep, but the dread in her tone is instant. A mother knows.

Michael kicks again, tries to spit out a plea for help. I jam my hand tight against his mouth, my chest tightening with every step I take across the soggy lawn. The rain picks up, each heavy droplet like needles against my scalp.

Inside, Penny's fear erupts into a sharp cry. She's reached his bed, found only rumpled blankets and the empty space where her son should be. Then her scream knifes through the night. "Michael! Michael!"

I grit my teeth. He thrashes in my arms, hearing his mother's voice. My lungs burn, and my arms ache, but I keep going, forging a path across the yard toward the trees. I'm counting on the roar of wind and thunder to mask our escape. Lightning flares, blinding me for an instant, revealing the stark silhouettes of the towering oaks. Their gnarled branches stretch overhead like a net, welcoming me into their cover.

I push forward, my grip never slackening around the boy. His muffled sobs vibrate against my palm. I can feel the frantic pounding of his small heart against my chest—it mirrors my own, each beat feeding a vicious cycle of terror and purpose.

Behind me, Penny's voice cracks, bordering on hysteria, reverberating in the open window: "Michael!"

I force myself not to look back. I've made my choice. I vanish into the shadows of the tree line, the storm swallowing up her desperate cries, her heartbreak echoing in the darkness. Thunder growls in a final, hollow note, sealing the bond I've chosen to make.

Michael's cries fade into a trembling whimper against my hand. My foot slips on the sodden leaves, but I regain my balance, forging deeper into the night. I cling to him, my teeth clenched, body locked tight with tension.

A muffled crash from somewhere behind me in the house signals Penny's frantic, futile dash to the window, maybe even out into the yard, searching. But I'm gone, her son cradled in my arms, the storm's heavy curtain shielding us from sight.

Just as the swirl of guilt in my chest threatens to slow my

steps, lightning ignites the sky again. In the flash, I see the outline of the path leading away from the Lark property. I'll follow it. I'll deliver Michael. And soon enough, the storm will pass—leaving yet another empty bed behind in Mount Dora.

I clutch Michael tighter, ignoring his feeble kicks. This has to be done. And like the storm itself, I'm unstoppable.

41

MARGOT, PRESENT DAY

George's confession sends a crawling chill along my spine the moment he begins. "I still remember how Michael trembled in my arms," he says. "The boy's fear was so visceral it almost gave me pause. It was an awful thing. A dark and monstrous act. But it was what Cecilia needed. It was what she wanted, and I would always provide."

I stand there, my heart hammering so loudly I'm half-convinced it will burst. The darkness in George's words grips me like invisible hands around my throat. I can't stop staring at him, this man I once considered harmless.

He glances at me, and the gravity of his admission hits like a battering ram. "The hauntings ceased after I added Michael's skull," he goes on, "and the restless spirit of my beloved wife was quieted for another year."

I want to shout for him to stop, but I'm frozen. Nausea wells up so fast I have to clench my jaw tightly to keep the bile down. George's eyes gleam with some wretched devotion I don't understand.

He takes a breath, gaze sliding toward nothing in particular, lost in some hellish memory. "I had come to understand the pattern after that third kill," he says. "Every year, Cecilia returns. The house grows cold, the shadows deepen, and Cece's cries echo through these halls once again. Each time, I oblige. I bring someone to the basement of Hawthorn House, waiting for Cecilia to show me if they're worthy. If she approves, I add their skull to the chest, then bury it again, and the hauntings end, her spirit pacified. If she doesn't approve, I still kill them—their bodies go into the lake like all the rest."

A tremor locks up my knees, and all I can think is: *This is a real person. The man in front of me actually did these horrible things.* It's one thing to be curious about a monster; the number of serial killer documentaries proves that. But it's a completely different experience to meet the monstrous truth face to face.

George's voice is low and almost pensive. "I learned to read her signs—how her presence shifts, that coldness seeping into my bones when she's displeased."

I can't do this. I can't listen to him calmly explain murder, the disposal of bodies, the notion of a twisted ritual with Cecilia's ghost at the center. My stomach seizes. A gag claws up my throat, and I stumble away, pressing the back of my hand to my mouth. The room swirls into a messy blur, and I crash into the corner just in time to heave.

My palms slam against the wall for support as I retch again, body convulsing until tears blind me. Humiliation scorches through me, but that shame is nothing compared to the horror twisting my guts. *This can't be real. It can't be.*

I sense George shift behind me. His footfalls are unsteady, and I realize he's stepping closer like he actually wants to help me.

Fury and disgust ignite in my chest, and I whip around, screaming at him, "Don't you *dare* come near me!" My voice rings out, snapping the tension like a gunshot.

George freezes, hands raised in some mockery of surrender.

But his eyes—God, there's something so emptily calm in them. I can feel every nerve in my body spiking to panic.

I press my forehead to the wall, breathing hard, fighting to gather the ragged pieces of my composure. At last, I turn back and face him. My voice is quieter this time, but the dread hasn't left. "Why make a map, George? Why record all of this if you already knew where to hide the bodies?"

George's posture relaxes fractionally, as though he's relieved I'm still speaking. "For years," he answers, voice hushed, "it was the same ritual. The same motions. I perfected them by repetition—knew how to move like a shadow through the woods behind Hawthorn Manor, how to bury that chest without leaving a trace. With time came age, though, and with age, forgetfulness."

I force myself to stand upright, keeping several paces between us, my fingers curling into the couch fabric to steady myself.

He drags a hand over his face. "One night, I realized I couldn't remember the exact spot. That sacred ground where I'd buried Cecilia's—company. It slipped from my mind like sand through an hourglass. I walked up and down the lake until frustration boiled into rage. The woods looked identical —every tree, every rock mocking me. So, I did what puzzle-lovers do: I devised a failsafe. I made a map. I hid it beneath the floorboards. In case I forgot again." He then produces a piece of paper from his pocket.

"Check the floorboards, Georgie" is hand-written in black ink. I look at him and he simply shrugs. "Just in case" he mocks.

My breath shakes in my throat. I recall that moment I found the rolled-up paper, never dreaming it could be tied to something so revolting.

Gathering my courage, I manage to speak. "What about

Penny Lark? You wanted her skull too, but she ended up in that lake. Why didn't you add it?"

A sneer curls George's mouth, as he waves his hand dismissively. "I never killed Penny Lark," he says. "Andy was always so worried about protecting himself. He'd always been so pliable, so easily twisted into doing what I needed from him."

His words rock me backward. My mind stutters, trying to latch onto a rational explanation: *The chief of police helped George commit murder.*

I swallow hard. My voice cracks when I force out, "So... it's true? Chief Miller knew about everything? The murders, the skulls... all of it?"

George chuckles, a hollow, humorless sound. "Of course he knew! I've had Andy Miller wrapped around my finger since we were kids. He was always the weak link, always cowering whenever life hit too hard, begging me to protect him. The idea that he's Mount Dora's 'finest' is laughable. He knew about Dot. He knew exactly what I did to my mother. And when Freddy Bahn vanished, I told him the truth, spelled it out, gave him the chance to turn me in and he didn't. I had him then. Imagine if the town knew their chief of police once covered up a homicide. He would've lost everything. So, he became my accomplice, hating every second, but too cowardly to stand against me. That gave me freedom to keep everything neat and quiet."

My heart thunders. I'm realizing the depth of this conspiracy is far beyond anything Shannon or I imagined. The entire place is a lie, a twisted carnival of illusions that make Mount Dora look idyllic when it's actually a goddamn nightmare.

I clear my throat, searching for my voice. "The skulls... that night... they just vanished from the station. You were with me, George. So how—"

George inclines his head mockingly. "Officer Jenkins. He arrived at Hawthorn Manor before Andy, before us. He took the skulls and stashed them in his cruiser. You were none the wiser. They were out there the whole time."

His casual explanation ignites something hot in my chest —a fury that dwarfs the horror pulsing in my veins. The puzzle pieces click into place. Everything in my life that's splintered traces back to this house and this man. I hate him with every single fiber of my being.

My voice is harsh with rage. "Why keep pretending? Why hide your identity if Miller and Jenkins already knew you were still here?"

George exhales, stepping toward the window. Rain slants across the glass in silver streaks. "Because I was done. They were all parasites. I dedicated my life to this town, gave every-thing—just like my father did before me. And once Cecilia was gone, I had no reason to keep playing caretaker."

He looks at me, eyes narrowing. "I let the business rot, stopped attending their ridiculous events, let them all believe I'd run off or died. Hawthorn Manor and I became one. I stayed here, reading, solving puzzles... waiting for Cece to stir."

There's a glint in his gaze that makes me shudder. He returns his attention to the storm outside.

I manage to speak. "Then what? How did we get here?"

George paces slowly, dragging his hand over the carved back of an antique chair. "Andy eventually brought me repos-session notices from the bank. My money was finally gone, investments tanked. The town was no longer under my thumb. The house was going up for sale. Even so, no one wanted to buy it—rumors of ghosts, you know." He smirks, as though the irony amuses him. "They posted realtors on the property. Sometimes I posed as the groundskeeper. Other times, I just waited in the walls, listening. If someone asked too many questions, or threatened the legacy I protected, their name joined the others at Lake Dora. They became part of the offerings that brought the both of us peace."

My stomach hitches again, a wave of revulsion sinking through me like poison. Tears burn my eyes as the hideous reality finally cements in my brain: he's responsible for every tragedy, every haunted moment tied to Hawthorn Manor. And Chief Miller's complicit.

He lets out a quiet chuckle. "Mount Dora thrives on ignorance, Margot. That ignorance is my shield."

My throat is so tight I can barely speak. I stand there, shaking, tears forging hot paths down my cheeks. George's confession tears my world apart.

The final question forces itself out. "So... all those missing people, all those years—this is just some twisted cycle of appeasing Cecilia?"

He nods, as though it's a simple, irrefutable fact.

I feel my stomach flip violently, and I press a trembling hand to my abdomen. Hawthorn Manor looms around me, dark and silent. The truth is a thousand times worse than any theory or ghost story.

Every dark revelation now assembles in my mind like the pieces of a puzzle. The truth is finally laid bare. George had been the puppet master behind every tragedy: the disappearance of Michael Lark, the cover-up by Chief Miller and Jenkins, the twisted pact with Cecilia, and the grotesque rituals of skulls buried by the lake. The Chief of Police was complicit; the town is nothing more than George's twisted playground, and every disappearance led back to this house and the monster who hid within it.

42

The storm outside thrashes at Hawthorn Manor as if it wants to rip the place apart from the foundation up. Thunder booms in waves, vibrating through the floor beneath me, and the wind hurls heavy sheets of rain against the windows, the force rattling them in their frames.

I force in a trembling breath, trying to center myself. My focus returns to George, his face half-lit by the fireplace's sputtering glow. My mind races with a dozen questions, each one jabbing at me like a knife. But only one forces its way out.

"Why Nate?" My voice sticks in my throat, turning the question rough, almost hoarse. "Why keep him alive this long? Why torment me with all the calls and messages? Why go through all that?"

George's gaze softens, and I catch a flicker of what looks like remorse crossing his features. Rain patters against the window, but his words drift above the storm, cold and deliberate.

"Nate was meant to be my next offering," he says, each syllable weighted with chilling finality. "It had been a year and Cecilia was restless again. When you and Nate moved in, everything changed," George continues, voice tight. "It complicated my usual routine. Harder to move unseen. Trickier to come and go as I needed to. So, instead I waited, and I watched. I watched you both. But he—"George's tone sharpens with a bitter edge "—treated you like you were a chore. A problem. It reminded me of my mother, the way she belittled me. And something inside me... connected with you. I wanted to protect you, the way I couldn't protect Amelia."

I feel my throat tighten as I catch the raw edge of George's words. His warped sense of devotion nauseates me, twisting my insides.

George's eyes flick to mine. "Eliminating Nate would give Cecilia what she needed—and I'd save you from him. Redemption, maybe."

A bitter laugh escapes my lips, barely audible under the storm's roar. He's delusional, spinning reality around his guilt and grief.

He shakes his head. "Then you found the map. Moved the chest. That disrupted the entire plan. I couldn't perform the ritual. Couldn't do my part to calm Cece. It forced me out of the tunnels, forced me to cover my tracks. And then I realized..." He hesitated, his gaze falling to the floor. "I realized I didn't want you to know. I wanted you to get to know Walter, the groundskeeper. I wanted you to know the man who was just here to help, to be kind, to watch over you. Not the monster my mother forced me to become."

I feel something snap inside me—a bolt of rage that electrifies my veins. I shoot up from my seat, face flush with fury. "You murdered my husband because you wanted a chance at fucking redemption?" I scream, my voice distance, like it's not even me saying it but someone else. "It wasn't about protecting me, or even satisfying a ghost that literally only exists in your head. It was your obsession to fix what you couldn't with Amelia. It could have been anyone else, and you chose him because you thought you could right the past by protecting me? You murdered him, George. You took away the love of my life."

Before I can stop myself, I reach for the table lamp, swinging it with everything I have. The lamp misses George's head by an inch, slamming into the floor and exploding into a spray of broken glass, metal, and sparks. A sharp hiss escapes as the bulb shatters and dies, throwing the room into even deeper darkness.

George raises his hands, words tumbling out in a plea. "Margot, please. You have to understand." His eyes flash with something that might be panic. "I do care about you. I've watched you for so long. I saw how you'd cry yourself to sleep, how your shoulders shook under the weight of everything that followed you from Maryland. After you'd fall asleep, I'd sit by your bed... talk to you... stroke your hair."

The impact of his confession is like ice water spilling down my spine. I can feel the blood drain from my face, a clammy dread settling over my skin.

"You've sensed it," he murmurs. "The glimpses in the dark, the whispers at night. Cecilia haunts these halls when she's lonely—she's real, and you felt her, too. But I was there, always, keeping you safe from everything else. Nate... he was unworthy. Removing him was mercy. You don't see that yet, but you will."

I clamp a hand over my mouth, fighting a wave of nausea. My eyes dart around the dim room, searching for an escape route, a weapon, *anything*. I realize now that every flicker of paranoia, every unexplained noise I dismissed as grief or madness, even the nightmare of the tub in the basement—*it was him*. George had inserted himself into my life in a thousand subtle ways and influenced the very way in which I thought.

His voice drops, heartbreakingly gentle. "I was your guardian, Margot. Your protector."

My lips part, but at first, no sound comes out. Then I manage a trembling whisper, "You're insane. You killed him. You... watched me. He was my husband. You—" I choke on sobs, my emotions tangled in devastation and wrath.

His eyes glimmer with sorrow, or maybe pity. "Nate was cruel," he insists, as though it's enough of a reason. "You deserve better."

Rage floods every inch of me, a molten heat fueling my limbs. My entire reality has been twisted by this man's lunacy, and I see only one path forward now: survival.

I grit my teeth. I need to make it out. I need to tell the world what George did.

He notices my shift—my posture tensing, my eyes searching. Panic flashes in his expression. "Margot, please—"

But I'm already taking a step away, determined to reach that door. I have to escape this place, blow the lid off his gruesome secrets, and ensure George never haunts another living soul again.

Lightning flares outside, illuminating his face in a stark flash—haunted, desperate, and scarily convinced he's right. The thunder crashes, shaking the floor under my feet.

George's twisted mind might believe he's saving me, but I see the real monster. No matter how terrible the storm raging outside is, I now know an even worse danger lives inside these very walls.

43

I lock eyes with George, who stands across the parlor. Even in the flickering firelight, I see every line of tension carved into his face. Then, slowly, as if playful, he turns toward the fireplace. My heart jolts as he picks up a broad kitchen knife I hadn't noticed before. The blade's length catches the glow of the flames, and a sickening wave of dread ripples through my stomach.

Every survival instinct screams at me to get out. I dart a look at the front door. The keys to the deadbolt are still missing. My chest tightens. The back door, I suspect, is locked in the same way. The window crosses my mind for half a second —hurtling through glass is suicide. One good shard lodged in my artery, and that's the end of the story.

My gaze lands on the grand staircase. Fear rears its ugly head again. The secret passageways inside Hawthorn Manor lurk somewhere up there. My nerves prickle at the thought of descending into those cramped tunnels again...but if that's my only option, I can't hesitate.

George steps forward, tightening his grip on the knife. Under his breath, I hear him murmuring again, except now I understand it's the ghost of his dead wife he's whispering to. Or that's at least what he believes. A shiver rattles my spine.

Then an idea snaps into focus. Maybe I can use George's twisted belief in Cecilia to my advantage. I stare straight past him, fix my eyes on a dark corner of the room. My own voice sounds genuine, "Cecilia?" I call, raising a trembling hand to point. "Please... don't."

He halts; knife still poised. He glances over his shoulder. That distraction is all I need. I dash for the staircase, ignoring the shriek of protest from my swollen ankle. My lungs burn, but I force myself onward, weaving around a table, sidestepping past a heavy armchair. George realizes the deception almost immediately—he growls my name, but I'm already at the first step.

My hand slaps the banister, desperate for balance, when I hear the sickening hiss of the blade cutting air. Pain detonates across my abdomen so fiercely I gasp. It's as if time slows. The jolt of it resonates through my entire frame; I see the red stain blooming across my shirt. The knife has carved a clean line directly across my body.

I collapse to one knee, choking on a cry. I haven't even fully registered the wound yet, and still, I scramble up the stairs. My body is in shock, but sheer adrenaline rams into me, keeps me moving despite the throbbing, molten sensation that's spilling warmth down my torso.

George is right behind me, driving me upward with each thud of his boots. My slippery palms clutch at the railing, fighting for traction. Somehow, I manage to kick backward, forcing him to flinch. A single blow in the right place might send him tumbling down. But I only connect with air.

"Margot," he hisses, voice rough with triumph—or madness.

My foot catches on the blood now coating the stairs, and I

crash onto my side. Another shard of pain spears up my leg as he slashes at my shin. Blood trickles hotly against my skin, and my thoughts spin in a vortex of panic. I try to scramble backward, pressing upward one tread at a time, but each movement drains more of my strength.

If I can just reach the second floor, then maybe I can retrace my steps through the hidden door and back to Hawthorn House.

I grab at the banister's spindle to haul myself higher. It snaps under my weight. I nearly tumble sideways down the steps, letting out a strangled cry. George lunges for me, practically throwing himself onto my body. We twist and claw at each other, the knife bouncing away down the steps. I watch it vanish below, out of reach for both of us.

"Please—George!" I snarl, twisting with every ounce of strength left. I succeed only in rolling onto my stomach, pinning my right arm beneath me. George's weight presses me into the hard edge of the step, and I taste blood where my lip collides with the wood.

He grabs a fistful of my hair and slams my face against the step, over and over, until I hear ringing in my ears. My skull vibrates, and I can't remember which way I was trying to go. A vague numbness creeps up my arms and legs, threatening to swallow me.

I'm fading fast when he shifts, maneuvering my head toward the jagged spindle that's broken. My mouth goes desert dry as I glimpse the razor-sharp wooden edge moving towards my face. Nate's face ripples through my mind—a heartbreakingly tender memory that gives me one fleeting moment of comfort. Tears blur my vision.

With a low, guttural grunt, George applies every ounce of strength he has left. The slice of flesh is the last thing I hear before everything slides into a dark, echoing silence.

44

NATE, 12 WEEKS AGO

I stand in the kitchen, the overhead light casting a dull yellow glow that makes everything look more tired than I feel. I'm staring at my laptop screen, which shows an account balance so far below zero it feels like a personal insult. The hush in the house is broken only by the hum of the fridge. That tiny sound seems to magnify how empty my life has become.

It's been months since I got laid off from CirroSystems. At first, I told Margot I was working from home on special projects, burying the truth that I was caught using my corporate card for gambling expenses. I remember the panic welling up in my throat when HR confronted me—signing my name on the termination papers with shaky hands. Since then, I've been piling lie on top of lie, hoping I could catch a lucky break, pay everything back, and Margot would never know.

But luck's a joke. I was always chasing that big payout, that one final hand of poker or last parlay bet that'd magically fix our financial crisis. The ledger in front of me now says otherwise—there is no magical fix. Just a cold, brutal bottom line.

A knock on the front door jars me from the miserable trance I've been in. It's early, and I'm not expecting anyone. I walk over, telling myself to act normal, praying it's not a bill collector in person. When I open the door, a courier in a uniform hands me a thick envelope.

"Certified letter for Nate Bennett," he says, monotone. I sign on his tablet with clammy fingers, and he leaves without a word. Closing the door, I return to the kitchen, the envelope feeling weighty in my hands. It's from a law office I've never heard of, the kind of mail that usually means lawsuits or more debts. My stomach clenches as I tear it open, half expecting to see the usual demands for money I don't have. Instead, I catch the words:

To: Nathaniel Bennett (Beneficiary – Son)

Re: Estate of George Hawthorn (Testator – Father)

My head spins. Father? I hardly know anything about him —he left before I was even born. Taking my mom's last name, Bennett, was all the inheritance I earned. And now, I'm apparently heir to his estate? I fight the urge to laugh. It's too insane.

I read on. George Hawthorn, deceased, owned various properties and businesses in Florida. Most of them sound like they need money more than I do, but a single property jumps out at me: a property called Hawthorn Manor in Mount Dora, Florida, which has been left to me. My mind whirls: is this some kind of sick joke? If it's not, how much is this property worth? I've never even set foot in Florida. This can't be right.

I re-read the letter again hoping to understand more about what's happening here, but the second read through leaves me even more confused than the first time. This documentation looks legitimate. And if it is, then– why me? If he was so sure about me existing, why had he never contacted me before? And why leave me this property? It could be a rundown shack or loaded with back taxes for all I know. It might not be worth a dime.

But here's the thing: I'm desperate. My debts are crushing

me, and creditors are sniffing around. I feel like a caged animal, lunging at any hint of an open door. If there's even a slim chance this place has legitimate value—enough to cover part of my gambling debts—then maybe I can keep Margot in the dark a little longer. The idea churns in my gut, making me sweat. But the alternative is telling her everything: that I've been out of work, that I lied, that I bet away our future on card tables and online sportsbooks.

I look again at the laptop, where my empty bank account still glows. I can't pretend this is some guaranteed windfall. An old house in Florida isn't necessarily an instant fortune. For all I know, it's a money pit, falling apart at the seams. Yet I feel a tiny spark of hope. If there's equity in it—if I can sell it, or at least convince Margot we should move in and somehow keep the collectors off my back—maybe we can reboot our lives.

I slide the letter back into its envelope with trembling hands. My thoughts dart to Margot. She's been through so much already—Lila, enduring that painful trial, and all the emotional fallout. She deserves peace and stability. She deserves the husband I promised her I'd be, not this liar with a gambling addiction.

I take a deep breath, trying to keep my guilt at bay. Maybe I can spin this. Frame it as a sudden inheritance—truthful enough—and then downplay the financial aspect. If I say I've used our "savings" to buy the house outright, she might not suspect there never was a savings account to begin with. It's risky, borderline insane, but so is letting her find out we're drowning in debt. So is waiting for the next round of angry phone calls and visits from collectors.

Clutching the envelope, I power down the laptop. My plan —half-formed and riddled with holes—takes root in my mind. I'll do what needs to be done to keep Margot safe from my mistakes. If this manor is worthless, at least I'll have tried something. If it's worth enough to put a dent in my debt, then maybe we have a future that doesn't end with my life in shambles.

For the first time in weeks, I feel the smallest flicker of determination. I'll take this inheritance, flawed or not, and see if it can save me—save us. Because the alternative is admitting I let everything slip through my fingers, and I'm not ready for Margot to see who I really am yet.

45

I settle onto the couch next to Margot, careful not to startle her. Her gaze is locked on the TV, but I know she's not really seeing it. The flickering light dances across her face, revealing the hollowness in her eyes. Ever since the trial, she's been like this—slipping further and further away, drowning in her own thoughts. She hasn't returned to work since they forced her out at CPS; not that they'd be calling her back, anyway. And leaving the house? Out of the question.

For me, though, this is a window of opportunity. If there's ever been a time to nudge her toward something new, it's now.

I lean in just enough so my shoulder grazes hers, my arm resting along the back of the couch. "You know," I say softly, pitching my voice like I'm holding back a secret, "I've been thinking. Maybe we could use a change of scenery."

Margot keeps her stare fixed on the screen. I sense her resistance in the way her jaw tenses. Change has never been easy for her, but I need her to believe this is all for her benefit.

"Is that so?" she answers after a beat, voice soft and brittle.

I ease closer, trying to match her tone—light, unthreatening. "Yeah, you know, maybe somewhere... different," I say. "We're not tied to Maryland anymore. I can work from anywhere these days. Plus, all these memories— they keep us stuck, Margot. Maybe a fresh start is exactly what we need."

Her eyes flicker, a hint of life behind that vacant expression, as though she's trying to piece something together.

I drop my voice, as if I'm letting her in on a personal confession. "We could go somewhere you can breathe again. Somewhere you won't walk outside and see ghosts on every corner." I let that hang for a moment, then offer a slight shrug. "We deserve it, don't we? A chance at a fresh start."

She stiffens, and I know she's not convinced. But I don't press too hard. Instead, I lean back, giving her a little space. "I hate seeing you like this, Margot. You deserve to feel alive again. I miss your laugh, I miss your smile, I miss– you."

She's quiet, eyes drifting. I stay silent too, letting her imagine what a new start could look like. I'm certain she's picturing the last few months—losing Lila, her forced resignation, the trial. All those painful moments pulling her down.

After a long, tense pause, she murmurs, "Somewhere warm?"

I nod, a careful smile creeping across my face. "You bet. A place with a big garden, a lot of sun. A place that feels like a real beginning for us."

Finally, she turns to look at me. Her gaze is weary, but at least she's looking. "Are you serious right now, Nate? Is that something we can even afford?" she asks.

Her question hangs in the air. It's the moment I've been waiting for. "It is," I say, steadying my voice. "I think we've been through enough to deserve a shot at something new."

She drifts off again, her expression torn. I wait, letting her process, then gently slide my hand over hers, thumb brushing across her knuckles. "Hey, no pressure," I add, keeping my tone easy. "Just think about it. We can look around, see what's out there. If we find the right place, great. If we don't, we stay put."

She bites her lip and nods slowly. That little gesture tells me my seed of an idea is taking root. A flicker of hope sparks in her eyes, and it mirrors the relief swirling through my chest. If she's open to leaving, then we're one step closer to the escape I need.

I let a quiet moment pass before I lean forward again, lowering my voice like I'm revealing a hidden gem. "I've actually done some research," I admit, keeping it casual. "There's this town down in Florida—Mount Dora. Supposed to be beautiful, near some lakes, warm winters. People say it's peaceful. Exactly the kind of place where nobody knows us."

Margot's eyes sharpen with a touch of curiosity. "Florida?" she echoes. "That's...far."

"It is," I concede, layering sympathy into my words. "But maybe that distance is what we need. So, we're not confronted with everything that's happened here. The trial. Lila..." I pause deliberately, letting the name hit her with its full weight.

She flinches like I thought she would, her face etched with pain. I can almost feel her resolve weakening at the memory.

"I've been looking at houses there," I say carefully, trying not to sound too eager. "Old ones with character—places that can be shaped into something new. Somewhere we could call ours."

Margot's eyes grow wet, the memory of Lila and the trial clearly tangled up in her mind. "You think...we could really leave it all behind?" she asks, her voice trembling.

"We can," I answer firmly. "We'll take it slow—make sure it's right. But I believe in us, and I believe in giving ourselves the space to heal."

She glances down, fingers clutching mine. "Okay," she whispers. "Maybe...maybe it's worth looking into."

That single word—okay—thrums through me like a bolt of electricity. I manage a gentle smile, nodding as if I haven't already planned half of this in my head. "Yeah," I say. "We'll see what's out there."

As I lean back, I notice a faint spark in her expression that wasn't there a minute ago. I don't let her see how triumphant it makes me feel. Instead, I press a soft kiss to the back of her hand and let the quiet settle again.

In the silence, my thoughts churn with the future I'm already constructing: Hawthorn Manor in Mount Dora, the warm sun on our shoulders, far from the creditors and mistakes chasing me. Margot can be free of her grief. I can rebuild our lives, finally provide for her again. I just need a chance, just a little luck on my side. I can be a good husband again, I know it.

For now, I keep my satisfaction tucked inside. I just squeeze her hand a little tighter, matching her weary gaze with a smile. But in my mind, I'm already gone, imagining the day we'll pack our life into boxes and drive south to Florida, leaving every specter of this place in our rearview mirror.

46

The first night in Hawthorn Manor is colder than I expected. A dampness clings to the air, and as soon as we step through the heavy front door, it feels like the house itself exhales—like it's been waiting too long for anyone to return. An uneasy hush settles around us, broken only by the rustle of cardboard as Margot and I unpack the bare necessities.

Margot gently trails her hand along the banister, a look of wary awe on her face. The place is undeniably grand: carved moldings, built-in bookcases, even stained-glass accents in some windows. Beneath the dust and cobwebs, you can still feel its former grandeur. I watch Margot closely, relieved that, despite everything, she seems excited to be here.

After an hour of wrestling with boxes in awkward silence, she tells me she's heading for a shower. I nod and watch her walk upstairs, her shoulders drooping with exhaustion. A second later, a sharp knock rings out from the front porch, echoing through the high ceilings. I freeze, heart kicking up a notch. I glance at the stairwell, hoping Margot's already out of earshot, then make my way to the door. *If some creditor already followed us here...* My heart sinks at the thought.

Standing on the porch is a stranger—tall, muscular, and exuding a kind of confidence that instantly sets me on edge. He has tousled hair, a shadow of stubble, and eyes that appear to be sizing me up the moment I open the door

"Hey there," he says, lifting a hand in a hesitant wave. "Sorry to bother you so late. I'm looking for... Nate Bennett?"

I hesitate, hand still on the doorknob. "That's me. Can I help you?"

He shifts his weight, offers a tight sort of smile that doesn't quite reach his eyes. "Yeah, uh... I'm Patrick. Patrick Brendamore. I heard someone moved into Hawthorn Manor, and, well, I live nearby. Thought I'd introduce myself." He rubs the back of his neck, glancing around the porch. "I know it's late, so I apologize. It's just... this might sound weird, but I think we have some things to talk about regarding this house—and George Hawthorn."

My stomach twists at the mention of my father's name. "Okay..." I say slowly, trying not to sound hostile.

Patrick breathes out, the exhale clouding in the chilly air. "All right. Look, I don't want to ambush you. I know you just arrived, and I'm sorry for catching you off guard. But I have reason to believe George Hawthorn was my father, too."

He glances past my shoulder, into the foyer where half-unpacked boxes line the walls. I can practically see him weighing whether he should push for an invitation inside. Before he can speak again, I step out onto the porch, pulling the door partially shut behind me.

"I see. Why do you think that?" I ask, folding my arms to ward off the cold and the tension crawling up my spine.

Patrick reaches into his coat pocket and pulls out a small bundle of yellowed letters. He keeps them close to his chest, not forcing them on me, but showing me they exist. "I believe George and my mother had an affair, many years ago before–

before his actual wife passed away." The tension on the porch makes every muscle in my face feel like it's being pulled towards the back of my head.

"My mom, Phyllis, saved every letter George ever wrote her. During the affair, he promised her things... a life together... that he'd acknowledge me. Unfortunately, for me and my mom, none of that ever happened before George disappeared. But it does mean that if all this is true, I might be George's oldest son."

I stare at him, my mind spinning. First day in a new house, and here's someone claiming we're half-brothers. It feels surreal. The air is so cold, my breath mists in front of my face, but sweat prickles at my temple. "That's... um, wow. That's a lot to take in on my first night here," I manage.

He nods, shuffling the letters carefully. "Trust me, I'm not thrilled about delivering this bombshell. But I figure you and I deserve a chance to talk before I go waving these around in court." He lifts the letters slightly, then tucks them away again. "If I'm older, I might have a stronger legal claim to this place than you. As uncomfortable as the situation is, I'm hoping we can handle this ourselves without needing to make it a legal thing."

He says it quietly, but I can sense an undercurrent of determination. I take a breath, trying to keep my voice even. "I'm sorry, but I've got paperwork showing George left the manor to me. I'll be honest, I never knew him—didn't even know he was alive until the inheritance stuff came up. I'm not sure what your letters say or what kind of validity they may have in any legal proceedings. All I know is, I have documents laying claim to this property."

Patrick's jaw tenses. "I get it. And, hey, we certainly live in a world nowadays where some crazy person could fabricate these

letters to try and scam you. It's understandable you're apprehensive. That's why I'm here, face to face." He glances toward
the front door. "Look, I don't want to intrude on your evening,
especially if you and your wife just got in. But I also don't want
to blindside you with a lawsuit down the road. This place means
something to me—and if George really intended it for one of us,
I want to make sure the rightful person ends up with it."

A draft cuts through the porch, and I shift on my feet. The
entire conversation feels surreal and way too big for this late
hour. "Listen," I say carefully, "I appreciate your approach here,
I do. But you're right, my wife and I just got here. She's
exhausted. I'm exhausted. I need time to figure out what you're
saying... Right now, I can't just—"

He lifts a hand in a calming gesture. "I understand. Look,
let me leave you my number." He fishes in his pocket and
hands me a plain white card with his name scrawled on it, plus
a phone number. "I'm not some scam artist, Nate. I'd rather
resolve this civilly than launch a full-blown legal fight. But I do
want you to know I'm serious. So, I'm hoping we can come to
an agreement like adults—figure out what George really
intended here."

I hold the card, feeling a tremor in my fingers. "Sure thing.
Give me some time and I'll be in touch."

Patrick nods once, the tension in his face easing a fraction.
"Good. Sorry again for dropping by without warning. I live just
outside the historic district, so just... reach out whenever you
can." He hesitates a moment, searching my face. Then, with a
small incline of his head, he steps off the porch and disappears
into the night.

I wait, letting the cold wind rattle the porch swing, before I
finally step back inside. The warmth of the foyer hits me, but I
can't shake the chill clinging to my bones. I lock the door with

unsteady hands, listening for any sign Margot might've heard something. Silence.

As I make my way down the hall, I'm already planning how to keep this from her—at least until I figure out what's real and what's just bluster. Because if Patrick's claim holds any water, my entire plan to start over here falls apart. I've staked everything on this manor. The idea that it could vanish from under me, or that I might have to share it with a stranger who calls himself my brother, makes my pulse thunder.

Heading toward the flicker of light in the living room, I pull out my phone. I aimlessly scroll socials as my mind works. I need to do a deep dive on this guy and maybe his mother. Are they legitimate or maybe just a pair of vagabonds or scam artists making their way through the town, looking to exploit our recent arrival? I open up a browser on my phone and type in his name: "Patrick Brendamore" followed by "Mount Dora, FL". No real hits. No socials, no LinkedIn, not even a mention of him in any local news article.

While that doesn't prove he's my half-brother, it also doesn't disprove that he's a scam artist trying to exploit my lack of knowledge regarding this town. I need time and opportunity to do a deep dive here. I need to put feet on the ground, ask around town about this guy, see what people can tell me.

I hear the shower turn off and my mind flips trying to figure out how to explain this to Margot. She's always been observant. If I'm out for hours asking questions about a random stranger, she'll poke and prod until she figures out what just took place on our porch. And then, eventually, she'd find out I didn't actually purchase this place with our savings like I told her but rather inherited it from my long-lost dead father. It's all so absurd. But with her in this fragile state of mind and my mile high list of lies and manipulations, she can't know. She can never know.

I run through possible scenarios in my head. A work trip—yes, that might buy me the time and opportunity I need. Margot still believes I'm employed and work from home. If I tell Margot CirroSystems needs me in DC for a customer meeting, I can slip away, do some digging into Patrick's story, maybe find a way to protect our claim to Hawthorn Manor. Yes, this could work. I used to travel all the time. She'll buy it.

I open a browser and start hunting for nearby hotels, my thoughts a chaotic swirl. The pressure closes in around me again, suffocating. I've lied this long; I can keep lying until I figure out how to deal with Patrick Brendamore. Because there's no way I'm letting him—or anyone else—take this house from me. Not when it's the one lifeline I have left.

47

I wake up to the dull roar of weather reports coming from the old TV in our bedroom. Every channel is focused on the hurricane barreling toward Florida, showing satellite images that look terrifying even from hundreds of miles in the sky. My heart sinks—I know exactly how Margot's going to react to me leaving under these conditions. But I don't have a choice.

By the time I slip downstairs, Margot's already in the kitchen, shuffling around with a pained sort of focus, like she's trying to keep her worries at bay by staying busy. She spots me, and concern knits her brow.

"You're still going?" she asks, voice tight. She's heard me mention "D.C." just once this morning, but she's latched onto it. "They're saying the storm could make landfall in the next day or two, and it'll be one of the worst ever."

Guilt prickles in my chest. She's right—flying anywhere in this mess is absurd. But I plaster on a reassuring smile. "They need me," I say, trying not to sound rehearsed. "I'll be back before it really hits. This house is solid, Margot. It's stood for decades, right? You'll be safe until I'm back."

She chews on her lower lip, scanning my face as though

she's searching for a reason to believe me. Eventually, she exhales, shoulders sagging. I can see the trust in her eyes, and it twists my stomach into knots. "Okay," she murmurs, voice barely above a whisper. "But please be careful. If the storm shifts—"

"I'll keep an eye on it," I promise, gently squeezing her hand. The tension in her fingers is palpable. I hate that I'm using her faith in me like a bargaining chip, but I have no choice. I need time away from Hawthorn Manor, away from Margot's watchful eye, to figure out the truth.

That evening, I park my car in front of a small, nondescript motel on the outskirts of Mount Dora. The neon sign flickers, half-burnt out, but the front office is open. I tug my baseball cap lower, press my sunglasses firmly onto my face—despite the dimness—and approach the desk.

"I've got a reservation under John Hayes, please" I say, voice casual but low. The woman at the desk barely glances at me before fishing a key from the drawer and sliding it across the counter.

"Cash or card?" she asks. When I hand her some bills, she takes them without even asking for ID. No fuss, no suspicion. Everyone in this town is too worried about the storm to bother with formalities. For once, I'm grateful for the chaos.

In my room, I lock the door behind me and toss my duffel on the single bed. It's a cramped space, smelling faintly of mildew and stale air freshener. A dingy lamp casts a weak yellow light over the walls. But it's perfect—I want to blend into the background right now, not draw attention.

Before long, I'm back out on the streets, driving slowly through Mount Dora. Even at a glance, the hurricane prep is everywhere. Plywood covers windows, lines snake out of grocery stores, and trucks loaded with sandbags clog the roads. The atmosphere crackles with tension, like everyone's bracing for impact. It gives me a strange shield—I can move around without anyone paying me a second thought.

The next few days become a blur of research. My first stop: the Mount Dora Historical Museum, housed in an old brick building downtown. From the outside, it looks more like the backend of a restaurant, it's entrance in an alleyway with a brick façade and a single door leading in and out. Inside is tight, with display cases randomly around the room, a huge assortment of trinkets and oddities like a horse-drawn wagon to put out fires, and three jail cells built into the building itself.

Before I'm five feet inside the tiny building, an elderly woman peers up from her crossword puzzle. "Morning," she says with a welcoming smile. "Two dollars for adults; unless you're a student?"

I fork over two crumpled dollar bills then clear my throat, fighting back nerves. "My name's John, John Hayes. I run a popular podcast about unsolved mysteries. One of my listeners recommended I look into a family named..." I paused for effect as if trying to recall the name, "Hawthorn? I couldn't find much online, so I figured I'd come down and take a look. Imagine my surprise when I found out this town had a historical museum. That's pretty rare, in my experience."

Her face brightens, but there's a flicker of curiosity behind her eyes. "You're the second one this week asking about the Hawthorns," she remarks, leaning forward. "Maybe there's something in the air."

My stomach drops. "Oh?" I manage, hoping I sound casual.

She nods. "Yes, the new owners of George Hawthorn's old house were just in. The lady of the house was eager to learn about its history." There's a fondness in her tone, like Margot made a good impression. "You should pop over and see her. Maybe she'd be willing to give you a tour!"

I force a smile. "Wow, yeah, that would be phenomenal," I

say, my throat painfully tight. My head spins with questions: Why is Margot investigating the house? Did Patrick come by? Did he say something that prompted her to look for answers?

With her guidance, I delve into the town's storied history, combing through fragile pages and sepia-toned photos. I discover references to George's philanthropic contributions, read about the citrus groves he inherited from his own father, and piece together how Hawthorn Manor came to be. Photos show George, clean-shaven with a healthy sized gut next to his wife, Cecilia, at various town events—always smiling.

No mention of Patrick Brendamore. No sign of any affair with a woman named Phyllis. But that doesn't ease my tension. George managed to hide me and my mother all this time, so why not hide Patrick, too?

Over the next few days, the monotony of digging through old records becomes my life. At the public library, I flip through property deeds, scanning for any hint of hush-hush transfers or secret trusts. Nothing. Zoning records, local gossip columns —still nothing. The official story is that George Hawthorn and Cecilia lived a quiet, well-respected life until Cecilia died of natural causes on Lake Dora, followed by George apparently vanishing from the public eye years ago. That's it. No mention of children, legitimate or otherwise.

Between the searching, I hunker down in my cramped motel room eating junk food and doing my best to keep my anxieties under control. I rarely sleep more than an hour or two at a time. I often wake-up nervous and apprehensive about my life, my future with Margot and how I navigate us through this challenging phase of our life together.

Part of me wants to check on Margot—my phone buzzes with her worried texts—but I can't bear lying to her anymore. It's affecting me more and more each day. I'm losing weight. My thoughts are cloudy and messy; I don't feel like much of a person at all these days. And the more I engage with her without a path forward, without a light at the end of this mysterious tunnel, the more I hate myself. No, I'll ice her out for now to manage my worries and then once I get it all figured out, I'll come back the husband she deserves.

But one specific question gnaws at me: Who sent me that letter claiming I was George's heir? I remember the envelope's local postmark. No official signature, no lawyer's letterhead, just a few pages stating that I was entitled to Hawthorn Manor. At the time, I was too stunned—and too broke—to question the gift. Now it feels like a trap, or maybe some twisted game.

If Patrick truly believes he's the older son, maybe he or someone connected to him set me up. But that wouldn't make sense if he wants the place for himself. Unless... it was a lure, meant to get me here so he could challenge me face to face?

My head throbs with the effort of it all.

I slam my notebook closed. Every minute that passes by is a reminder that time is running out—sooner or later, I'll need to confront Patrick about how to move forward. Unfortunately for me, that timeline is shifted forward significantly because I need to limit Patrick's visits to Hawthorn Manor. If he meets Margot there, he will probably tell her what he told me which would unravel everything.

I'm done waiting. I stand up and pace the small, dirty floor of my hotel room. I think back to the manilla envelope I had received a few weeks ago. Did I look at every single sheet of paper? Was it possible I had missed a critical piece of information that was simply stuck to another page?

My mind floats to the folder and where it was when we packed up the house in Maryland. My eyes absently flutter around as I cycle through my memories trying to recall where that envelope is now. I slam my fists on the desk in frustration.

Why didn't I bring the documents with me to begin with? How dumb can I be?

I sit on the edge of the bed, my right leg bouncing with nervous energy. I think I know where the envelope is now– a box of office materials I had moved to the foyer on our first night unpacking.

But going back means returning to the very house I told Margot I was leaving for D.C. If she sees me, my lies fall apart. If Patrick's there, it might get ugly. But what choice do I have? If I can get that envelope without being seen, maybe I can find a clue about who originally sent it to me. Someone in this town has answers, but I need to find them before Margot or Patrick find me.

I grab my hoodie and yank the hood low over my eyes. The door slams behind me as I step into the windy night. I slip into my car, pulse hammering. I'm going to break into my own home– in hopes that I'll find answers before the facade of my fresh start crumbles around me.

48

I crouch lower against the wind. Even after the hurricane made its way through, leaving behind significant damage in its wake, the residual wind and rain were exhausting. Through my pulled down hood, the downpour stings my cheeks. My sneakers sink into the mud behind Hawthorn Manor, and every squelching footstep sounds like a thunderclap in my ears. I've parked a mile away so no headlights or engine noise can give me away, but now I'm paying the price, soaked to the bone before I even reach the house.

Our house towers against the stormy sky, the windows lit faintly upstairs. Margot's still awake. I grit my teeth, ignoring the stab of guilt that twists my stomach. I can't let her see me. I only need one thing: the envelope. Then I'll be gone.

I hurry to the rear entrance, cursing under my breath as the wind whips across my face. My keys feel foreign in my hand—I've hardly used the back door since we moved in. The lock sticks. I fumble for the right key, heart pounding as I keep glancing over my shoulder, half expecting Margot to appear in a window.

Finally, the key slides home, and I turn it slowly. A faint click resonates over the storm's wind. I push the door open, wincing at the soft squeal of hinges. The hush inside hits me like a wall—a stale, cold silence that magnifies every breath I take.

I pause, pressing my ear to the gap. I don't hear Margot's footsteps, but the wind rattles the windows so it's hard to tell. I slip inside, letting the door drift shut behind me. Water drips from my jacket onto the kitchen tile, each plink sounding impossibly loud.

"In and out," I whisper to myself, scanning the dim room. "Just grab the envelope and go."

We never fully unpacked, so somewhere in this house is a box labeled "Office" that contains the letter that changed everything—the one naming me heir to George Hawthorn's estate. I have a general idea of where I left the box, but no idea if Margot moved it since I'd left. The thought of rummaging around in my own home like a thief makes my skin crawl.

Lightning flashes, illuminating the hallway. At night, this place looks twice as big. Shadows stretch across the high walls, and every creak of the old floorboards sets me on edge. I move carefully, listening for any sign of Margot. If she finds me here —finds out I never went to D.C.—this fragile lie I've built will shatter.

My shoes squeak as I inch deeper into the house. Margot must have reorganized the boxes, because the stacks I left by the foyer are gone. The study is the logical place for anything labeled Office, so I slip inside, my pulse pounding in my temples. The faint smell of damp leather and old paper hangs in the air—probably a leak somewhere we'll need to fix.

I scan the rows of half-open boxes, rummaging as quietly as possible through old receipts, dusty notebooks, random photos. My fingers tremble when they brush the thick manila envelope I remember. Even through the gloom, I can make out water stains along one edge—it must've gotten wet during the move down here.

I clutch the envelope, relief flooding me, and pivot toward the door. Just then, a muffled thud comes from overhead. I freeze. My heart feels like it stops entirely. Floorboards creak as Margot moves slowly across the room above me.

I can't risk meeting her. I hurry to the threshold, sliding into the hall, hugging the wall to keep out of sight. The wind blows rain against the windows; hopefully it's enough to mask my footsteps. Then I see a glow at the top of the stairs and hear her soft voice:

"Hello?" she calls, uncertainty lacing her tone.

She moves into view, a silhouette against the faint light. My breath catches. She's standing at the bottom of the staircase, hair loose around her shoulders, scanning the hall for any sign of an intruder. Me.

I press myself flat against the shadows, barely daring to breathe. If she steps forward another two feet, she'll see me. My pulse roars in my ears. Then, as if by some miracle, she turns toward the kitchen instead, drawn by a noise there.

I seize my chance, tiptoeing the opposite way. Each creak of the old floor feels like a gunshot. She pauses in the kitchen, and I see her tilt her head—sensing something. I hold my breath, gripping the doorknob of the back entrance. Slowly, I twist it. The storm howls, covering the whine of hinges as I slip outside. Cold wind whips the door from my hand, nearly slamming it shut behind me.

I half-stumble across the yard, feet sliding in the mire, until I'm safely out of sight. Only then do I let my lungs work again, heart thudding with terrified relief. Rain pours in sheets, soaking me all over again as I hurry the mile back to my car.

Back at my motel room, I'm still shivering when I drop onto the edge of the bed. My jacket's a sopping mess, my pants caked with mud. But I'm holding the envelope, triumphant and trembling at once.

Carefully, I peel it open. Water has blurred some of the print, but I can still make out the return address: 105 S Grandview St, Mt Dora, FL 32757.

My pulse is still racing from the close call with Margot, but now curiosity surges through me, along with a fresh knot of anxiety. This letter was how I learned about my inheritance in the first place. Why would it come from a random local address?

The adrenaline still thrums in my veins as I wrestle my laptop onto the battered motel desk. I punch the address into a search, teeth chattering slightly from the cold, and wait for answers. But none of the results on the screen make sense. Confusion settles over me like a fog.

Who is Andrew Miller—and why did he want me in Hawthorn Manor?

49

I'm hunched over my laptop in this dingy motel room, a place so dim that even the morning light seems reluctant to fight its way through the threadbare curtains. My gaze keeps flicking to the open envelope on the rickety table beside me, the edges weighed down by my half-full coffee cup. The name printed on the letterhead feels like a punchline to some cruel joke: Mount Dora Police Department.

It doesn't make any sense. Andrew Miller—Chief Andrew Miller—sent me that inheritance letter? The same one that turned my life upside down and brought me here to Hawthorn Manor in the first place. Why would the local police chief send me a manilla envelope, consisting of mostly informal documents, but not call or visit?

I nurse a few last swallows of lukewarm coffee, my brain on overdrive. Did Miller know George Hawthorn personally? How does he know about me, a long-lost son who'd never even met his father? Could this all be one big mistake?

By mid-morning, I can't stand the questions swirling in my head any longer. I button my jacket, tuck the envelope under my arm, and drive through the damp streets of Mount Dora until I spot the small, tired-looking building with faded letters spelling out "Police Department" above the door.

Inside, the station's lobby carries that stale undertone of cheap coffee, disinfectant, and polished wood that's seen better days. The walls, once cream-colored, have yellowed over time, and they're lined with old photos of retired officers—most of whom look like they served decades ago. A single fluorescent light overhead buzzes and flickers, as though it's tired of doing its job. I stand there, feeling like a trespasser in a relic from the past.

"You look lost," a gruff voice calls from behind me.

I turn and face a tall man in a police uniform. His salt-and-pepper hair is cropped short, and he carries himself like someone who's seen everything there is to see in a small town. The name tag reads Miller. His eyes narrow slightly as he appraises me.

I clear my throat and hold out the thick folder. "Chief Miller? I'm Nate Bennett. I believe you sent me this?"

His expression shifts almost imperceptibly before he gives me a brisk nod. "Let's talk in private."

I follow him down a hallway that smells like old wax and paper, passing a handful of small offices until we reach one that's cluttered but tidy in its own way—files stacked in neat rows on every surface. He settles behind his desk and motions for me to take the chair opposite. Folding his hands together, he fixes me with a level gaze.

"All right," he says, leaning back. "I imagine you've got a few questions."

I set the letter on his desk, struggling to keep my tone level. "A few, yeah. For starters, how did you even know about me? Did you know George Hawthorn? Am I actually entitled to that house or is this some type of prank?"

Miller exhales, and it's like I can see the armor in his eyes slip for a moment. "Because George told me about you," he begins quietly. "We were friends. Good friends, before he disappeared. I knew things about him that no one else did." He stares at me for a few moments. Then takes a big breath before continuing. "As far as the house goes, yes, it's yours– technically. After George disappeared, we weren't sure what to do with it. Some folks thought he'd show back up, while others thought he was gone forever. It sat unoccupied for years. In 2024 the state started the process of escheatment, which is just a fancy pants way of saying the property is taken over by the state. It's still going through that formal process today, but should be complete within the next month or so."

He leans forward and flips around an old picture featuring five young kids in it. "George was my friend. It didn't feel right for the house to be taken over by strangers; likely knocked down or sold off to be another hotel for the snowbirds. So yes, I stepped in, figuring you should at least have a chance. I couldn't stand by and let it happen without telling you. Or trying to, anyway."

My stomach twists as I process. "Okay, yeah– that makes sense. That's really kind of you to have done. Thank you." I say, while fidgeting with my hands. "You have to understand, Chief Miller– I never knew my dad, never knew a single thing about him. My whole life it was just me and my mom until she passed away. She refused to speak about him. When she died, I was placed into foster care until I aged out. So... I think I have some pretty negative feelings towards George. This is a lot for me to process."

He looks at me with sad eyes. "I completely understand, Nate. I do. Many years ago he asked me to keep an eye on you. Said he felt guilty for abandoning you and your mother, but he couldn't face the scandal. This is a small town, Nate. Appearances matter—even if the man behind them was flawed. George's money went to the local schools, to all kinds of community projects, and everyone thought he was a saint. But behind closed doors, he had secrets. Your existence was one of them."

My pulse hammers as I recall my mother never relenting, never sharing anything about my biological father, no matter how much I pleaded. "So, he just... left us to fend for ourselves?"

Miller's face tightens. "He did. I won't defend him for that. But he never fully forgot you. Even after your mother died, even when you ended up in foster care, he asked me now and then if I'd heard anything." He rubs a hand over his face, looking older than before. "This was his way, Nate. He did not have things figured out."

A strange heaviness settles in my chest. Part of me wants to despise George even more for trying to have it both ways—ignoring me yet keeping tabs from a distance. But another part of me is caught off guard, confused by the idea that I once had a father who cared at all.

I clear my throat, trying to maintain control of the conversation. "All right," I say, my voice wavering. "Maybe there's something else you can help me with then. The first night I was here, a man showed up at my door, Patrick Brendamore. He says he's also George's kid. That he's older than me and could take the house. Did George have more than one affair?"

Miller rolls his eyes instantly. "Phyllis. She always fancied herself some high-society type; never quite made it stick. I wouldn't be surprised if she claimed something happened with George just to elevate her own status. Unfortunately, he never told me about any other affair or any other children. My intuition tells me it's not true, but if he's throwing around legal jargon, it may be worth continuing to look into."

"Any idea where to find her?" I press.

Miller snorts softly, then opens a drawer, fishing out a worn notepad and pen. He scribbles an address and tears the page free. "Here. She lives outside the main part of town. Stays to herself, mostly. But be careful. While she is technically a local, that boy of hers is not. He's come and gone for years. Something is off about him."

I take the note and slip it into my pocket. "Thanks, Chief Miller. I appreciate your honesty. And... thanks for the letter to begin with. My wife and I have gone through a lot the past few years. We really needed a win. This might just be that."

Miller meets my gaze, and for a second, I see a hint of genuine concern. "Nate," he says quietly. "This place—Mount Dora—looks quaint, but there's a lot of tragedy behind the pretty facades. And Hawthorn Manor... Let's just say if you're going to make it your home, be prepared for ghosts. Not just the metaphorical kind."

A chill prickles my arms, and I'm not sure if it's from the air conditioning or his warning. But I force a tight smile. "I'll keep that in mind."

I stand, shaking his hand briefly, and head for the door. As I step back into the hallway, the scent of musty paper and fluorescent hum returns. My mind is racing. George, at least according to Chief Miller, is my biological father who abandoned me, yes, but also tried to keep tabs on me even after all the time. There's Patrick, who might be my half-brother, but again, according to Miller, is probably not.

And looming over it all is that manor—my chance at a new life with Margot. A new life already built on half-truths, secrets, and the shadow of a man I never knew.

I push open the front door of the station. Outside, the air is thick with humidity, and the sky threatens another downpour. As I walk toward my car, Miller's words echo in my head: Be prepared for ghosts.

I can't help wondering if I'm about to come face-to-face with them—and whether I'm truly ready for the truth about the man I believed to have been my father.

50

I pull my car onto the cracked shoulder of the two-lane road, the old engine ticking in the afternoon heat. The address from Chief Miller led me here—a faded, sagging house on the outskirts of Mount Dora. Its shutters hang askew, and the paint is so peeled it's almost colorless. A single, gnarled oak stands in the yard, its branches creaking in the breeze.

For a long time, I just watch from behind my steering wheel, waiting. I don't know for certain if Patrick currently lives here, but everything I've gleaned suggests he does. If he is here, I can't just stroll up and knock on the door. I'm not eager for a direct confrontation until I'm fully equipped with the necessary facts. So I sit, engine off, perspiration collecting in the stale air of the car, as the sun slides toward the horizon.

Eventually, the front door groans open, and I spot Patrick stepping out. Even from a distance, his tall frame is unmistakable. He hops into a battered pickup, the engine sputters, then he's gone in a cloud of dust. My pulse quickens. This is my opening.

I ease out of the car, scanning the yard for movement. No dogs bark; no curtains shift in the windows. Still, I approach slowly. At the door, I knock, and my heartbeat thuds in my ears when I hear footsteps approach.

An elderly woman appears, a red hair bob hangs close to her shoulders, her face etched by lines of weariness and something else—maybe a restless pride. She eyes me with open suspicion.

"Ma'am," I begin, offering a polite nod. "I'm sorry to bother you. My name is John Hayes. I'm researching the Hawthorn family for a cold-case podcast I produce. I wondered if you might help me."

Her eyes narrow, but she's not slamming the door in my face. "Sweetie, you're handsome which is the only reason I opened the door in the first place. But if you want me to understand what the hay you just said, you're going to have too speak slower. What in the world is a cold cast?"

I smile warmly. "No, no, ma'am. A cold case podcast. It's essentially a news program on the radio that tries to uncover new clues around old mysteries. I produce the program and was hoping to ask you some questions about the Hawthorn family, George and Cecilia?"

She hesitates, glancing past me at the empty yard, then gives a small sigh. Her gaze shifts, and a wry curve tugs at her lips—like she's about to play a part. She adjusts a vivid purple shawl draped over her shoulders, stepping back from the threshold. "Well, I can't say no to a radio show asking questions!" she says, an air of resignation coloring her tone. "Come on in."

Inside, the house smells like old incense and heavy perfume. Bright, mismatched furniture crowds the living room, dust lingering in corners. Framed photographs are everywhere—faded Polaroids, decades-old certificates, newspaper clippings. It feels like a museum dedicated to a life she's determined not to forget. Purple seems to dominate the décor, from the curtains to the cushions. She sinks onto a flower-patterned chair and gestures for me to sit across from her.

I settle gingerly, trying not to send up too much dust into the air with my weight. "Thank you for speaking with me. As I said, I'm diving into the Hawthorns and while it feels like I have a pretty decent understanding of Cecilia, I must admit, George is a harder character to nail down."

"Ah yes, George was somewhat of an enigma, you see. I think in times like these, he would have been considered odd, maybe even weird. But back in the day," she stares off, eyes glossing over, clearly deep in memory. "Phew, back in the day, George was the epitome of perfection. He had drive and class. He was book smart and didn't take crap from anyone. He was a giver and provider for everyone in this town." She looks back to me now before dropping her head towards her lap. Tears begin to fall and as she wipes them away, clumps of thick, clumpy foundation cling her hand. "I miss him very much."

I lean forward, my nerves on fire. I don't like the way this sounds.

"It seems as though many folks I've spoken with share your sentiment, ma'am. George Hawthorn sounds like a good man." I say as a surprising new emotion bubbles inside my chest: pride. If this man was my biological father, sure he did leave me abandoned which is pretty shitty, but... it also appears like he was a really good man later in life.

The woman looks at me and nods with a humble, gentle smile, but says nothing more.

I'm close, this is my opportunity to get what I came for. But I also need to press gently.

"So, of the many folks I talked to in town, your son, Patrick was one of them." I say causally, trying to monitor her response.

She stiffens a bit, her chin lifting. "Ah yes, Patrick is my boy. I'm sure he gave you a mouth full. He's an opinionated one."

I laugh to appease the joke and then draw a breath, bracing myself. "He, uh– he showed me some letters that he had found. Letters that he found... here."

"Here?" she repeats, looking me up and down with much more scrutiny than before.

"Yes ma'am. Letters that, apparently, George had written... to you."

Strangely, she didn't move at the bomb drop. Her face didn't change, her body language didn't give anything away. It's almost as if she hadn't heard me. So, I continue– "They mention an affair, a deep connection, and... a pregnancy. Patrick seems convinced George was his father."

She finally snaps back to attention. Her complexion pales, and the hand gripping her shawl trembles. "Those damn letters," she whispers. "Oh God." I can see her mind working through what this new information may mean for her. "They were never supposed to see daylight. And they sure as hell were never supposed to be seen by my boy." Slowly, she exhales, shaking her head.

I wait, letting her find the words.

She closes her eyes briefly, then looks at me with a haunted sort of defiance. "George never loved me. Hell, he barely noticed I existed. But I loved him—maybe from the moment I saw him on the schoolyard playground as a child. And when he cheated on Cecilia with that woman, that *bimbo*, Theresa Bennett... I couldn't stand it. I was so jealous I—" Her voice breaks. "I wrote those letters to comfort myself. A delusion to soothe the sting of being overlooked. They're fiction. Every word."

I'm rocked with a series of confusing emotions all in quick succession. My mother was just called a bimbo, which I suppose is fair when you sleep with a married man, but I still feel protective of her. Next, a huge wave of relief and vindication that it does sound like George Hawthorn was my biological father. And finally, intense nervousness that I now have the truth and need to confront Patrick with it. I think of his certainty when he arrived on my porch that first night here in Mount Dora, of the homemade letters he held close to his chest as proof. "So, to be clear, Patrick is *not* George Hawthorn's son?" I ask quietly.

She shakes her head, tears returning. "No. His father was... some nameless drifter passing through town. I latched onto him one night out of sheer heartbreak. Patrick was born nine months later. That's all. Those letters were just an escape, my own twisted fantasy. I never dreamed Patrick would find them."

Her face crumples at the realization of the damage, and I can almost hear her mourning the fallout. After a heavy moment, I stand, the floor creaking beneath my feet. "Thank you," I say, swallowing hard. "I appreciate your candor."

She looks at me with a plea in her eyes. "Don't tell him. Please. I'm begging you. Patrick has wanted a father his whole life—someone to claim him, to show him he mattered. If you strip that away, what will he have left?" Her voice cracks. "He's a proud man, but he's fragile in ways you can't imagine."

My thoughts reel. Patrick's claim is false, which means Hawthorn Manor stays rightfully mine. But telling him the truth could break him. I nod slowly, the guilt knotting in my chest. "I understand" is all I can muster. It feels disingenuous to promise anything more knowing I need to confront Patrick at some point.

I slip out of the house into the cooling twilight, relief tempered by a pang of sympathy for Patrick. All that conviction he approached me with was fueled by a lie he never asked for. And now I hold the truth that could shatter him.

Back at my motel room, the night air is thick and quiet. I drop onto the stiff bed and pull out a notepad, the overhead light buzzing faintly. *I have to deal with Patrick.* Letting him keep believing a lie is cruel, but so is tearing his identity apart. So where does that leave me?

My phone buzzes with a text from Margot, likely checking in. She's still at Hawthorn Manor, probably worried about me, about everything. A flush of shame spreads through me—I've lied so often it's second nature now. But if I can resolve this without hurting anyone else, maybe I can salvage the fresh start Margot and I are clinging to.

Grabbing a pen, I start jotting down a plan. I'll confront Patrick calmly, show him enough to make him let go of Hawthorn Manor without totally obliterating his sense of self. Maybe I can frame it so he doesn't have to know the devastating truth that his mother faked it all. But how?

My pen hovers uncertainly above the paper. I realize I'm caught between two precarious choices—lie to Patrick to preserve his dignity or reveal the entire truth and risk seeing his potential, yet understandable, fury.

The longer I stare at the page, the more I feel the walls closing in. I tap my pen nervously against the notebook, swallowing a surge of dread. The storms in my life are converging from every angle: Patrick's illusions, George's secrets, Margot's suspicions. Somehow, I need to navigate them all without losing the one thing I've been fighting for—my second chance to be a good man again.

51

The sun is dipping low in the sky when I return to Phyllis's bungalow, a tight knot of dread coiling in my stomach. The letter in my coat pocket feels heavier than ever—a quiet bomb waiting to detonate. I know Patrick will be furious at what I'm about to show him. Still, I can't see another way out. I've written and rewritten every word in an effort to break the truth gently.

When I knock, the door swings open to reveal Patrick standing there, confusion flickering across his features as he steps aside to let me in. Inside, the bungalow feels even more cramped than before—musty furniture, the faint smell of old perfume. My breath catches as I look at him.

"Patrick," I begin, forcing a calm I don't feel. "I just want to reiterate that I really appreciated your respect and patience as I worked through the bombshell you dropped on me when we first met." I smile passively to try and break the tension.

"During my research, I found some information that I think you need to see." My hand slips into my coat, pulling out the envelope. My palms are clammy with sweat, and I pass the letter over to him.

His expression hardens before he even reads a word. I can

sense the wall going up, a mixture of mistrust and anger. He slides out the pages, scanning the opening lines.

I step onto the small front porch, wanting to give him space. But I only get a couple of steps away when I hear the letter tear in two, echoing like a gunshot in the still evening air. Spinning around, I find Patrick glaring at me, shreds of paper in his hands.

"You think I'm gonna buy this garbage?" he snarls. "You think I care what you wrote down? This doesn't change a damn thing."

I flinch at the raw fury in his voice. My mind whirls back to my promise to Phyllis—she begged me to protect him from the ugly truth, to keep him from discovering her secret. But I've just made it worse. Fighting the urge to defend myself, I raise both hands, palms out.

"Patrick," I say quietly. "Easy. Listen, I'm not trying to shatter anything you believe. But it's important for me to provide you with the truth so we can both move forward."

"Fuck you!" he screams, spittle flying his mouth. I squint in a poor attempt to block some of the vile liquid spilling from his face.

"Okay, okay. We can't do this here. Not in front of your mom. She doesn't need to hear this." I say gently, trying my best to de-escalate the situation.

He flicks a glance over his shoulder, clearly wary that Phyllis might emerge at any moment. His jaw tenses. "Fine. There's a second house out on the Hawthorn property—it's a shit hole, but no one will bother us there. Take the gravel drive, keep right through the trees. I'll meet you there in twenty minutes."

He slams the door without waiting for my reply. Ripped shreds of my letter flutter across the porch, and a wave of nausea clenches my gut. Things are already falling apart and I don't know how to stop it from getting worse.

Twilight has fully settled by the time I navigate Hawthorn Manor's long driveway, passing the main house where Margot is likely inside. I keep my lights off and my speed at 5 mph to not attract any attention. Just beyond a bend, the gravel forks. I veer right, following Patrick's directions, and soon spot a secluded opening in the trees. Ahead stands a smaller, older building—Hawthorn House. Its siding is peeling, windows dusty, as though it's been neglected for decades. Perfect for a meeting no one else will overhear.

I hide my car along the tree line under a gnarled oak and climb out. Crickets drone in the thick summer air, and the faint hush of an approaching storm rustles the branches overhead. I sit and wait, well beyond twenty minutes. I get out and begin to pace, wondering what's taking him so long to get here.

Finally, after closer to an hour, I hear the growl of Patrick's truck. He pulls up directly in front of the house, the headlights raking across the house's chipped paint.

Patrick steps out, and even from a distance, I can smell the whiskey on him. His eyes are bloodshot, his movements jerky and unsteady. "Let's get this over with," he mutters, stalking toward the house.

I follow him to the porch, my heart hammering.

He reaches for the heavy handle first, but it refuses to budge, locked tight. I glance around, second guessing the nighttime rendezvous with an angry drunk man at an abandoned house. Moments later, I hear shattering glass behind me. Pulse pounding, I spin around—only to see Patrick grinning, a rock clutched in his hand.

"*One* of us owns it, right? What's the big deal?" he says as he unlocks the now broken window and then climbs inside. Seconds later the front clicks and swings open.

Reluctantly, I follow him, flipping on an overhead light that buzzes to life, illuminating a threadbare living room. Dust stirs in the stale air.

He spins on me before I can even close the front door. "So, this is where you try to tell me I'm not his son? That I'm some con artist? You want to take everything away from me. Is that it?"

I keep my voice low, forced calm. "I'm not taking anything. I just—"

"Liar!" he barks, and before I can move, he drives his shoulder into my chest, knocking me back a few steps. His breath reeks of alcohol and rage. "All my life, I've had nothing. I've been nothing. And then I learn about George! I finally have a chance to claim a legacy, to be someone. And you—some nobody from up North—show up to rip that away? Over my dead body."

I hold my palms out. "Listen, I—"

Patrick lunges. His fist rams into my cheek, and my vision bursts with white sparks. I stagger, fighting for balance. Another blow catches my jaw, sending me sprawling to the floor. Pain explodes down my spine, breath whooshing from my lungs.

He's on me in an instant, pinning me. "You think you're better than me?" he growls. "George abandoned you too, you know! He fucked your mother and then left her to die. He didn't give a shit about you!" He lands another punch, and my head snaps back, the world going fuzzy at the edges.

With the next hit, I taste blood. Panic surges—he's going to kill me. "Patrick—please!" I gasp, trying to bring my arms up. He batters them away with surprising force.

"I'm so sick..." another fist connects to my cheek bone, "of everyone else..." one more crack to the same spot, "looking down on me!" He head butts me this time and with a crack I know my nose is broken. "And finally, instead of being stolen from, I'm going to do the stealing." He screams, with literal heat pulsating from his body.

"I'm taking your damn house," he hisses, hooking a fist into my ribs. I gasp in agony. "Your money... your inheritance..." Each word is punctuated by another brutal blow. Darkness swims in my vision, and I now know I made the worst mistake I've ever made in coming here.

Then something changes in his gaze—an ugly sneer. He grabs my left hand, yanks my wedding ring free. "Might take your wife, too," he snarls.

Fury and desperation swell, but I'm too disoriented to fight back. Another hit crushes my temple, and blackness sweeps in.

When I come to, my head throbs as though a jackhammer is burying itself within my brain. My mouth is filled with coppery blood, and I barely register the coarse floorboards under my cheek. Patrick is hunched over my wallet and phone, rifling through them with shaking hands. He's so focused, he doesn't notice me stir.

I grit my teeth, bracing against the pain, and force myself upright. My limbs feel like lead, and my eyes are struggling to focus in the low light. I look at the violent man in front of me, wondering how I'm still alive. Then a glint glances off his hand and I see my ring, my wedding ring, on his finger. The sight shoots adrenaline straight through my veins and I lunge, without thinking. I knock into him and he staggers, swears, and tries to swing at me again. But this time, I'm ready for it and instead, I use his momentum against him, grabbing hold of his incoming wrist and swinging him off-balance towards the still open door.

I follow in pursuit, with no plan, just rage. We crash out

onto the porch. My back slams against the railing and he rushes towards me: I twist, shoving him away. Patrick stumbles down the three steps leading up to the porch, his head cracking against one of the stepping stones with a sickening thud. He collapses in the dirt below, unmoving.

Gasping, every nerve aflame, I stare at him. Did I just kill him? Heart hammering, I scramble down the steps and check for a pulse at his neck. It's still there, faint but steady. Relief trembles through me. I hoist his dead weight by the arms, dragging him back inside the house, this time closing the door.

I drop him unceremoniously onto the living room floor, my muscles screaming. My head spins, spots dancing in my vision from pain and fear. But I can't stay here. The moment he wakes, we'll be right back at each other's throats. I slump against the wall, pressing shaking fingers to his neck again— yes, still breathing.

Then I hear it—a low rumble of an engine outside. Headlights flash across the dusty windows. Panic floods me. If someone finds me here with an unconscious, bloody Patrick, there'll be no explaining. Slowly, I climb to my feet, searching for any escape route that doesn't involve stepping right into those headlights.

I stumble down a short hallway, nervously looking from left to right for an exit. I head towards the back of the house intending to use the backdoor, but it's nailed shut with several old two by fours. A hear a car door slam and panic floods my thoughts. I turn and see a door. The handle squeaks in protest, but it opens. I slip inside, pulling the door nearly shut behind me just as the front door opens and heavy footsteps enter. My pulse thunders in my ears.

Crouched in total darkness, I listen to the newcomer walk through the living room. There's a muttered curse, then a scraping noise, followed by a grunt. Suddenly, I realize they've found Patrick's limp form. My mind churns with panic—who is it? Did Phyllis follow him? What if it's the police?

The footsteps grow heavier, and I realize in horror the newcomer is dragging Patrick across the floorboards. I hear the person move into the hallway towards the kitchen and every cell in my body screams to hide. I turn towards the blackness leading down into the basement and silently feel my way down until my feet touch hard floor. I take a deep breath and try to identify where the footsteps are now when the basement door creaks open. Dim light spills down, illuminating the bottom steps where I press flat against the wall.

Then a terrible thud echoes. Patrick's body cartwheels down the stairs like a discarded doll. He lands in a crumpled heap right in front of me, limbs bent at awful angles. I have to clamp my hand over my mouth to smother a scream.

Slowly, a man descends behind him, each step unnervingly calm as I silently push deeper into the basement. My stomach churns as he comes into view: Walter, the landscaper we hired to help maintain the house. His face is set in a strange calm, eyes distant, almost as though he's in a trance.

"I don't remember taking this one, my love" he mutters, voice low and oddly conversational. "Was this *really* the next offering?" I wait for a response, confused as to who he's talking to. I hear no more footsteps, no responses. There's no one else here.

Confusion and terror tangle in my gut as my mind struggles to make sense of what I'm seeing. Walter stands over Patrick's body, head tilted in puzzlement. Then he murmurs, "Georgie, Georgie. Tsk, tsk. You're getting worse!" A chill runs through me—*Georgie*? Does he think he's talking *to* my father?

Before I can move, Walter grabs Patrick under the arms, hoisting his limp form and dropping it into an old clawfoot tub deeper in the gloom of the basement. Horror grips me as

Walter rifles through a battered toolbox and extracts a wicked-looking saw.

My stomach heaves. I know what he's about to do—and I can't bring myself to move, to scream, to do anything. I'm paralyzed. The jagged rasp of metal on bone splits the silence, and I press myself against the wall, shutting my eyes. Nothing can erase the wet, grinding sounds that follow.

When the noise finally stops, I force my lids open in time to see Walter lift Patrick's severed head from the tub, blood spattering his overalls. He gazes at it with an eerie detachment. "This one's quite handsome, darling. I have to say, I'm a bit jealous! If you weren't so convincing, I'd say pick someone else!" he cackles with genuine enjoyment.

My heart nearly stops. My teeth clamp so hard on my lip, I taste blood, fighting the urge to vomit or pass out.

Without warning, Walter strolls back upstairs, carrying Patrick's head in one hand. The basement door closes, plunging me into near-darkness. The only sound is the slow dripping of blood from the tub. I sag against the stone wall, every inch of me shaking.

I crouch there, too shocked to move. Tears find their way out of my face even though my entire body is numb. Eventually, my survival instinct kicks in. Police. Call for help. It's beyond hiding at this point. Someone is dead. I reach for my phone and realize it's missing. My mind races and I think about Patrick going through my pockets when I was unconscious.

I have to get out. Make it to the police station. Tell them everything. I push to my feet, ignoring the burn in my ribs. Each step through the gloom is agony, but I manage to creep up the stairs. I crack the door and glance into the living room.

Walter is outside, rummaging around near Patrick's truck. I look to the floor where our scuffle happened, and I can't find any of my belongings. My head snaps up as Patrick's truck roars to life with Walter behind the wheel. I duck as headlights tear through the house. I listen, face pressed flat on the floor, as the truck makes its way around the property towards the rear where the engine then dies. I remain frozen, unsure of Walter's movements or intentions. I think I can hear his footsteps growing closer again. I prepare to run back into the basement when I hear a second engine start up and then roar off into the night.

It feels like forever before I find the strength to push up off the floor. My legs wobble, and bile claws up my throat. I barely make it to the sink before I'm violently sick. When the retching subsides, I collapse to the floor, tears running hot down my cheeks. *How did we get here?*

As I struggle to stand, headlights sweep past the windows again. My entire body seizes. *Shit. Why is Walter back?* But then I hear the faint murmur of a familiar voice drifting in through the broken window. *Oh my god, that's Margot.* My gut twists. She's come looking for me. She knows. Or maybe she's still trying to satisfy her own curiosities about our new property. Either way, I can't let her find me.

The front door creaks open. Panic rages inside me. I don't have time to bury the evidence or hide the gore in the basement. My only choice is to vanish before she sees me. My eyes land on the basement door. *No, no—I can't go back down there.* But the footsteps grow louder, drawing near. I have no choice.

I dart back down into the darkness, pulling the door shut just as Margot and someone else step inside the old house, calling out tentatively. Pressed against the cold stone wall, I clamp a hand over my mouth to stifle the ragged sob building in my throat.

52

Above me, I hear the heavy groan of the front door closing, followed by the creak of floorboards. Margot and another voice, sounds female—are moving inside. I don't dare move.

Their muffled voices filter down as they fumble for a light switch, and my stomach drops. They're here, probably searching for answers, the same way I am. But why?

A weak, jaundiced glow flickers to life overhead, barely reaching into the corners of this grim basement. Margot's voice stands out, tense as she responds to some kind of joke I can't quite make out. I can picture Margot's face—her eyes darting around, her expression wary. My chest aches just knowing how close she is. But I can't reveal myself. Not now. Not like this.

Their footsteps draw closer, every groan of the old floorboards a threat. I swallow hard, searching the basement with my eyes. I have to stay hidden. If they find me near Patrick's body in that tub, drenched in blood, they'll assume I did it—that I'm some sort of monster. I need to protect Margot from this but what can I do?

Then I hear the basement door creak open, and a cold ripple of dread slides through me. I press myself flat against the wall, eyes squeezed shut, struggling to stay invisible. Margot's voice trembles– she's scared. The smell of blood is overpowering down here. The air is damp, and it clings to me. I feel the wet , hard ground against my palm and I curse Chief Miller for ever bringing us to this town.

I realize suddenly that I might not be hidden enough. Panicking, I pace one step, then another, searching desperately for a better spot. My hip bangs into the edge of the tub. Patrick's body shifts, and I cringe at the disgusting slosh of blood swirling through the water.

Margot goes quiet. I can almost feel her hold her breath for a better listen. She heard that sloshing. I know it. My teeth clench, and I silently beg them to turn around and go back upstairs—anything to avoid seeing what's in this awful basement.

"Shannon, do you see that?" Margot's whisper cuts the silence like a gunshot.

I follow her line of sight and realize my own shadow stretches across the wall like some monstrous shape. My heart hammers so loudly, I'm sure they can hear it. I'm trapped, and they're only a few feet away.

Before I can think, I notice the breaker box within arm's reach. Desperate, I flip the main switch, plunging the house into darkness. Instantly, I can't see a thing. But I can hear them —Margot's breath, Shannon's quiet gasp—and I can hear myself, panting, ragged, terrified.

I force myself to move along the wall, careful not to scrape my shoes against the floor. It feels like every slight shift echoes a thousand times. My stomach churns as Margot calls Shannon's name in the dark, her voice tight with fear. Footsteps approach—slow, deliberate.

We're stuck in a cruel dance in the dark. Them on one side of the tub, me on the other. We're rotating now, but I can't tell which direction they're taking. I'll either move clockwise with them or run directly into them which petrifies me.

I can see a speck of moonlight to my right and I recognize I'm now close to the stairs. We've managed to swap places, and I realize this is my only chance. Keeping low, I tear up the stairs. My pulse is pounding in my ears, and I silently pray that Margot and Shannon won't follow. The basement door slams behind me, and I press my ear against the wood, straining to listen.

I hear someone stumble, a dull clang against metal, and my blood runs cold. The tub. Did Margot touch it? I can imagine her hand brushing the slick, horrific surface of Patrick's remains. I want to scream at them to leave, to run away, but I'm frozen in place, terror and guilt binding me.

Shannon's shaky voice drifts through the door, and a second later, the lights flicker back on. Even though I can't see it, I know exactly what's happening. Margot's soft cry, Shannon begging her to look away—they've both seen the bloody tub, the missing head, the gore that covers everything. And now Margot is seeing the ring—*my* ring– on Patrick's hand.

I can hear her muffled sobs, Shannon's attempts at comfort, and it tears me apart. I want to run to Margot, to hold her and explain how wrong everything is. Tell her I didn't do this. But she wouldn't believe me. Not now. Not after this.

With my heart in my throat, I flee. I run through the house, hearing my footsteps echo across the creaking boards, the walls seeming to close in on me. Margot's voice calls out, desperate and afraid, and it nearly breaks me. But I keep going, out the door, out into the night, into the suffocating darkness.

My lungs burn and my legs ache, but I don't slow down

until I'm far from that cursed house, hidden in some patch of shadows. I collapse, chest heaving, tears burning my eyes. Everything is wrong—so terribly wrong. I need to fix it somehow. I need Margot to understand. But I don't even know where to go from here.

53

I crouch low among the citrus groves, though the leaves have long died. So instead they cast long, skeletal shadows on the ground. The air is thick with humidity and the branches scratch at my skin. I ran until my legs gave out, and now I'm here, surrounded by neat rows of trees.

My body trembles as the last drops of adrenaline drain away, leaving only bone-deep exhaustion and a suffocating wave of guilt. Patrick is dead. I watched it happen—hidden in the darkness, helpless to stop the horror. And now Margot has seen him—what was left of him in that tub, my ring, all that blood. She saw it, and I wasn't there to protect her. I didn't prevent any of it. What will she think if she discovers I was there the entire time, lurking in the shadows?

I press my forehead against my knees and inhale, trying to steady my breath. I have to tell her. About Walter, about Patrick, about my gambling addictions, about the lies and manipulations, about everything our lives have become. I recognize I can't keep running. Margot deserves to know, no matter how twisted or impossible it sounds.

The thought of seeing her again, of touching her, almost

doubles me over with longing. But fear quickly follows. What if she doesn't believe me? From her perspective, I was there and watched Walter murder Patrick. I incapacitated him in the first place. He had a pulse when I last checked, but maybe he died before Walter even threw him down those steps. Am I positive that I'm not the murderer here?

I lift my head, peering through the branches at Hawthorn Manor, a ghostly shape in the distance. Lights flicker weakly in the windows, like the house itself is alive, exhaling some malevolent gasp. It calls to me, tugging at my heart. Suddenly all my lies and schemes—the web of deceit I spun over the years—feel meaningless. None of it matters next to what I witnessed down there.

Patrick is dead, and Walter killed him. My throat clenches as I remember the crack of bone on the basement steps, the sickening thud when Patrick's body landed in the tub. Margot saw him. She saw him and thought it was me lying there. The idea twists my stomach into knots. She thinks I'm the one in that tub, missing a head, blood everywhere. And here I sit, in the safety of these groves, while she's inside that awful house. My chest tightens under the weight of it all.

I just want to hold her. To hear my name on her lips again. To tell her about the addiction, the secrets, the reasons I hid so much of myself from her. I wanted to be the man she deserved, but now all of that is ash. As much as I crave to cross that threshold, I know I can't face her yet. Not without a plan.

"I'm sorry," I whisper, my words vanishing into the warm, night air. My hands shake; shake from everything I've done, everything I've failed to do.

I can't go back to that house—can't step foot inside that vile place, not even to get my car. It's cursed, and whatever dark force lives there has stained me as well. I need time to think, to rest. Maybe food. Anything to keep my mind from splintering apart.

Leaves and twigs crunch under my shoes as I head toward the main road. The manor fades behind me, swallowed by the black night. Am I doing what's right, or am I just running away from the hardest choice?

When I finally reach town, it's quiet. The streetlamps cast weak puddles of yellowish light onto empty sidewalks. My limbs feel like lead, but the thought of stopping sets my nerves on edge. I duck into a rundown gas station, the fluorescent lighting buzzing overhead. The clerk barely glances at me as I grab a few sandwiches, a bag of chips, and some water. Just enough fuel to keep moving.

I trudge to my cheap motel, where the door groans disapprovingly at my return. The stale air inside reeks faintly of mildew, but I'm too spent to care. I sink onto the bed, ignoring how the thin mattress sags beneath me. I choke down part of a sandwich, forcing it past the nausea clawing at my gut. I need the energy. I need to think.

My eyes land on a battered spiral notebook on the nightstand. I flip it open and force myself to write, the pen scraping across the paper in uneven strokes:

Walter killed Patrick.

Margot thinks I'm dead.

Get my story straight for Margot and the police.

Prove I'm not responsible.

My hand stops, the pen hovering above the page. I'm not a saint. I've done terrible things—lied to Margot, manipulated her trust, stolen from her even. But I am not a killer. I won't let anyone believe otherwise.

I try to scribble more, to figure out how I can make Margot understand. But my head sags forward, the pen sliding out of my grip. Exhaustion claws at me, dragging me under. I slump onto the bed, breathing in slow, ragged pulls. The notebook lies open beside me, its final words scrawled in a desperate, looping script:

I'm not a monster. I'm not a monster.

54

I lie in the motel bed, drifting into dark, restless dreams. Whispers hiss at the edges of my consciousness—soft, relentless sounds that slip through the cracks of temporary peace. I'm back at Hawthorn House, standing at the top of the basement steps. The air down there is thick with decay, every breath sticking in my throat. I descend one step at a time, limbs leaden and slow, until the smell of blood slams into me. My stomach clenches in revulsion, but no matter how hard I try, I can't force myself to turn back.

A sickening splash echoes from somewhere below. Something heavy shifts in water. "Come see," a voice whispers, so quiet it might be the wind. "Come look, Nate." My bare feet peel away from the clammy floor with each step, sending chilling squelches through the silence. Dim light flickers, illuminating an ancient porcelain tub in the center of the room. Patrick's body floats there, the water black and still. His arms are twisted at impossible angles, head lolling to one side like a ruined doll.

A strangled cry catches in my throat as Patrick's head snaps upward. The face is bloated, discolored, his eyes locking onto mine. His lips move, and a grotesque rattle comes out: "Why didn't you stop him?" His voice sounds like it crawled out of the grave. Blackness sprays in all directions as Patrick's arm lashes out, fingers clutching for me. "Why didn't you stop him?"

I stagger back. The whispers swell, merging into an angry crowd of unseen accusers. The basement walls begin to close in, pressing against my shoulders. Hands burst out of the concrete, gripping my arms and legs, dragging me toward that tub.

"You can't hide from this, Nate," they chant. "You can't hide..."

I bolt awake, screaming. My lungs ache, and I clutch at the thin motel sheets, eyes darting around. The flickering neon sign outside casts jittery shapes on the walls, and I'm drenched in sweat. It's a struggle to remember where I am. Slowly, my mind catches up. It was just another nightmare.

The old school clock on the nightstand reads 7:42 PM.

I stare, disbelieving. Twenty hours—nearly an entire day—slipped away from me. How? How did I sleep for so long?

My insides clench as reality crashes down around me: Margot. Walter. Patrick.

"Jesus Christ," I mutter, shoving the sweaty sheets aside. My shoes, my jacket—where did I leave them? My body is frantic, my mind a swirl of panic as I stumble around the small room. Then I remember the car. It's still hidden back by the tree line near that other house.

I can't lose more time, so I run out into the storm-dark streets. Rain lashes at my face, the wind roaring in my ears. I force one foot in front of the other, each step hammering through puddles as I push toward Hawthorn Manor.

. . .

By the time I reach the long gravel driveway to Hawthorn Manor, I'm gasping for breath. The Florida heat smothers me, and I'm drenched in sweat, but I can see the manor's peaks jutting over the tops of the trees. My legs threaten to buckle, but I keep going.

My senses go into overdrive as I draw nearer. No alarms, no screams, no doors left ajar or windows shattered. Everything looks too ordinary, and that normalcy sets me even more on edge. I slow as I approach the house, chest heaving, prepared to enact part one of the plan I hastily threw together on my way here.

I know I can't just barge in, spill the entire tangled mess, and expect Margot to handle it calmly—especially with Shannon here. Shannon never cared for me, and everything I say, no matter how true, will sound suspect.

I need first to confirm Margot's safety.

I edge around the side of the house until I reach the kitchen window. The curtains are partly drawn, but I can see Margot inside by the fireplace, her posture stiff and anxious as she glances around. Shannon is nowhere in sight. Relief floods through me just seeing Margot alive and apparently unhurt. No sign of Walter, no obvious signs of violence.

With validation that Margot is safe, I feel better about moving onto the next part of this plan, which is to get my story straight for the police.

I start moving again, heading toward the other house, the one where everything went so very wrong. My pulse thumps wildly as I recall Patrick's fate. He was violent, yes, but something about him was also desperate and broken—like a man drowning in his own insecurities, battling to find his place without a father figure. I know the feeling well. A wave of pity emerges as I think of him lying in that tub, alone and disfigured.

As I step onto the porch, echoes of last night's struggle come rushing back: the smash of a breaking window, the cracking of bone on stone. Pushing past the sick memories, I open the front door, letting myself back in. The air inside is exactly the same, heavy with the metallic stench of blood and decay. A shudder runs through me.

I make my way downstairs, flipping the light switch, half terrified my nightmare will come true and Patrick's body will lunge at me. The tub still sits in the center of the room, Patrick's body slumped in it. My stomach lurches at the sight. A faint buzzing sound reaches my ears—odd, hollow. I step closer, realizing it's coming from Patrick's pants pocket. His phone.

I gag, fighting the urge to vomit, forcing myself to approach the tub. The body is so close now, the smell overwhelming. My gaze snags on my wedding ring—the ring I once wore. I slip it off Patrick's finger and place it back on mine. It feels like a small reclamation of myself, but it also feels dirty.

Hands trembling, I reach into Patrick's pocket and ease out a battered flip phone, still vibrating with missed calls. I flip it open, my heart sinking when I see "Mom" on the screen— Phyllis. She's desperate to reach her son. She has no idea he's lying here, murdered, head severed and stolen.

I swallow hard, feeling the crushing weight of what I must do. I punch in the numbers. The line rings, echoing painfully loud in this dark chamber. Finally, a voice answers. I can barely steady my breath enough to speak.

"Hi," I say, my voice cracking in the silence. "My name is Nate Bennett, and I need to report a murder."

55

I stalk back and forth across the basement floor, my pulse thudding in my ears so hard it almost drowns out the sick gurgle of my stomach. A thousand times, I consider bolting for the stairs—away from the rank smell of congealed blood and the heavy feeling of death pulsing in this place. But I can't leave Patrick a second time. Even though his head is gone, the sight of his torso sitting in that tub still makes my insides twist with guilt. The last thing I want is to abandon him down here like a discarded piece of trash, so I hover at the bottom of the steps, grimacing at the sticky residue of dried gore that coats each riser.

Every few seconds, I rehearse what I'll say to the cops. The words tangle in my throat. Who's going to believe me? This entire situation, from the moment that manilla folder arrived on our doorstep, feels like the plot of an Agatha Christie novel. While Chief Miller will be able to vouch for portions of the story like that envelope, I imagine what his face will look like as I stand here, half delirious, trying not to throw up while I relive every dark secret and every fatal decision that led us here.

It's then that I hear it: a faint, distant noise, so soft I almost mistake it for my own thumping heartbeat. I freeze, head tilted. Could it be the police outside? Or maybe someone else entering? No—this sound is different. The hush of dripping rain seeps through the walls. The threatening clouds I saw on my run here are now crying over Mount Dora. But still, somewhere, deeper in the gloom, there's another sound.

I pivot, the hair on the back of my neck standing up as I wander toward the far corner of the basement. I've always assumed these walls were it—the boundary of this godforsaken space. But I discover a shadowed alcove that recedes beyond the flickering light. My lungs constrict with a fresh wave of dread as my shoes sink into frigid water that's pooled along the floor. The force of the storm overhead must be sending water down here, turning this corner into a shallow lake of icy muck.

That's when the sound tears through the silence again—louder, distinctly human. A scream. A woman's scream, carrying the unmistakable edge of terror. My entire body goes cold. I glance back at the main room, where the single yellow bulb sways, illuminating Patrick's final resting place. Only a few feet separate me from my makeshift vantage by the steps. I clench my teeth, summoning every ounce of courage just to lift one shaky foot deeper into the dark.

I flick open Patrick's ancient flip phone. The green glow is pathetic, but it's enough to see the jagged outline of a tunnel, hunkered low under the foundation. Water trickles down the walls, the dank smell of wet earth flooding my nostrils. From somewhere in that black maw, another scream reaches my ears —this time impossibly clear. The kind of scream that chills your blood.

I spin back, heart slamming against my ribs, torn between charging in and waiting for the police. My mind snaps to the memory of myself frozen in this same basement last night—

immobile while someone was murdered in front of my eyes. I feel the shame all over again, the hot burn of regret in my throat. I won't let that happen a second time.

"All right," I whisper, voice shaking so badly it's hardly audible. "All right... you can do this."

The phone's meager glow dances across the water. Fear floods my senses with every step I take into that low tunnel. Darkness closes in, wrapping around me like a living thing, but I keep going, because there's a voice—someone who needs help. And for once, I'm not going to run. For once, I'm going to be the man Margot once believed in, the man I lost somewhere behind years of secrets and mistakes.

My lungs struggle to pull in enough oxygen in this tight space, and my skin crawls at the cold water soaking my ankles. Every inch of me screams to turn back, but I push forward, because if I give in now, if I cower again, that scream might stop. And that would be the worst sound of all.

56

I push farther down the tunnel, and I can't be positive, but it feels like the water is rising the deeper I go. Initially, it was just my feet sinking into cold puddles, but now it sloshes around my ankles, making my skin prickle. Every drop of water that drips from the low ceiling mingles with the beads of sweat on my neck, and I can't tell which is which. Fear or rain—either way, it's soaking me in a clammy dread.

The darkness hangs onto me like a living thing. With no idea how far this tunnel goes, I can't shake the mental image of floodwaters creeping higher until I'm forced to swim. And while I was a lifeguard back in high school, it's been many years since I needed to swim for any significant period of time.

That scream—God, that piercing, female scream echoing through these walls—it could be coming from anywhere. My breathing grows labored, my heart hammering like a caged animal as I inch forward unable to see more than an inch or two in front of me.

Eventually, I feel the space in front of me shift. I pull out the phone to see if I can make sense of the shapes ahead. The tunnel splits in two. I could continue forward or take a hard left that leads to what appear to be steps; how many or where they lead, I have no idea. But the sight of those stairs makes my heart skip with hope. Stairs mean an exit—maybe a way out of here.

I stand there, drenched and trembling, listening for that scream again, but I only hear rainwater echoing through the rocks. Deciding to follow my gut, I choose left and start climbing. My relief is short-lived. After a few steps, I plant my foot to rise onto the next stair—and my boot lands on empty air. I lurch forward, panicking as my arms flail. Instead of dropping into another pit, I smack onto a sloping floor that cuts right off from the step I missed.

I stay crouched for a moment, breath catching in my throat. Then I notice tiny pinpricks of light up ahead. The weird angles and absolute blackness mess with my depth perception. My brain spins, imagining what I must look like to anyone watching. I shuffle forward in a half-crouch, arms out, trying to avoid invisible drops or sudden obstacles.

The glimmers of light grow larger, like bullet holes in a wall that let splinters of illumination through. Seeing them calms me for a moment. Even if they're not an escape route, they're the marking of life outside of this blackness. That tiny comfort vanishes the instant another scream pierces the silence. This time, it ricochets from behind me, not ahead.

My pulse spikes again. How could the disembodied voice be behind me now? Is there another hidden entry, another secret path carved into these walls? I freeze in place, torn between the faint hope of what's ahead and the undeniable fact that my gut, once again, steered me in the wrong direction.

I stare at the pinholes of light. They beckon me with the potential of warmth and freedom. It would be so easy to keep going, slip through some hidden door somewhere, and escape this watery crypt. But I know why I'm here. I'm not the same coward who stood paralyzed in that basement, watching as Walter murdered Patrick. This time, I'm the man who's willing to wade into terror for the sake of saving a life.

My jaw clenches. One last glance at the light, then I turn around. The steps behind me loom like an ominous descent, each step back down darker, wetter, more dangerous. I brace myself, practically sitting on the edges of each stair so I don't miss another break in the floor. Once I'm down, I steer myself left, heading deeper into the unknown rather than returning to the main basement I came from.

The water's higher here—maybe it's pouring in from the storm, or maybe this section is just lower ground. Regardless, I push forward, steps noisy as the water drenches me up to mid-shin now. Then another scream rings out, closer this time. My blood turns cold, but at least I know I'm on the right track. Someone needs help, and I'm getting closer

Clutching the flip phone, the pallid glow trembling with my shaking hand, I walk on. Water drips, fears swirl, and that desperate cry for help drives me forward through the rising flood, faster and faster.

57

My lungs burn with every breath as I wade deeper through the flooded tunnel, and my chest tightens with a fresh stab of panic. Just a few minutes ago, I felt a surge of courage—ready to play the hero, to save whoever might be screaming in the dark—but human resolve is a fragile, ever-shifting thing. I can sense mine dissolving as the water creeps relentlessly higher.

Two new developments set my nerves on edge. First, I see flickers of light reflecting off the water—not directly ahead but bouncing off the curved walls as if there's a source somewhere around the bend. Second, the water is no longer just lapping at my shins. It's up to my chest. I can hear the storm outside, pounding the ground above, sending torrents of rain through grates overhead. That run-off is funneling in, threatening to fill every last pocket of air in this tunnel.

Fear tries to claw its way up my throat. I swallow it down and keep moving, repeating a mantra in my head like a desperate prayer: *Be the man she thought you were. Be the man she needs you to be.* I picture Margot's face, haunted by Patrick's death, maybe hating me for the role I played or didn't play.

Even if I can't right that wrong, I can do some good here. I can be the man who rescues someone instead of letting them die.

The light I saw before is growing now, but so is the water. I'm forced to hobble forward on tiptoe, my chin lifted to keep from gulping in the rising tide. Another grate looms above me, spilling a sheet of water across the entire tunnel. I grit my teeth, close my eyes, and force my way through. The torrent slaps against my head, flooding my ears. I shake them clear, blinking water from my lashes. For the briefest second, I hear not one but two voices echoing somewhere in the darkness. Two women, maybe. My heart gives a violent lurch. Could it be...Margot? Shannon? No, that makes no sense. Why would they be here?

But something in my chest tells me it's not such a crazy thought after all. A burst of adrenaline grips me, yanking me from my stupor. I shove forward, half swimming now, each push of my legs lifting me off the tunnel floor. The ceiling looms just inches above the waterline. Another corner— another bend—and up ahead, a massive, grated opening. Dim light from who-knows-where outlines the bars. Beyond it lies the open air, presumably Lake Dora. My thoughts spin in frantic circles, trying to piece it together, but the tunnel's current surges forward, and I'm swept under.

Water covers my head, and I swallow a mouthful of salt water before I manage to resurface. Spluttering, I crane my head back, discovering I have only a sliver of space between water and stone—a few precious inches for air. I smash my face against the slick ceiling, gasping for oxygen, knowing that if I don't get through that grate, I'm dead. I push out all the carbon dioxide in my lungs, taking the biggest breath I can manage, then plunge beneath the surface.

Underwater, I kick wildly. My hands stretch out in front to avoid slamming face-first into the iron bars. But instead of metal, I collide with something soft– human skin. I try to open my eyes, but the water is dark and brackish, stinging my vision. My heart pounds as I sense a body drifting. I claw for the surface, desperate for air.

Breaking through, I find maybe an inch of breathing room. I gulp another shallow lungful and angle my head sideways. In the murky gloom, I spot a floating shape. It's Shannon. Her face is pale, her eyes closed, her body limp. She's on this side of the grate. I don't know if she's breathing. I don't know why she's here. Terror lances through me—what if Margot's down here, too, pinned somewhere by the current?

I force the thought aside and dive again, palming the rusted bars. There has to be a hinge, a lock—anything—but my fingertips graze only solid, unyielding iron. The water level pushes upward, swallowing precious inches of air. My mind reels: This is how I die. This is how Shannon dies. And if Margot loses both of us, after losing Lila, after everything that's happened—what will it do to her?

The images slam into my brain in a series of brutal flashes: Margot, alone, devastated, with no hope left. I picture her broken. I see her on the bathroom floor again, the same horrific scene I stumbled upon a year ago– crimson red escaping from the long, straight line on her left arm. The horror of it all ignites a new flame in my chest.

I thrust off the tunnel floor, wresting another shallow mouthful of air from that last sliver of space. Then, with a roar of defiance echoing in my head, I grab Shannon around the waist. Her body is limp, but I cling to her, refusing to let go. The water roars in my ears, pounding like blood rushing through my temples. I will find a way out.

I'm not dying here. Not like this. And neither is Shannon.

58

I plant my feet against the grate, gripping Shannon tightly in my arms, and kick off with every bit of strength I have left. For one dizzying moment, we're moving forward, carried by momentum through the churning water. Then, in a heartbeat, she's ripped from my grasp.

Panic engulfs me. I fling my arms out, trying to grab onto anything—her clothes, her hair, some part of her—to keep us together. My momentum propels me forward without her until, in desperation, I brace a hand against the mossy tunnel ceiling. That sudden friction slams me onto my back, half of my face above the water, half below it. I gulp down more liquid than air, choking as my lungs scream for oxygen. A nasty burn clenches my throat. This is what drowning feels like. I force the thought away. Not now. I can't let it happen now.

With my feet scrambling for traction along the tunnel's slick bottom, I twist around until I make contact with her again. My fingers glide over her waist, then down to her arms —and there it is, cold, unyielding metal. She's handcuffed to something. Probably the grate. My heart's in free fall, but there's no time to question it. The only hope we have is to get her free.

I tip my head up, trying to inhale, but I take in more water than air. I cough, vomiting the briny liquid. I try once more with my lips pressed tight, managing only a shallow, pitiful breath. It'll have to be enough. I plunge below the surface, hands searching in the blackness until I find her cuffed wrist. Eyes squeezed shut, I position my palm against the back of her hand, line the other beneath her joint for leverage, and press down with all the strength I have left.

A sickening crack reverberates through the water, and for a split second, I pray Shannon will scream, because that means she's alive. But there's only silence. Terror knives through me. I maneuver the newly broken joint, forcing the cuff to slide up and over her hand.

I shoot back up, slamming against the tunnel ceiling. Once more I try to inhale, water stinging my throat, hacking and spitting. I've run out of time. No more illusions—this is it. I clamp Shannon to my side, kick off that cursed grate again, and feel us surge forward in the current. My single free arm claws at the water, but the storm's runoff pushes us back. I'm exhausted, and we're sinking.

My momentum ebbs. I bounce off the tunnel floor and realize I have no last-ditch burst of adrenaline left. No help is coming. The pipes are designed to keep debris out of the lake. Well, here we are, pinned into the grate just like debris. In the heavy darkness, a hollow resignation settles in me. Before I can stop myself, I check Shannon's pulse. My fingertips graze the side of her neck. To my disbelief, there's the faintest flutter. She's alive.

A sick laugh bubbles in my chest, barely contained. The universe is mocking me. We came so close, and now there's nowhere else to go. At least I tried. At least I wasn't a coward this time.

Then, in that haze of complete hopelessness, something

changes. Or rather, something rests. The roar of rain overhead softens, replaced by a damp hush that resonates through the grates. My mind latches onto that sudden silence. The rain— it's finally stopped.

59

The roar of the water dulls to a trickle, and with the onslaught of rain finally halted, the main run-off tunnel recedes by at least a couple of inches in what feels like mere seconds. One moment I'm pinned against the ceiling, convinced we're both dead and the next I'm able to lift my head and suck in a full breath. Mount Dora's drainage system may be old as sin—dating back to the late 1880s—but it's incredibly effective. I nearly weep with relief as the current slackens around me.

I holler at Shannon to hold on, though she's unconscious and can't hear a word. I hoist her to my side, hooking my arm beneath her armpits and kicking with every bit of strength I have left. Water sluices around me, still waist-deep in places, but at least I'm not drowning. Each kick sends fire through my calf muscles, but the knowledge that this might just be enough to save us drives me forward.

Keeping my eyes peeled for that stairwell I found once before, I nearly overshoot it—the water is much higher, distorting the shape of everything around me. But I spot the dark maw off to the right and push off the tunnel floor, lifting Shannon entirely over my shoulder as I stagger up the slick, narrow steps. My teeth clack from the strain, but I don't slow until we reach a flat, muddy patch of ground.

With shaking arms, I lower Shannon onto the slope. Her body is limp, and every second that passes stabs deeper into my chest. I clear her airway, pressing my mouth to hers and forcing precious air into her lungs. My own lungs feel shredded from near-drowning, but I keep going. I can barely speak now —my throat is ragged, my voice a desperate rasp—so I focus on the rhythmic compressions, praying with every push.

Just as my vision starts to blur from exhaustion, Shannon coughs, a splatter of dark water dribbling from her mouth. Her entire frame jolts as she turns onto her side, retching up the remains of the flood. Relief smacks me so hard I almost collapse against the stone wall. I lean over, patting her back in the most urgent, gentle way I can, my voice little more than a whisper at her ear.

"Breathe, Shannon," I croak, my own lungs rattling. "Just breathe."

She's alive—but the moment I start to believe we've caught a break, she mumbles, barely audible: "Margot." My heart stutters, and a new rush of panic shoots through me. If Shannon was cuffed down there, that means someone left her to die. God knows what that someone might've done to Margot.

I want details, want to shake Shannon until she can give me a full sentence, but she's still half-conscious, blinking in confusion. Then I hear a deep, resonant thud echo somewhere farther down the tunnel. I turn and see faint pinpricks of light flickering—someone's crossing in front of them from the other side of the wall.

I scramble upright, ripping Patrick's phone from my pocket. It still glows when I snap it open—a small, blessed miracle all thanks to the Motorola brick. With trembling fingers, I wipe the screen on my sopping shirt. I punch in 911 and press the phone to my ear. After the first ring, I drop it into Shannon's lap. "Stay here," I tell her, or I try to—it comes out as more of a wheeze. Then, because there's no time and my heart is thundering, I spin headlong into the darkness.

60

I sprint through the darkness, slamming into cinderblock walls more than once in my haste, trying to get my bearings. My vision wavers, my lungs still ragged from the ordeal in the tunnel. I'm convinced this passage led into Hawthorn Manor via the old run-off tunnel I took. My thoughts momentarily flash back to the dirty basement, hoping by now the police have arrived to discover Patrick's body, to search for Margot...to search for me.

Muffled voices seep through the stone around me. I try to yell, but all that comes out is a raspy whisper. Whatever life was in my vocal cords is gone; after near-drowning and screaming through the tunnels, my throat is done.

The tunnel keeps snaking around in wild, erratic turns. I glimpse small holes in the walls and think I see glimpses of furniture and floorboards, but the house lights must be off, making it impossible to orient myself. I just keep going, guided by the subtle changes in air pressure and the scattered patches of moonlight that occasionally slip through cracks.

Then more steps appear. Some rise only a step or two; others climb five or six. A couple slope downward, disorienting me further. Eventually, I have no idea where I am—upstairs, downstairs, or somewhere in between. My heart starts to pound again, panic rising like bile.

And then, finally, I see it: bright, brilliant light shining from somewhere ahead, flooding the corridor. Relief hits me like a battering ram, and I break into a run, weaving past an old treasure chest with a rusty, half-open lock, dodging dusty chairs and an old bed, until I burst through the exit.

The rush of clean air nearly knocks me sideways. I double over, hands on my knees, gasping for breath. When I straighten up, the confusion nearly topples me again. I'm in our bedroom. The bed Margot and I once shared stands in the same place, the desk shifted at an angle to reveal the opening I just emerged from. Shock ties my thoughts into knots. Why the hell is there a secret passage here?

Before I can piece it together, I hear the voices again—this time clearly. Margot. She's alive. Hope and dread fuse in my chest, because there's a second voice: Walter. My pulse roars in my ears. He's here, and my wife is in danger.

I don't know if he's armed. I don't know if he's threatening her with a knife, a gun—anything at all. If I move carelessly, I could lose her in a single heartbeat. She's yelling now and I track the sounds to somewhere downstairs. Trying to dampen each step, I tug off my soaking boots, gently dropping the first.

I'm halfway through removing the second when I hear it: the crash of a struggle. Someone's running up the stairs just outside the bedroom door. My heart leaps, and I creep closer, ready to pounce on Walter the moment he appears. My blood sings with adrenaline, images of Patrick's murder fueling a desire for retribution.

But then the noise dies—replaced by a strained tussle. I inch around the doorway until I can see the top of the staircase. My eyes go wide at the sight. Margot, face pressed against the step, pinned down by Walter. He's leaning his entire weight onto her, forcing her head toward a broken banister spindle. A sharpened splinter of wood waits to impale her throat if he pushes an inch farther.

My muscles coil, and I fling myself into motion. I slip in the mud my soaked boots have tracked inside, almost go down face-first, but manage to plant a hand and vault forward. Margot's chin is fractions of an inch from that lethal shard, and while I can't directly see them, I know what Walter's eyes are like: burning with the same frenzied hatred he wore when he removed Patrick's head.

I barrel into them, hooking around the banister's main post on my left. I hurl my body forward, letting gravity carry me. My left palm slams into Walter's nose, a grisly crunch confirming the cartilage is shattered. In the same instant, I wedge my right hand under Margot's neck, shielding her throat from the spindle.

White-hot pain flares through my palm. The shard tears into flesh, sending splinters spraying across the steps, but it's my hand, not Margot's throat, that's skewered. My voice is gone, so the roar of agony I try to unleash emerges as a ragged whisper. Walter howls for both of us, letting go of Margot so he can grab at the ruin of his nose.

He stumbles backward a few steps, blood streaming, then surges forward, murder in his eyes. I'm pinned down by my wounded hand, wincing as it throbs, and can barely muster my left arm to protect Margot. But she doesn't need my help. Her leg lashes out, striking him squarely in the chest.

I see Walter's body heave backward, no part of him touching the stairs anymore. He flies past the railing, arms and legs splayed. I cringe as he hits the floor far below with a sickening thud, and the house goes eerily silent.

61

MARGOT, MOMENTS BEFORE

I lay at the top of the staircase, chest heaving, my pulse hammering in my ears. Though I'm about to die, I can't help but think back to the first moment that sent me on this journey; that night not so long ago when I came down these very steps and uncovered a hidden map in the floor of my beautiful new home. If I had only known then what I know now, I would have left the paper in the floor, and quietly walked out the door, to never set foot in Hawthorn Manor again.

Unfortunately, I didn't know what I know now and instead, I started down a path that has led to the deaths of the people I care about most.

I hear George's grunts, feel his muscles straining on top of me. I feel my neck muscles growing weaker, my throat growing closer to the needle like wood protrusions jutting out of the stair, yet all that I can think of is Nate.

He stands bathed in the warm, golden light of a fading afternoon. I see him with beach blown hair, covered in sand and salt from a day on the coast. He's sporting his signature half-smile, so effortlessly kind and smooth. His eyes—always the color of polished mahogany—reflect me back at myself,

ELLIS HART

and for the briefest of moments I remember how safe I felt whenever his gaze settled on me. There's a gentle lift to his chin, a playful tilt of his head that says he's about to tease me, or coax me into his arms, or make some silly joke he knows I'll pretend to hate but secretly adore.

The edges of everything else blur: the house, the stairs, George. Nate is what remains, in perfect focus—his broad shoulders that carried the weight of our problems when I couldn't, the faint scar above his eyebrow he once got skateboarding as a teenager, the compassion in his face that endures even through tragedy. It's the details that catch my breath: the tiny flecks of gold at the center of his irises, the smattering of freckles trailing along his collarbone, the way his smile lines deepen when he sees me.

In the hush of my mind's eye, I can almost feel his hand at my waist, his low, steady voice beckoning me closer. Everything else drifts away, dissolving into memory. This final vision of Nate is all warmth and light, the very best of him—love made manifest in a single, precious moment. And as I cling to that image, I let it carry me back to every promise we ever made, every laugh we ever shared, knowing it will stay with me far beyond my death here.

And yet, even when I open my eyes, prepared to look out over the house that was supposed to change everything for the better, I still see him; I still see Nate. Except this Nate is rushing towards me with wet hair, and muddy lips, and terror in his eyes. He rests his hand on my chin and releases the heavy pressure on top of my body.

George screams and it shocks me back to attention. He's leaping towards me again and instinctively my foot goes out, kicking him in the chest.

Time splinters. George's eyes fly wide, reflecting pure

disbelief. He topples backward into empty air, arms flailing, and for the briefest of moments, I think I see him smile.

In the momentary silence, there's a sharp crack that snaps through the house like a gunshot. George hits the hardwood floor in a heap, his neck twisted at an impossible angle.

I freeze at the top of the stairs. The world narrows to George's shattered body sprawled on the floor below. My lungs constrict, and everything blurs, except for the sudden certainty that the twisted Hawthorn legacy ends here, in this place.

George Hawthorn's death is grotesquely poetic: a fall, a broken neck—exactly how his mother killed Amelia, exactly how he'd ended her life in return. Three Hawthorns, three falls, three broken necks. And now I watch the final chapter, the last violent page in a lineage stained with cruelty, come to a brutal close on these very steps.

I curl into a ball, and Nate's still there. He looks at me, and I can't believe what I'm seeing. Neither of us moves for an endless moment. The Hawthorn curse—this terrible line of heartbreak and darkness—lies broken and lifeless below.

EPILOGUE
ONE YEAR LATER

I sit on the wide front porch of what was once Hawthorn Manor, sipping from a chipped cup of tea, and I can hardly believe how different everything looks now. The late afternoon sun casts a warm golden glow across the yard, and laughter drifts through the open windows. It's bright, joyful—the sort of sound I once believed would never come from a place like this.

To my right, a little girl sits on the edge of the porch, her scuffed shoes swinging just above the floorboards. She reminds me so much of Lila—same untidy braids, same curious eyes—that my chest aches whenever I look at her. But it's a good ache, one full of purpose.

"Mrs. M?" inquired the tiny voice next to me. She points toward the newly painted sign near the gate, the name carved into the wood in smooth, looping letters. "Why's it called Cece's House now?" she asked.

I take a slow breath, letting the memory of the old manor fade behind fresh coats of paint and bright windows. "Because once upon a time," I say, "a very kind woman lived here named Cecelia. She had a dream to turn this big house into a beautiful home full of children." I turn to meet her eyes so my words carry weight. "But sadly, she passed away before that happened. So, we've worked hard to keep her dream alive by making it a safe place for children, just like–" I take my index finger, drawing narrowing circles towards her face and then gently touch the tip of her nose as I say, "you."

She giggles, her eyes now tracking a group of children running across the yard. Their laughter float on the breeze, and my heart swells. Where there were once dark hallways and hidden passages, there's now light and openness.

The same night George Walter Hawthorn died, we'd made the call to the FBI. The agents had arrived in Mount Dora swiftly, like a fresh storm sweeping through the sleepy town. They'd arrested Jenkins and dragged him from his home, his face a mask of shame as he was led away in cuffs.

The investigation into the skulls was long and exhaustive, but in the end, it brought closure to families who had waited far too long for answers. The FBI combed through every inch of the house, pulling out what remained of George's twisted legacy, leaving behind only empty echoes that, in time, would fade.

When they finally left, Nate and I hired a crew of men and women who hadn't known the place's history and saw only an old house needing repair. They'd torn down Hawthorn House and sealed the hidden tunnel below. We then completely renovated Hawthorn Manor, closing up the tight tunnels hidden along the walls, and the entryway into the run-off tunnels prohibiting anyone from ever being stuck down there again.

Piece by piece, we stripped away any remnants of George Hawthorn until nothing was left of him. And when it was done, Nate and I had stood in the center of the yard, staring at what we had remade. I felt a new sense of peace, and more importantly, a new sense of purpose.

Today, the main house, along with the smaller cottage we

had built out back, forms the heart of our foundation: "Shield and Shelter Promise." Working together, we've turned what was once a place of secrets and fear into a refuge for children who need a safe haven most. Shannon's legal expertise has been instrumental in securing the grants we receive from Mount Dora and the state of Florida, while we work to create something good from our shared tragedy.

We focus on filling the gaps in the overburdened, under-funded child protective services system in America—sub-contracting social workers, sponsoring therapy, and providing food and shelter to any child, including those who've aged out of foster care with nowhere left to go. We do this because we've witnessed what happens when no one is there to protect a child. George Hawthorn grew up under the shadow of domestic violence and neglect, and by the time anyone noticed, it was too late. We can't undo his story, but we can prevent others like it. Bit by bit, child by child, we're creating a new legacy on this land: a place where love replaces loneliness, and hope triumphs over the darkest histories.

A low rumble from the driveway catches my attention. My fingers tighten around my teacup on instinct, but I exhale as soon as I see the Mount Dora police cruiser. A moment later, Nate steps out, his uniform catching the dying rays of the sun. His right hand is still stiff, permanently scarred by the injury he received that night on the stairs, but he's learning how to live with it. Sometimes I catch him wincing when he forgets his limits and tries to open jars or lift heavy boxes, but he never complains. He just keeps going—keeps proving that he can be the man I always believed he could be.

My pulse flutters when he makes his way onto the porch. Even now, after everything we've been through, the sight of him in uniform brings tears to my eyes. He sets his hat aside and leans in for a kiss. I taste a hint of coffee on his lips—familiar, comforting.

"Hey, Margot," he says softly, then bends to press his mouth to my growing belly. "Hey to you, too," he adds, smiling at the life growing inside me.

I brush a hand across his temple, pushing back a stray lock of hair. "How was work?"

He shrugs, wincing slightly as he adjusts the angle of his right wrist. "Quiet." A small grin touches his lips, though there's a shadow in his eyes that never fully fades. "Quiet is good—it means we're keeping the worst people away. For now, anyway."

I kiss his scarred hand, my heart warming at the thought of Nate working in law enforcement here in Mount Dora—the very place that nearly destroyed us both. "You're doing good work," I say, holding his gaze. "You're doing exactly what this town needs– honest and transparent police work."

His lips twitch, a mix of gratitude and lingering guilt. "I'm just trying to do better," he answers simply.

From inside the house, a chorus of young voices shouts for "Mr. N," and I catch Nate's smile widen. Children spill onto the porch, arms outstretched for him, and he sets down his hat to pull them into a loose embrace. My heart melts at the sight, because for so long, I thought I'd lost him, lost us. Yet here he is, battered hand and all, cradling these kids with the same tenderness he once showed me.

I let out a long breath and glance over the yard. Shannon steps out from her own little cottage located catty-cornered to Cece's House, phone in hand. She notices me looking and waves, her expression already poised to discuss some legal matter we're working on. We've been partners in this new life, turning heartbreak into a home for those who need it most.

And she's thriving, too—no longer haunted by the tragedies that once threatened to drown us both.

Everything feels lighter now, like the air itself is filled with possibility. I catch the little girl beside me smiling, her gaze drifting from Shannon to the children tumbling around Nate's legs. The battered citrus grove in the distance has started to bud once again, the vines not as gnarled, a fresh patch of green bursting through the old roots.

Hope in the unlikeliest of places, I think to myself, my heart swelling. And somehow, despite it all, that hope belongs to us. It belongs to these children—safe now, free to laugh in the sun without fear.

"You know," I say, speaking to the girl at my side but also to the ghosts that once haunted this place, "I think things are finally going to be okay."

She nods; her eyes bright. "Me too."

This house once held us like a secret—Cecilia and me. One trapped in death, the other in life. We were both caught inside George's design, ghosts of different kinds, each kept by a man who couldn't let go.

I still wonder if she was ever really here at all. The whispers, the dreams, the weight in the air—were they signs of her spirit, or just byproducts of George's manipulation and my own guilt? I'll never know for certain. But this I do believe: if she was here, if some piece of her was ever caught inside these walls, she's free now. Her story is no longer mine to carry.

The doors no longer whisper warnings, and the walls don't watch me at night. This house holds my family, yes—but not as prisoners. Not with hauntings. It holds space for us. For healing. For quiet. For everything that comes after survival.

For the first time since arriving in Mount Dora, we are not held captive. We are free to stay—or leave—as we choose. And as for me, I'm choosing to stay.

ACKNOWLEDGMENTS

To my wife, **Kate**—words can't capture how much your unwavering support means to me. Whether I'm writing a novel, lifting heavy objects and setting them back down, experimenting with new coding projects, or remixing the same song for the fortieth time, you stand beside me through every wild idea. You are my rock, my guiding light toward becoming a better person. You're Nora Krank to my Luther Krank and I can't imagine this life without you.

To my children, **Brooks**, **Wesley**, and **Teddy**—each day with you is a fresh adventure, and watching you learn and grow is my greatest joy. Thank you for reminding me that life is full of magic and possibility.

To my **parents** and **grandparents**—thank you for encouraging me to write my first book all the way back in high school. It paved the way for this journey, and rediscovering my love of writing has been an unexpected gift in adulthood. Without your early enthusiasm, I might never have made it here.

To my "early readers" and biggest supporters, especially **Sara Powers**, **Hannah Umbra**, **Emily Jones**, and Emily's phenomenal reading group—**Jenna, Tyrah, Becca, Tiffani, Jess, Emily, Nicole, Kandra, Ashley, Bethany, Miranda, and Kaitlyn**—your enthusiasm gave me the energy and confidence I needed to finish (and re-finish) this book. Nothing fueled my creativity more than your feedback, encouragement, and genuine excitement for each new version of the manuscript.

Thank you to **Andrew Lowe** for your brilliant editing, poking, and prodding. You challenged me to dig deeper, think harder, and restructure this story—and I wouldn't have it any other way. Your dedication turned these pages into a story I'm proud to share.

To the nutty **Psychological Thriller Readers (PTR) Facebook group**, thank you for reigniting my passion for reading. I really, really hope you guys like this book.

To the many **agents** I queried who ignored me, turned me down, or sent that oh-so-familiar lines, "Submissions are so high right now" or "it's just not a good fit"— thank you. Your rejection spurred eight total rewrites, four different endings, a switch from third-person to first-person perspective, and revived several "dead" characters (you're welcome Shannon lovers)! This book is stronger because you pushed me to hone every detail, and I'm grateful for that spark of perseverance you gave me.

Finally, to **you**, the person actually reading this—I appreciate you more than you know. Sharing songs as a musician is one thing, but letting someone live in your head for months (over hundreds of pages) is a unique kind of trust. Thank you for spending your time with these words. I'm eternally grateful you've joined me on this journey. Am I an author now? Wild stuff indeed.

Here's to the next adventure!

A PERSONAL NOTE

Writing **The House That Held Her** was both a cathartic and challenging journey for me. While I have never been a victim of domestic violence, I'm no stranger to trauma. I'm a survivor of childhood sexual abuse, and there were times when the weight of shame, fear, and isolation felt unbearable. When I finally found the courage to speak up and seek professional help, it was like a lifeline had been thrown out to me. Therapy and the support of trusted friends not only saved my life—they helped me rediscover parts of myself I'd locked away for years.

So, I know firsthand that suffering in silence can be suffocating, and it's my deepest hope that nobody reading these pages feels alone. If you see parts of your own pain in any of these characters, please understand you deserve compassion, care, and healing. There are many roads that lead to hope: sometimes it's therapy, sometimes it's a trusted confidant, sometimes it's time spent in quiet reflection or with people who remind us we are more than our scars.

As you turn the final pages of this novel, please remember that your story isn't finished. There are people, organizations, and safe spaces ready to guide you, whether you're facing trauma, supporting a loved one who is struggling, or simply wanting to help. In the following pages, I've included a list of resources—both for those in need of immediate help and for those looking to get involved in good causes. It's my wish that every reader who needs these services finds them in time, and every reader who can give back does so wholeheartedly.

From the bottom of my heart, thank you for being here and for caring.

Yours,

Ellis Hart, 2025

WHERE TO GET HELP AND HOW TO HELP

Life can be as unpredictable and turbulent as the storms and shadows in **The House That Held Her**. If you or someone you know is experiencing difficulties, please remember that support is available. Below are resources you can turn to for help or to make a difference in someone else's life.

IMMEDIATE DANGER OR EMERGENCY

- **Call 911 (USA)** or your local emergency services if you or someone else is in immediate physical danger.

- **General Distress, Anxiety, and Grief**
  - **Crisis Text Line (USA)**: Text "HELLO" to 741741

- **Domestic Violence, Abuse, or Sexual Assault**
  - **National Domestic Violence Hotline (USA)**: 1-800-799-SAFE (7233), or text "START" to 88788

- Rape, Abuse & Incest National Network
  (RAINN; USA): 1-800-656-HOPE (4673)
- Childhelp National Child Abuse Hotline
  (USA): 1-800-4-A-CHILD (422-4453)

- **Mental Health and Suicide Prevention**
  - **988 Suicide & Crisis Lifeline (USA):** Call or
    text 988
  - **SAMHSA (Substance Abuse & Mental Health
    Services Administration; USA):** 1-800-662-
    4357
  - **National Alliance on Mental Illness
    (NAMI; USA)** Helpline: 1-800-950-NAMI
    (6264)

- **Gambling Addiction and Financial Crisis
  Support**
  - **National Problem Gambling Helpline (USA):**
    1-800-522-4700
  - **Gamblers Anonymous:** http://www.
    gamblersanonymous.org/
  - **National Foundation for Credit Counseling
    (NFCC):** https://www.nfcc.org/
  - **Financial Counseling Association of America
    (FCAA):** https://fcaa.org/

- If you reside outside the USA, you can find global
  hotlines here: https://findahelpline.com/

If the content of this book or events in your life leave you
feeling overwhelmed, please reach out to one of these professional crisis lines or contact a trusted medical provider or
counselor.

IF YOU WANT TO HELP

Just as the characters in **The House That Held Her** take steps toward building a better, safer future, you, too, can make an impact by supporting organizations that address the issues explored in this story:

- **Domestic Abuse and Sexual Assault**
  - **National Coalition Against Domestic Violence (NCADV)**: https://ncadv.org/
  - **Futures Without Violence**: https://www.futureswithoutviolence.org/

- **Child Welfare and Protection**
  - **Childhelp**: https://www.childhelp.org/
  - **CASA (Court Appointed Special Advocates)**: https://nationalcasagal.org/
    - CASA/GAL volunteers advocate for abused and neglected children during court proceedings, striving to ensure they find safe and loving homes.

- **Mental Health & Suicide Prevention**
  - **National Alliance on Mental Illness (NAMI)**: https://nami.org/
  - **Mental Health America (MHA)**: https://www.mhanational.org/
    - Offers information, tools, and direct support for individuals seeking to manage or improve their mental health.

- **Grief and Trauma Support**

- o **American Foundation for Suicide Prevention (AFSP)**: https://afsp.org/
- o **The Dougy Center (Children's Grief Support)**: https://www.dougy.org/

- **General Community Engagement**
  - o Look for **food banks, shelters**, and **community centers** in your local area where you can volunteer your time.
  - o Donate to **local nonprofits** or **church programs** supporting at-risk children, domestic violence survivors, and individuals in crisis.
  - o Participate in **fundraising events** or **charity walks** that raise money for mental health programs or crisis hotlines.

ABOUT THE AUTHOR

Ellis Hart is an independent author who lives in Orlando, Florida, with his wife, three children, and delightfully curious cat, Jovie. **The House That Held Her** is Ellis's debut novel, and he's already immersed in writing his second. Always eager to connect with fellow book-lovers, if you'd like to chat about this novel or swap reading recommendations, you can reach out via any of his official author platforms.

www.ingramcontent.com/pod-product-compliance
Lightning Source LLC
Chambersburg PA
CBHW030246120726
47903CB00005B/1638